Web of Silence

Kathleen Dutton

Olympus Story House

Dear Readers,

I want to thank all of you for reading OUT OF HABIT and appreciate your feedback and support. I have enjoyed the craft of writing since childhood as a way to enter a world of unlimited possibilities. I retired from the professional world as a clinical engineer, training cardiologists in the US to support products which make a difference in cardiac procedures. I now enjoy life in Michigan with my husband, and family, especially in northern Michigan where Hemmingway spent time writing his early novels.

Best Wishes, Kathleen Dutton

PROLOGUE

May 2020

A loud pounding sound disturbed Rose's slumber. Her heart thudded as she jumped from the bed to grab her robe and rushed down the hall to the front door. Again, an insistent knock alerted her that something was amiss as she unlatched the dead bolt. "Lena! What's the mat…"

"Rose, come quickly," Lena exclaimed. "Beth's hurt. We must get her to a hospital."

Still in a daze from the abrupt awakening, Rose stared at Lena in disbelief. "Hurt? How?"

"She's in the car. Please hurry."

Rose glanced at the car parked in the driveway. "Go wait with her. I'll be right with you," she said as she rushed toward her room to dress.

Her hands trembled while she fumbled to fasten her jacket buttons and a sinking sensation engulfed her as she rushed out of the house to the car. A small whimper escaped her lips when she opened the door to find her granddaughter lying motionless on the back seat.

"Beth?" she whispered as she slipped in next to Beth and gently touched the young woman's hand. Rose closed the door and frantically called out directions to the hospital for Lena.

In the darkness, she couldn't assess the injuries, but felt Beth shake violently, as if she were in shook. Rose moved closer and gingerly pulled Beth against her. Rose felt her stomach muscles knot when Beth cried out at the slightest touch. "I'm sorry, honey. Where are you hurt?" When Beth didn't reply, she met Lena's gaze in the rearview mirror. "Why didn't you take her the hospital in Aidan? Why did you drive all this way in her condition?" Rose stifled the near panic in her voice and struggled to remain calm.

"Beth insisted I drive to your house. I don't know why, but she refused to stay in Aiden?"

"What happened?" She wondered out loud, as she gently held Beth's cold, clenched hand.

"I don't know!" Lena exclaimed. "She was hysterical when she called me, but when I arrived, she wouldn't tell me a thing."

Rose's eyes misted with tears. "Do you think her mother did this to her?"

"No. Linda was at work," Lena said.

Beth cried out softly when the car jolted over a bump in the road and Rose refrained from screaming at Lena to drive more carefully. Instead, she held her granddaughter tentatively in an attempt to protect her.

"We're almost to the hospital, Beth. You'll be okay." She moved closer when she heard a faint whisper and strained to listen. "What is it?"

"Promise me you won't let anyone know where to find me," Beth said in a raspy murmur.

Rose frowned, confused by Beth's words. "What do you mean? Why?"

Lena pulled the car to a halt at the emergency entrance of the hospital, opened the door and rushed inside for assistance.

A shudder of unknown fear spread through Rose when Beth's fingers clasped tightly onto her jacket. "I need to hide," Beth pleaded.

Rose glanced out the window in time to see Lena directing a hospital attendant toward the car.

As Beth was lifted onto a stretcher and covered with a blanket, Rose searched her granddaughter's face for meaning while Lena parked the car.

"What's your name, young lady?" the attendant asked as he wheeled Beth toward the triage of the emergency room.

Beth didn't answer, so he turned to Rose. "Are you a relative?

Only Rose saw the glint of terror in Beth's gaze. "My friend and I were driving home from Bingo when we found her lying on the side of the road." The words stuck in her throat and her heart sunk to her stomach, but when she detected relief on Beth's face, she continued. "I don't know who she is."

CHAPTER ONE

November 2022

Alisa Rose bit her lower lip and stared out the frosted windows at the deserted playground. Always on alert, she searched the line of trees in the distant and half expected a terrifying entity from her past to suddenly materialize.

She visualized herself running through the halls of the elementary school, where she taught second grade, howling like a rabid animal desperate to escape the madness that picked at her sanity like a bird on a suet ball.

Alisa counted to ten, exhaled slowly and blinked her eyes to extinguish the images of her past. She was safe. There was nothing to fear. Then why were her hands unsteady and her stomach turned to knots?

Alisa glanced at the school clock situated above the chalkboard. How could it possibly be two o'clock already? With a resigned sigh, she closed her lesson plan to observe the students seated in her classroom. She was pleased to discover most of the children were concentrating on their assigned math lesson.

Of course, there were always a few exceptions. Bret and Kurt were engaged in a spitball war. When Miss Rose took several steps toward them, they quickly buried their noses in the pages of their math books. Alisa turned back toward her desk in time to intercept a folded note Amanda passed to Lauren. Amanda glared indignantly at Miss Rose.

"Miss Rose, that's private."

"Young lady, you know the rules about passing notes." Alisa ripped the note in half. "I don't read them, but I won't give them back."

As she made her way over to Robbie who was waving his hand in the air to get her attention, the classroom door opened and the school secretary entered.

Alisa frowned when she noticed the serious expression on Mary's face. "What is it, Mary?" she asked.

"I have an urgent message for you." Mary passed a slip of paper to Alisa.

"Thanks," she said and swallowed hard as Mary closed the door behind her.

Alisa read the note and fought the urge to bolt from the room. Her grandmother never called her at work unless there was an emergency. With light speed, her senses jumped to full alert and she grabbed the doorknob with a sudden stab of dread.

"Take your math work home if you're not finished, we'll correct it tomorrow." She called out, surprised her voice remained calm. "It's time for gym class."

Alisa crushed the note as she made a fist while the children pushed to form a single line and when all was quiet, she led them to the gym where Mr. Siddon waited to take over the class.

She refrained from running down the hall toward the office. Relieved to find the office empty, she dialed Gram's number and paced as each unanswered ring increased her anxiety. Alisa tapped her fingers on the phone and wondered if Gram was ill or had bad news from out of town.

Two, three four. . . Alisa felt her pulse race with each ring. "Answer the phone," she muttered. After the sixth ring, Alisa closed her eyes with relief when she heard her grandmother's voice.

"Hello?"

"Gram, it's me. Are you alright?" "I'm fine, dear."

"Oh, God." Alisa exhaled slowly. "What's wrong then?"

"Honey, your mother. . .she died this morning."

Alisa frowned, torn by an array of conflicted emotions. "What?"

"I'm sorry." Gram's words were calm, but Elisa detected apprehension in her voice.

"Dead. How?" she whispered and pressed her fingers to her lips.

"Your Aunt Lena found her." Rose wavered. "She died in her sleep." Alisa started at the wall clock in a daze.

"How did it happen? Was she hurt? Did she fall?" She cleared her throat to steady her voice.

"It's too early to know the details, but Lena wants you to go home to take care of the funeral and to settle whatever legal details there might be." Rose's voice grew tender. "I know you can't go back there, dear. I'll go in your place to take care of everything."

Tears filled Alisa's eyes. "I have to go back, Gram. In spite of everything, she was my mother." She rubbed her temple to soothe the beginning of a headache.

Worry sounded in Rose's voice. "I don't want you to go back there."

"I know, Gram. It's just something I have to do."

"Then I'll go with you to help you get through the ordeal of whatever made you run away in the first place." She paused as if to allow the idea to settle. "Besides, Linda was my daughter-in-law. It's only right."

The noisy sound of children's voices erupted in the hall. "Gram, I have to go. I'll call you later."

Alisa placed the phone on the receiver and wondered how she could manage the strength to go home. After all she'd been through to rebuild her shattered life. She clenched her damp hands into fists and inhaled unsteadily to keep the panic at bay as she walked into the principal's office.

Mr. Gordon's secretary, Shelia, stopped typing when Alisa approached her desk. Shelia's smile faded when she looked up. "What is it, Alisa?" Shelia watched after the young teachers like a mother hen. She passed a box of tissues to Alisa.

"My mother died this morning," Alisa said and wiped her eyes. "I need to go to travel back to my hometown." She wondered if Shelia could guess the tears were out of dread, not of grief for her mother's death.

"I'm so sorry." Shelia stood and hugged Alisa. "I'll let Mr. Gordon know you need to see him right away."

As Shelia's footsteps echoed on the hard tile floor, Alisa rested her head against the wall. Eyes closed, she inhaled deeply, but the tension remained.

"Miss Rose." She opened her eyes to find Mr. Gordon, his forehead furrowed, his expression concerned. "Come into my office where we can talk."

Alisa followed and hoped for once, this discussion would be brief. She eased into the chair across from his desk and explained the circumstances regarding her mother's death.

"Take whatever time you need," he said as he shifted through papers to find the proper form. Alisa studied his cluttered office. She decided organization was not one of his strong points. There were books stacked everywhere, along with papers and files placed in no apparent order. She closely examined photos along one wall. Many of the pictures were candid, fun snapshots of various youngsters and pets. Touched by the kindness he had displayed during the past year, tears filled Alisa's eyes once more. Mr. Gordon and her grandfather had been close friends and associates. She wasn't sure she'd have survived if Mr. Gordon hadn't presented the opportunity to teach.

He passed the form across the desk. "Shelia will fill out the details." He cleared his throat awkwardly. "I'm sorry about your mother. Be sure to give your grandmother my regards."

"I will," Alisa said and stood to leave. "Thank you."

In the outer office, Shelia completed the form. "I've already sent someone to cover your class. You're all set to leave for home."

Thoughts of home caused a shudder to creep through Alisa as she stepped outside to the crisp November air. She turned away from the school and clutched her coat against her shivering body. Was it the cold that caused her tremble or the harsh realization she must return to a time and a place where she was someone else? She whispered the name she had blocked from her mind for almost two years. "Elizabeth Rose Brockton." How strange it sounded. How foreign. Beth Brockton was the woman she left behind in the small town of Aidan, Michigan. Beth Brockton ceased to exist long ago.

Beth inserted coins into the pay phone located outside the drug store across from her apartment to make the dreaded call to her aunt.

"Hello, Aunt Lena."

"Beth! I was beginning to wonder if you were going to call or not," Aunt Lena stated rather coldly.

Beth griped the phone and cringed at the sound of her name spoken out loud. "This is the first opportunity I've had." She bit her lower lip to keep from grinding her teeth.

"How are you, Aunt Lena?"

"How do you think I am? It's been a horrible day." Lena sniffled and paused for a moment. "I need to know if you want any special arrangements for the funeral, Beth. There is so much to do, but you're the next of kin and need to make some of the decisions."

Beth pressed the back of her cold hand against her throbbing forehead to soothe the ache. What she wanted most was for the funeral to be over. With all the tolerance she could gather, she spoke softly, "Make whatever decisions you think are best. I won't arrive until tomorrow afternoon."

Her checks flushed, most likely from the guilt. Most people would drop everything to hurry home for such an occasion. Then again, most circumstances were much different than hers. Beth detected a clucking sound of disapproval from her aunt.

"You make it sound as though your mother's funeral is an inconvenience for you."

Beth cringed and wanted to scream nothing could be closer to the truth. She struggled to maintain a civil tone as she twirled the phone cord around her finger. "I'm sorry, Aunt Lena. This is difficult for me, too." Beth heard a loud sigh. "I'd be grateful if you could take care of the arrangements." The sniffling grew louder and Beth closed her eyes.

"Maybe you'd like the visitation and the service at the same time so you can hurry back to your busy life," snapped Lena.

Beth felt the sting of sarcasm in Lena words. "I'll come back only because she was my mother. Not because I want to, but because I'd never feel right if I didn't."

"I'm sorry, Beth." Lena's voice softened. "I was hoping you had forgiven your mom."

Beth pinched the bridge of her nose to ward off the sting of unshed tears. "I wish I could."

After she hung up the phone, she rested her head against the icy glass of the phone booth as she dialed her grandmother's number.

"Gram. Lena agreed to handle the funeral arrangements."

"How long did she make you suffer before she said yes?" Rose asked.

Beth managed a slight smile. "I had to do some groveling."

"You know darn well, even if you were back in Aidan, Lena would take charge of the plans anyway," Gram responded.

"I guess." Beth's sigh was wistful as she erased several smiley faces she had doodled on the foggy glass. "I'll come over to spend the night at your house so we can leave for Aidan first thing in the morning." Beth paused to catch her breath. "Aunt Lena expects us to stay at her house. Do you mind, Gram?"

"I don't care," said Rose. "How are you feeling, dear?"

"I'm fine," she lied, not wanting to share the full extent of her fears with Gram. "I'll feel better once the funeral is over."

* * *

As Rose Brockton placed the phone onto the receiver, a sensation of impending doom settled over her. She just didn't know how to help her only granddaughter, for Beth guarded her secrets well.

Her fingers shook as she reached for a framed photo of Beth at the age of six. Even then, Beth's wistful smile did little to camouflage the sadness in her large brown eyes.

Tears blurred her vision as she glanced at a picture of her son, Joseph. What a tragedy he died twenty-four years ago in an accident overseas at the army base in Germany. He died before his baby girl was born, so he never had the chance to hold her in his arms. Rose wiped away the tears as she examined the photo. How handsome he was in his uniform. How proud he was to serve his country. Beth resembled Joe. The same dancing brown eyes. Deep brown like rich chocolate. The same wavy brown hair with a reddish cast, the color of wild chestnuts. Even her sweet personality was like Joe's. Patient and kind to a fault they were. Cut from the same mold. Rose was thankful Joe lived on in the daughter he never knew.

"How would Beth's life be different if you were here for her?" Rose wondered out loud as she tenderly set the photo on the table.

She opened her book in search of the spot where she'd left off.

These thoughts only raised her blood pressure. She'd learned long ago there was little she could do when Beth refused to talk about what happened the terrible night she was rushed to the hospital.

* * *

Beth stopped at her apartment long enough to grab things she'd need and was on her way to her grandmother's. The drive from Beth's apartment in Cabot's Cove to Rose's house in Pineville was short and it wasn't long before Rose greeted her at the door with a warm hug. Beth noticed the questions in Gram's hazel eyes and smiled as the familiar scent of rosemary calmed her senses.

"Beth," Gram hesitated, "is it all right to call you that now?"

Beth nodded and bit at her lower lip. "I'll have to get used to it again for a while."

"You look tired," Rose said as she took Beth's coat. "Come into the kitchen. I've fixed you dinner." As Beth was directed to have a seat at the kitchen table, it was clear Rose would not be denied. "Just look at you! You're so thin."

Beth rolled her eyes, but smiled at Rose's ability to fuss. It was what Beth expected and adored most about her grandmother. Beth watched while Rose heated her meal on the same stove Beth remembered as a small child. Her heart swelled as she realized Rose was the only stability in her life. Always predictable, always a pillar of strength. Rose's white hair was fashioned in the short curly style she'd worn as long as Beth could remember. Her pink chenille robe had the same ancient bare spots at the elbow. The robe had been a gift from Beth's father years before and she knew Rose would never part with such a cherished possession. Finally, the scent of chicken with dumplings invaded her senses.

Not able to resist the pleasures of Gram's cooking, she shoved a spoonful to her mouth and then another.

Rose watched with mixed emotions. "Good Lord, child! When was the last time you had a decent meal?" she demanded.

Beth shrugged, but couldn't answer as she ate the meal with delight. She smiled while Gram lectured and placed a pot of tea on the table along with a plate of freshly baked oatmeal cookies.

"You should be ashamed of yourself." Rose glared while shaking a teaspoon at her. "You shouldn't neglect your heath."

Beth remained undaunted by Gram's scolding as she nibbled on a cookie. "I'm fine," she said and looked out of the window at light flakes of snow.

Gram laid a hand on Beth's arm. "I don't mean to nag, but I'm so darned worried about you all the time."

Beth gave her a quick hug. "I know, Gram, and I do appreciate your concern."

Gram poured two cups of tea, passed the cream and sugar to Beth. "Are you dating anyone these days?" she asked with a twinkle in her eyes.

Beth lowered her gaze as she stirred her tea. "I haven't met anyone I want to date."

"Could you describe the type of man you think you might be interested in? Does he even exist?"

Beth looked away, afraid the pain in her heart would be transparent. At one time she had the perfect man and could describe him to the last detail. Now her heart was filled with a painful void.

Rose patted her hand. "When you meet the man you are meant to be with forever, you'll know." She sipped her tea. "How are you dealing with your mother's death?"

Beth's mind flashed with confusion. "I don't know how to feel," she said with a touch of contempt. "I can't stop thinking this is another way for her to punish me."

"You don't need to feel ashamed. No one would blame you if you didn't attend the funeral, Beth."

Rose squeezed her hand.

Beth stood to clear the dishes from the table to change the subject of the conversation.

"Have you heard anything from Aunt Lily and Samantha?" The last reserve of her strength slipped away when she thought of her baby so far away. Although it was a comfort to know Samantha was safe with Rose's sister in Maine, she felt a constant emptiness because she hadn't seen her daughter since her birth.

"I talked to Lily last week. Your baby is fine." Rose reached to hold Beth when she saw tears well in her eyes. "When are you going to tell me what happened? It's not right you're apart from your child."

A raw grief overwhelmed Beth and she allowed Rose to hold her close. "I'm sorry, Gram. It's all I can do to keep her safe. I won't let anything happen to her."

Rose dabbed her eyes with a tissue and handed one to Beth. "I wish you'd let me help."

Beth squeezed Rose and turned to wash the dishes before she retired to her father's bedroom.

Once inside, she leaned against the wall to appreciate the familiarity of the surroundings which had always been a safe haven for her. She searched the familiar bookshelves cluttered with the treasures from her dad's youth. A little league baseball trophy was exactly in the spot she remembered, there was his well-worn catcher's mitt and an autographed hockey puck. Beth reached for a dog-eared copy of a super hero comic book and cradled it against her. A comforting reassurance embraced her as if her father's presence was alive in his belongings and although she never met him, she always felt a connection to him her whole life. If only he could help her face the uncertainties of what was yet to come.

* * *

When Beth insisted they drive a rental car to Aidan, Rose stared at her granddaughter curiously, but thought it wise not to ask questions.

The three-hour drive was uncomfortably quiet. As each passing mile brought them closer to their destination, the more tension filled the car.

"You're going to explode if you continue to keep everything bottled up inside," Rose said. Beth gripped the steering wheel and continued to drive in silence. "Honey, please talk to me."

Beth glanced at Rose and lifted her chin stubbornly. "We've been over this before, Gram. It's best you don't know."

"Just tell me why you left Aidan. Tell me what you're hiding from."

Beth felt trapped from the weight of secrets, but swallowed the bitter taste when she saw the hurt in Gram's eyes. "I'll get through this week. You can help by keeping Aunt Lena from turning the funeral into a grand social event. I'd like to keep it simple, make an appearance and leave town as quietly as possible."

Rose disguised a chuckle with a cough. "You know Lena. You're asking me to do the impossible." She offered Beth a stick of gum. "I'll be glad to keep Lena under control if you promise to let me know if you run into any problems." She stared at Beth with conviction. "I mean it. If anyone bothers you, I want to know."

A smile touched the corner of Beth's lips. She was sure her Gram could take on the largest of foes, but there was no way Beth would involve her. She squeezed Gram's hand to appease her. "I promise."

CHAPTER TWO

"This is the right exit, but I'd swear we took a wrong turn." Beth stared in amazement at several new buildings which lined Main Street. "I hardly recognize anything."

Gram shrugged. "Honey, the last time I was here, I picked you up to visit Lily in Maine when you were ten." Gram frowned as if deep in thought.

"I loved that trip. We saw the ocean and whales and I loved the small shops in the harbor towns." As Beth drove by the bar where her mother worked on the outskirts of town, she looked the other way and barely managed to fend off waves of nausea. As they approached the town of Aidan, she focused all effort to fight the irresistible urge to turn the car around and head back to Cabot's Cove.

"I can get through this," she muttered in an attempt to give her sagging spirits a mental pep talk. She noticed a look of concern on Gram's face. "What is it, Gram? You look like I'm going to break into a million pieces."

"Well, aren't you?"

"No. I just need to get used to all the changes. Everything will be fine," she repeated, trying to convince herself as much as Gram.

"Oh, really? Then why are you as pale as a ghost?" Gram questioned.

"I'm tired. It's going to be hard."

At Aunt Lena's house, Rose and Beth removed the suitcase from the trunk.

"Leave mine, Gram."

Rose looked at Beth with a puzzled expression. "You aren't thinking of going back home and leaving me stranded here with Lena, are you?"

Beth completely missed the twinkle in Gram's eyes and remarked defensively, "Of course not." She shut the trunk. "I think it would be better if I didn't stay here." Beth nervously stared at the suitcase to avoid Gram's gaze. It was impossible to explain that if someone threatened her, she didn't want Gram involved.

"What's the real reason, Beth?"

"Please don't ask," was all Beth could offer in response.

Rose released an exasperated sigh. "I know from past experience that arguing with you is a futile waste of time."

Lena welcomed them at the door as she hugged Beth and smiled at Rose. "It's been such a long time, Rose! Let me see," she paused, "the last time I saw you. . ." She stopped mid-sentence and searched Rose's face.

"I remember it well, Lena. The less said the better," replied Rose with a warning tone.

As Lena picked up the suitcase, Beth studied her aunt's petite form. Although Lena was pretty, her harsh features made her appear cold and untouchable.

"Come in and let me show you to your room." Lena led them down the hall to the guest bedroom and set the bag on one of the twin beds. "I hope you don't mind sharing a room. I'm in the process of changing the other bedroom into an office."

Uneasiness filled Beth as she glanced at Rose then faced her aunt. "Only Gram will be staying here. I've booked a room at the motel for myself." She turned to avoid Lena's glare.

Lena followed Beth to the living room. "I was hoping you'd spend the time here."

"I'll spend most of my time here," Beth assured her. "We can still visit." Lena placed her hands on her hips and appeared as if she had more to say about the subject, but stiffly announced lunch was ready.

Seated at the table, Lena passed a basket of warm rolls to Rose.

Beth fidgeted in her seat and thought of how to break the silence by approaching the subject they'd avoided so far. "What was the cause of death?" she asked as a cold knot formed in her stomach.

"Evidently your mother's heart was damaged from years of alcohol abuse." She paused and inhaled an unsteady breath. "Linda never let anyone know how sick she was." Lena looked away from the table as her eyes glistened with tears.

"What arrangements need to be done, Lena? Beth and I are here to help now," said Rose with a note of sympathy.

"We need to be at Sawyer's Funeral Home by six-thirty for visitation this evening. I scheduled a short memorial service for tomorrow from one to two o'clock. There won't be a traditional funeral. Linda wanted to be cremated."

Beth set her fork on the table and twisted her hands together, no longer able to eat.

"Are you alright, Beth?" asked Lena. Beth wasn't able to form any words around the lump in her throat, so she shook her head. "If you object to the cremation, you need to call Mr. Sawyer right now to make other arrangements."

"No, whatever Mom wanted," she said softly.

Lena reached forward to hold Beth's hand. "If you want to say good-bye, we can rush over there right now before. . ."

Beth shuddered, imaging the effects alcohol and illness must have had on her mother. "I don't need to see her." Too abruptly, Beth removed her hand from Lena's and checked her watch. "It's going to be a long day, so I'd like to settle in at the motel before this evening." Beth stood to clear the dishes.

Rose took the plates from her. "You go ahead and try to get some rest. I'll take care of this. It will give me something to do."

Beth smiled at Gram's tender words. "I will." She hugged her grandmother close. "I'm glad you're here."

Lena joined Beth at the door and held out a card. "This is the number of the attorney who is handling the estate. You need to call him right away to confirm an appointment at one o'clock the day after tomorrow."

Beth read the information on the card that stated,

Stephen A. Wittford

Attorney and Counselor at Law.

"His office is on Market Street across from the hardware store." Lena glanced at Beth and searched her face.

"Thanks, Aunt Lena. I'll call from the motel."

As Beth drove the few miles to the motel located by the interstate, she wondered how she'd be able to make it through the remainder of the visit. If only she could manage to catch her breath without the heaviness which tended to manifest itself into full blown hysteria.

Beth checked into her room, dropped her suitcase and fell onto the bed. She drifted in and out of a light, troubled sleep and struggled to be free from the worry about events yet to come. If only for a few precious moments.

* * *

Sam Andrews ripped open a box of one-quart paint cans and proceeded to rotate the stock on the shelf. As usual, his imagination was taking him to places far from his father's hardware store.

"Hey, Sam. Come here and read this."

Sam set down the can and joined his father, John Andrews, at the counter where he was talking with two other local merchants.

Sam took the newspaper from his father's outstretched hand. "Did you read the paper today, Sam?" asked Bob Dobson.

Sam shook his head as he scanned the print. When his attention rested on the name Linda McCray Brockton, he folded the paper in half and handed it to his dad without reading the details of the obituary. "I know all about it," he said and turned away to resume the task of stacking the merchandise on the shelves.

"What's the matter with him?" Bob asked John, his voice loud enough for Sam to hear.

Sam scowled as he lined the cans on the shelf with more force than was necessary and felt three sets of eyes watch him in silence. Then Bob continued the conversation. "It sure is a shame Linda Brockton drank herself into the grave."

"Yeah, a damn shame. Remember what a looker she was in high school?" asked Jim Finch, as he inhaled deeply to suck in his rotund mid-section. "She was never the same after Joe Brockton died in a helicopter accident in Germany."

Bob nudged Jim. "Don't tell me you had the hots for the prom queen, too." Bob ran his fingers through his thinning gray hair and straightened his grubby sweatshirt.

"Well sure I did. Just like every other guy in town."

Sam rolled his eyes and coughed back a laugh as he watched the middle-aged men suddenly transform into overgrown adolescents at the mention of Linda Brockton's name. He regarded his dad's tall, fit frame and thick silver hair. Even still, John removed his reading glasses, squinted and held the newspaper at arm's length to read the details of the service. "It says visitation is from seven to eight-thirty at Sawyer's."

Sam found it impossible to tune out the conversation, so he headed for the office at the rear of the store to refill his coffee.

"What ever happened to Linda's daughter? She seemed to disappear from sight.

Jim called out to Sam, "Did you ever find out where Beth Brockton is at?"

Sam didn't turn to face them, but kept walking toward the office and mumbled something incoherent in reply.

"What's the matter, Sammy? Still carrying a torch for her?" asked Bob.

Sam stopped so fast, cold coffee spilled over the edge of the cup and dripped onto his work boots. He gritted his teeth before he turned to face the guys. "Not a chance. I haven't seen her in almost two years."

"No one has seen her for two years," said Bob. "I'll bet you're looking forward to meeting up with her again." Bob snickered like a schoolboy and nudged Jim.

"I don't think she'll show up for the funeral," said John with a worried look at Sam. "Seems like she left for good."

"I think your right, Dad," Sam said and set the coffee cup on the counter. Suddenly the thought of coffee on his grumbling stomach didn't sound like a great idea.

"I wonder why she left town so suddenly in the first place," said Jim. "It's odd she's never been back, especially as sick as her mother has been the last six months."

"You know what the gossip is about her, don't you?" added Bob. Jim shrugged and John continued to glace at Sam. "Her mother finally pushed Beth over the edge and she's now a permanent resident of Haverhill Institution."

John discounted the rumor with a wave of his hand. "You don't believe that crap, do you?"

"I don't know what to believe. Like I said, it's a real mystery why she vanished without a trace. Her Aunt Lena doesn't even know where she is."

Sam shrugged his shoulders in an attempt to loosen the forming knots. Just the thought of Beth brought back memories better left forgotten. He ignored a familiar sinking feeling in his chest to make a real effort to sound bored with the whole subject and casually shrugged as if her appearance didn't matter one bit. "Yeah, my guess is she won't show up at all."

* * *

When Beth, Rose and Lena entered the reception room at Sawyer's Funeral Home, Lena sighed deeply and dabbed her eyes with a tissue. "Just look at all the beautiful flowers!" she gushed and plucked a card from the largest floral arrangement. Rose followed Lena, but her attention was drawn to Beth who paced at the entrance. "This one is from the Kowalski Family with their thoughts and prayers." Lena turned to Rose. "They run the grocery store over by the highway into town."

"That's nice." Rose was still distracted watching Beth, who stared out of the window. "Beth, what are you looking for?"

"It's snowing harder now. Look at how pretty everything looks with a blanket of snow."

"Hmm," Lena paused, "don't you think it's odd this card isn't signed?" Beth focused her attention to the card Lena referred to. "It was attached to this bouquet," she said and pointed to a vase filled with delicate pink roses.

Beth didn't need to look at the card to know who sent the flowers. She examined the card and read the familiar handwriting and the neatly written words; *You are in my thoughts forever.* She gulped back a sob, clutched the note against her chest and rushed from the room.

When she was safely behind the closed door in the rest room, she fought back tears, afraid if she began to cry, she might never stop. She reread the card and the hidden meaning of the words ripped at her heart. "Oh, Sam," she whispered.

The first of the visitors had already arrived when Beth rejoined Rose. "I don't recognize most of these people, Gram."

Rose leaned over. "You know how small-town folk are," she whispered. "They show up because they don't want to be the main topic of conversation."

"For once I'm glad Lena likes to be the center of attention." Beth stepped back and deferred the socializing to her aunt.

Lena motioned for her to join her. "You know the Wilson's, Beth? They live across the street from me."

Beth smiled politely. "Yes, of course." She hoped her tone was convincing. It seemed as if she'd been away for an eternity.

She glanced at her watch. Thank heavens only a short time remained. She felt less shaky and the throbbing in her head eased a bit. Maybe this wouldn't be so hard to endure after all.

In an instant, the false sense of calm shattered the moment Sam Andrews entered the room with his older sister, Suzanne, and her husband, Jack Walsh.

Beth felt the room spin and she fought to focus her attention on the Wilson's.

Rose leaned over and whispered, "You look like you're going to pass out. Why don't you sit down?"

"I'm okay," she murmured. Her stomach muscles tightened and her mouth felt so dry she was afraid her lips would crack.

Suzy Walsh was the first to greet her. "I'm so sorry about your mom, Beth," she said. "But I'm glad you finally made it home so we know you're alive!"

Suzy was the picture of perfection. She had flawless, olive completion, which was accented by her thick brown hair. Beth's gaze lingered on Suzy's pregnant form. She grabbed her friend's hand, overcome with happiness. Suzy's gaze met hers. Her eyes were the deepest shade of blue accentuated by thick, dark lashes. Beth felt a smile lift the corner of her lips, yet the heaviness of regret lodged in her heart. "Look at you" Beth exclaimed and reached to hug her friend.

Suzy smiled. "Another one on the way. Can you believe it?"

Beth turned her attention to the young boy at her side. His hair was light brown, the same color of faint freckles spattered across the bridge of his nose. "This can't be Bradley," she said. "You're tall for your age." She knelt down and smiled at the child. "You look just like your dad."

"Bradley, do you remember Beth?" Sara asked. "She and Uncle Sam let you tag along everywhere with them." Bradley moved close to his mom and looked down at his shoes.

Beth felt her smile waver, finding it impossible to hide her sadness.

"You'd better not leave town again without saying goodbye," Suzy whispered as she hugged her. "Stop by the house latter so we can talk. Everyone's been worried sick about you."

Jack stepped over and pulled Beth into a crushing hug, which swept her off her feet. "It's about time you showed up around here, Lizzie."

She smiled at Jack's good-natured teasing. "You know how the nickname bothers me." She paused to gaze at him affectionately. "But right now it sounds like heaven."

Jack released her. "Where have you been hiding yourself?' he asked, his tone no longer teasing.

As if seeing it for the first time, his police uniform stood out and reminded her to be wary. Beth felt her cheek's flush. "I. . .well. . .," she stammered. She stared at Jack's stern expression and struggled for an answer. Her gaze rested on his shiny badge, then to the gun in his holster and she turned away.

"I need to talk to you before you leave town again," he stated formally. His voice grew distant, replaced by the buzzing sound of panic.

Beth fought to control her voice. "Why? Is there a problem?"

"This isn't the place to talk. I'll catch up with you later."

Why did he need to talk to her? What could he possibly know? Beth wanted to grab him, but when she reached out to stop him it was too late. Jack stepped away leaving her alone with Sam.

At over six foot tall, Sam had always towered over her, but standing before her, his presence seemed larger than life. She felt nothing but the burning sensation of Sam's gaze upon her. She attempted to run, but she was frozen. She glanced down when tears stung her eyes.

"Hello, Beth." His deep voice caused her heart to beat erratically. When he leaned forward, electricity radiated between them. "You still smell like a fresh spring morning," he whispered.

Beth's chest tightened. She backed away from him slightly. She needed distance and air to fill her lungs.

"Hi," she barely managed. His unrelenting gaze continued to hold her captive. Her body stiffened as she stared at his broad chest and fought the urge to crumble against him, to fall into his warm, protective arms and close the world away.

When he took her hand, she felt a shiver travel deep within her. Did he feel it, too?

"You're cold." He slowly lifted her hand to his lips and kissed the ruby ring he had given to her the day she graduated from college. "I'm surprised you still wear this ring." A note of sarcasm hung on each word.

Beth stared at the contrast of his strong hand cradled around hers and bit her lower lip to stop the trembling. Sam traced his thumb along her chin and her skin burned beneath his touch. Still, she was powerless to move. He pulled her closer until she felt warmth radiate from his body.

"Beth, can't you look at me?" His words were soft, but she easily detected the undertone of bitterness. She didn't answer as a fat tear spilled down her cheek and splattered on her wrist. "Everyone is watching."

Suddenly aware of her surroundings, she scanned the eerily quiet room. Most of the visitors watched the young couple.

Sam placed his finger under her chin and gently guided her face until her gaze met his. Nothing in her wildest dreams could have prepared her for the impact of seeing the hurt and bitterness etched upon his handsome face. His deep blue eyes normally sparkled with warmth and humor, but were now cold and accusing. He wore his dark hair longer, but it only enhanced his roguish good looks. She pulled her hand free from his grasp to keep from reaching out to touch him and cursed under her breath. "Sam. . . "

The hush of her tone carried the sound to Sam's ears only. She forced herself to turn away, the spell of the moment broken. She gathered what little courage she possessed and rushed past the people who closely watched her disappear from the room.

Once more, she sought the solitude of the ladies' room where she splashed cold water onto a paper towel and applied it to her burning face. Why did it hurt so much to breathe? She scolded herself for almost losing her grip and stepped into a stall to grab some tissue paper to wipe her eyes. She placed her hand on her chest to calm the beating of her heart so she could catch her breathe.

Interrupted by the clinking sound of the door lock, she stepped out to see who joined her in the room.

When the lights went out, her heart lurched to her throat and she knew instinctively who was in the room.

"Have you changed your mind and finally come to your senses about us, Beth?"

In the darkness, Beth covered her mouth with her hand to keep from screaming. A strangled cry escaped her lips as she was grabbed from behind and slammed against the wall. "No!" she gasped.

"I thought you and I made a deal."

His hand around her neck squeezed tight. She was trapped between the wall and his body pressed against the length of her. When she raised her knee to connect with his groin, she heard the sharp click of a gun and felt the coolness of metal pressed to the side of her face.

He whispered into her ear. "Did you come back because you missed me, darling?" The combination of his warm breath and the familiar, sickening scent of after-shave revolted her. "Do you need a little reminder of what happened the last time you refused me?"

Frantically, she shook her head. When he crushed her against the wall once more, she cried out. "I'll be gone in two days. I'm not staying."

"Shut up!" His grip tightened around her throat. "If I find out you've talked to anyone, I swear I'll kill you this time for sure." Roughly, he spun her to face him. In the small amount of light that filtered from under the door, she barely made out his menacing handsome features.

" I haven't told anyone." She felt faint from lack of air and pushed at his hands.

He traced his finger down her tear-stained cheek and stopped at her lips. "You better keep your word. I don't want you screwing things up."

Beth closed her eyes and prayed she would wake from this nightmare. "I had to come back for the funeral. Even you should understand." She lifted her chin and met his icy stare.

Roughly, he kissed her, but she pushed him away. When he held her against him, she knew her stiff resistance only fueled his fury. "You know the only reason you're alive is because of me, don't you?"

She forced down the bile which rose from her stomach and left a nasty taste in her mouth. "I want you gone by tomorrow." He jolted her roughly to emphasize each word. "Do you understand?"

"Yes."

As he looked into her eyes, a cruel smile twisted across his lips. "That is," he paused, "unless you choose to stay under the terms I offered before."

Beth's fear was heightened by repulsion, but she said nothing while he observed her. "I could easily crush the contempt from your face." He released her and stepped to the door. "I'll be watching."

As the door closed, she wilted to the floor and hugged her knees tight against her.

* * *

Rose searched for Beth after the last of the visitors departed. She opened the door to the rest room and discovered her weeping softly. She extended her hands and helped Beth to her feet.

"What did the young man say to you?" Beth wiped her eyes.

"What man?"

"The one you were talking to before you left the room in such a hurry. Sam Andrews." Rose studied her skeptically.

"Nothing important. Really, Gram. I want to go home."

"You won't sleep any better at the motel all alone, will you?"

Beth looked at her grandmother blankly, the effects of the day had diminished all of her strength.

Rose took Beth by the arm and marched her out of the room. "Come with me. You're staying at Lena's house tonight."

Beth began to protest, but Rose wasn't going to allow it. "I don't want to hear one word of argument," she insisted.

CHAPTER THREE

Bradley studied his grandfather's next move on the chessboard. His eyebrows almost touched from the deep furrow that marred his eight-year-old face. "Come on, Grandpa! I didn't mean to move the rook there."

John Andrews hid a smile from his grandson. "Well, kiddo, you're getting much too good at this game for me to cut you any slack." He scooped the captured chess piece from the board.

Sam glanced over and chuckled. It wasn't long ago he was Brad's age and played chess with his dad at the same table. He turned his attention back to the television. He felt restless and couldn't concentrate on the weekly comedy his sister and mom watched.

"I think Beth looked sad and lonely tonight," said Suzy during a commercial break.

"Hmm, maybe." Sam opened the newspaper and scanned the sports section to check on the stats of the Detroit Red Wings.

"Well, she's been away for so long, I suppose she has a right to look out of place." Helen Andrews looked up from her needlepoint. "What did Beth have to say to you, Sam?"

He glanced over the top of the paper. "Not much," he said and continued to lose himself behind the paper as he reread the same paragraph for the third time.

"Come on, Sam!" Suzy pleaded. "Tell us what she said. Did she say why she left town?" She grabbed the paper then grinned at his look of disgust. "I'm being noisy, but I really want to know. It's all such a mystery."

He clenched his lips tightly. "It's hard to be mad at you when you have the decency to admit you're such a pain." Being two years his senior, she had always played the bossy older sister to perfection. He tapped the tip of her nose with his finger and stood to reach for his coat. "You know about as much as I do, Suz. You talked to her longer than I did."

Suzy smiled. "It was so obvious you two are still in love,"

While he slipped on his coat, he stopped at the table where Dad and Bradley were deep in the throngs of battle. "You'd better be on your toes, Dad. Brad will be beating you before long." Sam playfully tousled his nephew's hair.

John peered over the top of his glasses at Sam. "You know Brad, it's been so long since your Uncle Sam and I played chess, he's probably afraid he won't remember how."

Sam grinned. "I can still give you a run for your money anytime, Dad."

"Where are you off to?" asked his mother.

"I'm meeting some friends. I'll be late."

As he walked to his car, Sam inhaled deep to fill his lungs with the cold, night air. Behind the wheel of his car, he gazed at the canny glow the moon cast over the houses on the street. A few doors down, Christmas lights already twinkled at the Emerson's house. He shook his head. It wasn't even Thanksgiving.

He hadn't planned to meet his buddies at the bar, but too many questions about Beth were making him feel claustrophobic. His lack of resistance to hold her at the funeral home left a nasty taste in his mouth. Didn't he have any self-respect? Hell, it took him so long to bury his feelings for her, only to have them dredged up the moment he saw her. He didn't need this distraction. Not when he was finally on the verge of moving his life forward in a positive direction. He was almost twenty-seven years old for God's sake! He'd been hampered with too many setbacks to allow anything else to put a wedge between the goals he'd set.

He increased the volume on the radio, wanting nothing more than to drive away all thoughts of Beth. He hit the steering wheel with his fisted hand and cursed the ill-fated timing of her return.

In a few months he'd be on his own in some big city. His dreams of climbing the corporate ladder, fighting for environmental issues were almost within sight.

Again, he attempted to erase the image of her sad, beautiful face and stepped on the gas pedal to head out of town. Suddenly the idea of having a few beers with his friends sounded damn good.

* * *

The next morning, when Beth discovered Rose and Lena were still asleep, she jotted a quick note to let them know when she'd pick them up for the service.

She drove around town several times, backtracked and turned until she was sure no one followed.

Once she was locked inside her motel room, she called the lawyer's office, but was told by the receptionist she couldn't change her appointment.

"Isn't there some way you can make an exception in my case? I must leave town tonight." Beth refrained from screaming into the phone.

"Mr. Wittford's schedule is full today and he has court all afternoon. I'm sorry, but it's not possible."

After she hung up, Beth mulled over the list of documents the receptionist asked her to bring to the appointment. How could she step foot in her mother's house to retrieve them?

She showered, quickly dressed in jeans and a sweatshirt and towel dried her hair.

Over coffee in Lena's kitchen, she shared the list with her aunt and Gram. "I don't have a clue where these papers are, do you?"

Lena studied the list. "No, but I'm sure the lawyer can help you get copies if needed."

Beth sighed and felt her patience wear thin. "I need everything today. I'm leaving right after I meet with the lawyer."

Lena refilled her coffee. "I don't know why you're in such a rush to leave. You can stay a few more days to take care of everything."

Beth stared at her aunt. "No. I can't."

Lena's face was flushed when she faced Beth. "Look, I'm not going to get stuck with the expense of the funeral and the hassle of selling the house so you can benefit from it. Do you understand?"

Beth's mouth dropped open. She wanted to laugh at the ridiculous notion. "I don't want anything from the sale of the house. I'll sign everything over tomorrow, but these documents are needed first.

As if she were thinking over the idea, Lena was silent for a few moments. "Well, I guess if that's the case . . ."

Beth turned to Gram with a sense of urgency. "We have three hours until the service. Will you please come with me to the house? I need to get this over with."

Gram stood up to place the coffee mugs into the sink. "I'll be glad to help," she said with ice in her tone as she glared at Lena. "I need a change of scenery anyway."

At the door, Lena handed the house keys to Beth. "The house is a mess. I don't know how you're going to find anything."

In the driveway of her old home, Beth's mouth was suddenly dry and the palms of her hands were clammy. She turned and took Gram's hand. "Let's get started. We won't accomplish anything sitting here thinking about it."

Beth's hand shook so badly, she couldn't fit the key into the lock, so Rose took the keys and the door swung open. Gram stepped inside first while Beth reluctantly followed. "Wow! This sure is a mess."

Beth pulled her jacket up to cover her nose and mouth. The musty scent of sickness soured the coffee in her stomach. She scanned the living room. "I wonder if anything has been cleaned since I was last here." She hesitated in the hallway. "I suppose we should start searching in the spare bedroom upstairs. That's where Mom kept all the bills and paperwork."

Beth moved toward the stairs, but abruptly came to a stop.

Rose nearly bumped into her, and then stepped in front of her to coax her along. "Come on, honey. I'll go first. There's nothing to be afraid of now."

Beth's gaze followed the steps to the top of the landing. "I can't do this, Gram. I can't go up there." Her eyes felt as wide as saucers.

"I don't have the faintest idea what you want me to look for. You have to come with me," Gram insisted.

Beth slowly took one step up, then another. Her heart pounded relentlessly the closer she approached the top of the stairs. She gripped the guardrail, managed another step and frowned to focus on Gram's face.

For a flash of an instant, it wasn't Gram she saw guiding her up the stairs. It was someone else's face. He dragged her up the stairs, his eyes full of rage and drunken madness. She saw Gram's lips move, but the thundering of her heartbeat smothered the words. Shear panic drove her away from Rose and down the steps. She ran outside and leaned over the porch rail to catch her breath. Gram stepped next to her and tenderly placed an arm around Beth's trembling body.

"It's no use. I can't go up there." Beth wiped beads of sweat from her forehead with the sleeve of her coat.

Gram led her from the house. "Let's sit in the car to keep warm while we think of something."

Gram turned the key in the ignition while Beth rested her spinning head against the passenger seat. "Hand me the list," said Rose. "You stay here while I try to find these papers."

In no condition to protest, Beth watched the door close behind her grandmother. She flipped through the radio stations to distract her thoughts. Again, she closed her eyes to concentrate on John Legend's voice as he crooned a lonely ballad about love lost. She switched the dial, in need of something more upbeat and settled on the traffic and news channel. She breathed in and out to focus on relaxing her tense muscles and nearly jumped a foot when the car door opened.

"That didn't take long. . ." She was startled to discover Jack seated next to her. "Hi, Lizzie. What's going on?"

She frowned and turned away from him. "I'm waiting while my grandmother looks for something in the house." Out of the corner of her eye, Beth noticed how intense Jack's gaze was. "Is this an official investigation?"

Jack shook his head. "I'm off duty. Unless you have something to hide." She fidgeted in her seat but couldn't meet his gaze. "What's wrong, Beth?"

"I have a headache." Her eyes squinted against the glare of the sun's reflection off the snow.

"You look like you're scared out of your mind." His face registered concern.

"I'm also tired of questions."

He continued to watch her. His jaw set with determination. "It must be hard to come back home after all this time."

She didn't reply as she again searched for a radio station.

"Why did you leave in the first place?" he asked and rested his arm on the seat behind her.

"I don't want to talk about it. Okay?" She searched his worried face and felt her own determination falter.

"Whether you believe it or not, some of us care enough about you to ask why you walked out of our lives without a trace."

"Jack, I'm not going to talk about it."

"Come on, Lizzie. You used to tell me everything." She couldn't resist a smile and his grin deepened.

She stifled the urge to purge her mind from every tormented detail. "Why are you bugging me?" she asked.

"Because I'm good at it." He flashed another smile. "It's a great trait to have as a cop."

Beth bit her lower lip. "I bet you are a good cop. I'm happy you're doing what you dreamed of." She blinked back tears that stung her eyes.

When she looked out of the window, she discovered a parked car down the street with a dark figure sitting inside. Beth tried to hide the instant wave of nausea. "Jack, could you go up to the house and tell my grandmother we need to hurry?" She glanced at her watch. "It's getting late."

"Why can't you go into the house, Beth?" His smile faded to a scowl. "Why are you so pale and why are you shaking?"

"I told you I have a headache." Once again, she watched the car as it approached slowly. "Please hurry, Jack."

He stepped out of the car but bent over to look at her. "I'm not done bugging you yet, you know."

Jack made his way to the front door and Beth held her breath as the car passed by, continued to move slow to the end of the street and then disappeared around the corner. Her breath came out in a long unsteady sigh. She watched Jack disappear into the house.

"Damn it!" She jumped out of the car after him. The last thing she wanted was for Jack to go snooping around the house. He was on a mission and who knows what he might find. She rushed up the steps to open the door.

"Gram," she called out, "we need to get moving." Jack and Gram appeared at the top of the stairs.

"We have plenty of time yet, Beth. So far I've found two of the four papers you need." Gram held up file. "Your friend has offered to help me sort through everything."

"Great," Beth muttered and reached for the door. "Just great."

"Go wait in the car. This won't take much longer with the two of us." Gram called out.

Beth stepped onto the porch once more, cursed the taut control, the dread and fear had on her. She wasn't normally the skittish type and it grated on her nerves she felt so vulnerable. She sat on the step and rested her head on her knees to concentrate on her breathing.

* * *

Rose sorted through one box, while Jack tackled another. He surveyed the room for anything out of the ordinary. What he was searching for he wasn't quite certain, but something in this house had

Beth acting peculiar enough to tweak his cop intuition. After he sorted through the papers, he placed everything back inside the box. "I didn't find the house deed in any of those boxes, Mrs. Brockton. I'll check out the other rooms. Maybe papers are stashed somewhere else."

Rose smiled over the top of her glasses. "Thanks for helping out, Jack." Jack entered the first room he came to, which was the bathroom.

He noticed the faded, discolored floral wallpaper curled at the edges and the rusted tub. He found the vanity drawers jammed with makeup and dirty hairbrushes. The cupboard under the sink was stocked with cleaning supplies and toiletries. He found nothing out of the ordinary in the linen closet.

On to the next room, he turned the doorknob only to discover the door was warped shut. With a quick step, he rammed the door to open it with a loud bang. The room was dark and musty. When he turned on the light, he smiled at the row of stuffed animals on the shelf above the bed. He knew this was Beth's room. His smile faded when he discovered the walls and dresser riddled with holes. The dresser mirror was shattered into hundreds of pieces, each glistening like diamonds on the dresser and surrounding carpet. He inspected a hole in the wall and concluded the cause was from the impact of a bullet.

He picked up a framed photograph, broken and shredded. He folded what remained of the photo and tucked it into his jacket pocket. He felt a sudden chill in the room as a wariness settled over him. Something alarming occurred in the room. Something so dreadful it drove Beth away two years ago. He was determined to discover exactly what that something was.

The sound of Beth's grandmother calling from the other room disrupted his thoughts. Impulsively, he unlatched the window lock and opened the pane a few inches before he stepped from the room.

"What did you say, Mrs. Brockton?" he said as he secured the door behind him.

Rose met him in the hall and waved several papers. "I found all the documents."

Jack helped her return the boxes to the closet. "Thank you again, Jack, I'm sure this will be a huge relief for Beth."

"It was my pleasure," Jack said as he touched the tattered photo in his pocket.

Together they descended the stairs and found Beth seated on the porch steps.

"You'll catch a cold sitting out here," Rose scolded.

Jack walked them to the car and crouched down to address Beth. "I still need to talk to you before you leave."

He caught the tentative flash in her eyes before she averted her gaze. She looked ahead to avoid his stare.

"Good bye, Jack," Rose called out.

Jack watched the car slowly move down the street. He turned his attention to the house and started at the dark window of Beth's bedroom. Deep in thought, he walked toward his house a few blocks away. Why did she leave without telling anyone what had happened? Why was she terrified to enter her own house? Could someone he knew be involved in whatever happened to make her run away? The questions continued to plague him as he tuned up his collar to shield the bitter wind. In the gray, dreary sky, he sensed the beginning of an early winter storm.

* * *

From the cluttered office of the hardware store, Suzy called out to Sam. "I made a fresh pot of coffee. Want a cup?"

"Sure," answered Sam as he unpacked a new shipment of tools that arrived at the store that morning.

Suzy brought Sam the coffee. He smiled after taking a sip. "Thanks. This is great."

Suzy positioned herself on top of a large box. "So, have you decided whether you're going to Linda Brockton's service?"

A cold knot formed in his stomach and he set the coffee on the desk. "I'm not sure."

"Why not? Mom and I think you should go."

Sam unpacked the remaining hammers, but didn't want to give her an answer.

"At least you can attend for Beth," Suzy said. "I think she needs you there."

Annoyed, Sam felt his lips tighten as he spun around. "I don't owe her a damn thing. I'll probably go to the service, but it won't be for her sake!" He made a feeble attempt to control his temper, but his blood pressure was another matter.

"Okay! Geez, I'm only trying to help."

Sam detected the hurt in her voice and felt like a jerk. "I didn't mean to bite your head off. I'm just tired of everyone trying to make something more out of the situation."

"I understand how you feel, Sam." She stood and squeezed his arm. "Probably better than you do."

When the front door swung open, the entrance bell rang and a blast of frigid air followed Jack into the store. "Man, it's freezing out there." He rubbed his hands together and smiled as Suzy walked to greet him. He gave her a quick kiss. "I thought you'd be home getting ready for the service."

She looked at the saw shaped clock on the wall behind the counter. "I didn't realize how late it is." She grabbed her coat and purse and waved. "I'll see you there, Sam."

An acute sense of emptiness overcame Sam as the bell announced their departure.

* * *

In the reception room at Sawyer's Funeral Home, Beth listened as Father Kenner eulogized her mother. Surely, his kind words were meant for someone else.

Her gaze lingered a moment on Sam's hard stare, but she abruptly looked away.

As the service came to an end with a final prayer, Beth closed her eyes and whispered a prayer of thanks the service was finally over. She jumped to her feet with a surge of energy, knowing she could keep her composure intact until the last of the well-meaning visitors departed.

Mr. Sawyer, the funeral director, stood in the center of the room to make a final announcement. "The Brockton-McCray families would like to thank you for attending the service. Lena McCray has extended an invitation to join the family and friends for a luncheon at her home. You will find address cards on the entrance table."

Beth's eyes opened wide in surprise as she looked at her aunt, who was busy socializing with a group of people on the opposite side of the room. Beth sought out her grandmother who already looked guilty.

"Gram, did you know about this?" Beth whispered. "I thought we were going to keep it simple."

"I didn't have anything to do with it. You know Lena better than I do. Most likely she had all the arrangements made before we arrived."

Beth muttered an oath, but smiled and braced herself against the onslaught of guests that approached to bid farewell. She glanced at the back of a petite, blond women and let out a cry when her childhood friend, Carrie Simpson, rushed to greet her. "Carrie! I can't believe it's you." Beth's eyes glazed with tears as they embraced.

"Don't you dare cry. You'll get me started." Carrie hugged her again. "I've missed you so much."

"Are you coming to my aunt's house?" asked Beth.

"Of course." Carrie smiled at Beth once more. Beth released Carrie's hand. "I'll see you there."

* * *

Beth studied the appetizing array of salads, entrees and desserts arranged buffet-style on the dining room table and wondered how Lena could possibly organize this feast on such short notice. No one had arrived yet, so she surrendered to a soft easy chair next to the fireplace. Mesmerized by the dancing orange, yellow and blue flames, she watched the fire and secretly wished no one would attend the luncheon.

Her hopes were dashed when the doorbell chimed. She slipped on her heels and joined Lena at the entrance. A tall, buxom woman stood in the foyer.

"Beth, this is Sally Cantrell. She worked with your mom at Max's Tavern." Lena said.

Sally glared at Beth and scrutinized her with obvious distain. "We've met before," Sally commented and marched past Beth.

Beth wondered what she'd ever done to provoke such a cold response from this woman. She followed the offensive scent of heavy perfume to find Sally seated on the sofa.

"Can I get you something to drink, Sally?" Lena asked.

"I'll take a beer."

Lena frowned and glanced at Beth. "I can offer you some tea or coffee."

Beth stifled a smile when she noted the disapproving look in Lena's eyes.

"Coffee's okay, with extra cream and sugar."

Beth sat across from Sally. Both women sized each other up, but neither spoke.

Lena returned and set a cup in front of Sally. "If you'll excuse me, I'm just finishing up in the kitchen."

Sally excused Lena with a wave of her hand, but didn't take her gaze from Beth. After she sipped her coffee, she broke the silence. "Your mom didn't talk about you much. She once told me you got away from this miserable little town. I got the feeling she wished she'd done the same years ago."

Beth waited for her to continue while Sally fumbled through her purse and pulled out a pack of cigarettes and a lighter. Beth searched the room for an ashtray, but knew there wasn't one in the entire house. Her eyes opened wide with surprise when Sally reached for a crystal candy dish, dumped the pastel mints onto the coffee table and flicked an ash into it. The whole time, her gaze did not leave Beth's.

"You're much thinner than I remember," Sally said with an undertone of superiority. Beth noticed how Sally puffed out her oversized bosom, as if it were a trophy, and resisted the urge to dump the coffee over Sally's head.

"Linda certainly was a strange one all right. I know the two of you weren't close. Like I said, she hardly talked about you at all."

"What did she talk about?" Beth wondered out loud.

"She always talked about things in the past she wished she had done. It seemed like she lived with a lot of regret." Sally exhaled a stream of smoke. "She never appeared happy."

Beth was relieved when Lena led Carrie into the room and announced the buffet was served. Beth watched surprise flicker in Lena's eyes as she cracked open a window and waved her hand to dissipate the smoke. Sally crushed out the cigarette in the crystal candy dish and followed Lena to the dining room.

Seated beside Beth on the sofa, Carrie waited until the others left before she spoke. "Do you realize how sick with worry everyone has been since the day you left? I've never stopped wondering what happened." Beth studied Carrie's expressive green eyes shadow with concern.

"I know you want answers to many questions, but I can't tell you anything," Beth said.

Carrie's mouth dropped open in astonishment. "I'm your best friend in the whole world. We've known each other since kindergarten. I can't believe you won't tell me anything." Carrie's eyes flashed a darker shade of green.

Beth understood Carrie's frustration. "You'd be the first person I'd talk to if I could." Beth lowered her gaze, not able to stand the hurt in Carrie's eyes.

"I don't understand all the secrecy. Something awful must have happened to make you disappear without a word to any of us." Carrie's tear-filled eyes searched Beth's.

Beth's lips trembled as she attempted a smile. "Tell me what you've been doing since college."

Carrie frowned when Beth changed the subject. "Jeff and I got married a year ago. You were supposed to be the maid of honor, remember?"

Beth flinched from one more reminder of dreams and plans gone awry. "I would have been there if I could. You know that don't you?"

"I know," said Carrie, her voice softening as she squeezed Beth's hand. "We moved to a small town in Virginia. Jeff practices at a law firm in Washington, D.C. I'm a housewife and love it. Why don't you plan a visit? Jeff would love to see you again."

Beth smiled when Carrie's face lit up with pleasure as she talked about her life. "You look happy, Carrie. I'm so glad."

"I wish you were as happy. You seem so sad." Carrie sighed. "What have you been doing these past few years? "

Beth bit her lower lip and hesitated. It was second nature to guard her life, yet she saw no harm in talking about teaching.

A few more guests trickled in, but they were Lena's friends, so Beth and Carrie spent the time reminiscing about memories they shared growing up together.

When Carrie stood to leave, she grabbed Beth and hugged her protectively. "When will we see each other again?"

Beth searched the room for a pencil and paper. "Write down your address and phone number. I promise to keep in touch."

At the door they were reluctant to say goodbye. "Sam asked me to stop by the hardware store. Do you want to come?" Carrie asked eagerly. "It would be like old times. Remember when we hung out at the store after school to flirt with Jack and Sam? I don't know how they put up with us."

Beth remembered all too well and the memories tightened around her chest like a vice. "Aunt Lena would never forgive me if I left."

She watched Carrie walk to her car before she closed the door. With a heavy heart, she passed the dining room where Lena chatted with friends. Beth was sure she wouldn't be missed, so she sought shelter in the guest room. Gram was napping, so Beth lay down and buried her face in the pillow to stifle her sobs.

* * *

Carrie entered Andrews's Hardware and found Sam busy with a customer. Smiling, he gestured toward the back of the store. "Suzanne's in the office, Carrie. I'll be right with you."

Carrie returned his smile and found her way to the office. Suzy's face lit up when Carrie entered the room. "Hi Carrie. I'll be just a minute. I need to finish this account."

Carrie glanced around the office until her gaze rested on the graduation, wedding and family photos which told a story about the Andrews's family.

Carrie watched Suzy with fondness and was instantly flooded with memories. She and Beth would imitate everything about Suzanne Andrews. After all, Suzy was sixteen when they were twelve. Suzy was dating Jack and well on her way to a life they had only begun to dream about. When Suzy styled her hair, they would follow suit. When she wore a new color of lipstick, they would do the same. At the time, the only goal they hoped to achieve was growing up to have a storybook life exactly like Suzy's.

Suzy looked up from the ledger and closed the book. "You look great, Carrie. Married life sure does agree with you."

Carrie smiled. "I love everything about my life with Jeff. How about you? How are Jack and Bradley?"

"They are fine. Our life is hectic, but I wouldn't change one thing. Bradley is eight years old and a bundle of energy. Jack works the midnight shift at the Aidan Precinct."

"I can't believe Bradley is eight already. When is your baby due?" Carrie asked with a slight note of envy in her voice.

Suzy patted her extended belly. "Not until May."

Carrie smiled wistfully. "I'm anxious to start a family, but Jeff wants to wait until everything is perfect."

Suzy laughed and rolled her eyes. "Jack and I never plan anything. We just deal with whatever comes our way."

Carrie glanced at the open door of the office and lowered her voice. "How is Sam doing? I can't quite put my finger on it, but he's different somehow."

Suzy looked at Carrie with a puzzled expression. "Of course he's changed. None of us are the same as we were in high school."

Carrie shrugged. "I stopped over to see Beth after the service. I'm really worried about her." Carrie stopped talking when she discovered Sam standing in the doorway.

"Carrie was just telling me about her visit with Beth," said Suzy as she motioned for Sam to enter the office.

Sam casually leaned against the doorframe, but appeared tense. "What did she have to say?" The intensity in his eyes clearly betrayed the indifference he attempted to portray.

"She teaches third grade elementary school. " Carrie glanced at Suzy, then Sam. "She wouldn't tell me where she's living."

"Did she give you any clues as to why she left?" asked Suzy.

Carrie shook her head. "It was perfectly clear she wouldn't talk about it."

When the entrance bell clanged, Sam moved to answer, but Suzy waved him off. "I'll take care of it," she said.

Suzy left the room and Carrie frowned when she faced Sam. "Do you think something terrible happened to Beth before she left?"

Sam's blank expression revealed no emotion. "I drove myself insane imagining every possibility. She has her reasons for leaving and they aren't my concern anymore."

His uncaring attitude aggravated Carrie further. "I don't think she can tell anyone what happened. She's in some kind of trouble. Don't you want to help?" Carrie's eyes, which silently pleaded with Sam, were filled with tears.

"I can't afford to help her. I stopped asking questions long ago," he said as he stepped to the door.

Carrie reached for his hand. "I know how frustrated you must be, but I don't understand how you can turn your back on her like this. Not when she meant so much to you."

He rested his head on the door jam and looked almost on the brink of tears himself. He took a deep breath and steadied his voice. "She's the one who turned her back, not me."

* * *

Darkness fell as Beth watched the last of the faded shadows dance on the ceiling of Lena's guestroom. She waited for the last of the visitors to depart.

Gram stirred in the next bed. "Why didn't you wake me?" Good heavens, I've slept through the luncheon." She sat at the edge of the bed and glanced at the alarm clock.

Beth ran her fingers through her mass of hair and smoothed out some of the unruly curls. "Most of the guests were Lena's friends."

"What now," Gram asked while yawning.

"We can leave tomorrow after the appointment with the lawyer."

"Do you mind if I stay a bit longer? Lena agreed to drive me home at the end of the week."

Beth looked at Gram surprised. "Why do you want to stay longer than you have to?"

Gram's voice grew soft with emotion. "When I sorted through the boxes at your mom's house, I found some of your father's belongings. I'd like to keep whatever was his."

Beth slid onto the next bed and took Gram's hand as pangs of guilt tugged at her. Had she been so immersed in her own problems that she'd forgotten how to be sympathetic? She kissed Rose on the cheek. "Of course I don't mind."

A quick rap at the door interrupted the conversation and the door swung open. "Come and eat something," Lena called out.

"Is everyone gone?" Beth asked guardedly.

"Yes. The last group to leave was from the bar where Linda worked." In the kitchen, Lena passed a plate with food to each of them. "There was a man asking about you, Beth."

Beth's heart skipped a beat and she nearly dropped the plate she held. "Who?' Her voice was barely above a whisper.

"I don't know. He arrived with the group from the bar. I didn't catch his name." Lena continued to scoop mounds of food into storage containers. "But, I have seen him in the paper before,."

"What did he want?" No longer hungry, Beth set the plate on the counter.

"He didn't say much. He asked when you were leaving town, where you currently live. Just small talk." Lena replied.

"What did you tell him?" It was hard for Beth to hide the desperation in her voice. She dreaded the answer.

"I told him you plan to leave after an appointment tomorrow." She looked at Beth with a frown. "I didn't say anything about where you live now."

Beth rushed from the room feeling trapped and exposed. She covered her mouth with her hand as she realized he'd been in Lena's house. A room away from where she'd slept. The thought screeched in her brain.

Exasperated, Lena looked at Rose "What did I do now? I swear that girl is too emotional for her own good."

Gram followed Beth into the bedroom. "Come and eat something."

Beth turned to Gram. "Not now, Gram. I have to go back to the motel to get my things." Beth paced, wondering how to escape this mess. She ran her hands up and down her arms for comfort. How she despised this feeling of helplessness.

"Your things can wait." Gram placed a reassuring hand on Beth's arm. " You need to eat."

CHAPTER FOUR

Before Beth entered the motel room, she surveyed the lighted parking lot for anything or anyone suspicious. The snow had not let up all day. The weather report warned of at least seven inches of new snowfall by evening. All she needed was a blizzard to prevent her from leaving until the spring thaw.

She unlocked the door and checked for any clues the room was the way she'd left it. She locked and bolted the door, and quickly gathered her belongings and threw everything into her suitcase.

Her heart lurched to her throat when she heard a noise outside the door.

When the door knob moved, she placed her hand over her mouth to silence a cry. "Oh God!" she whimpered, as she searched the room for another means of escape. She rushed to wedge a chair under the doorknob. When a loud knock sounded, she jumped back in terror.

"I know you're in there!" a low voice growled.

"Go away!" Beth yelled. She sank to the floor and lost track of time, paralyzed by the horror awaiting her on the opposite side of the door.

* * *

Sirens brought her back to reality. She waited and after what seemed like an eternity, a knock on the door startled her back to reality.

"Go away! I won't let you hurt me again!"

"Open up! It's the police."

Beth stumbled to her feet. "I need to see some identification," she called out warily. She switched the light on and watched a laminated identification card appear under the door. She quickly examined it and nervously laughed when she read the name, Lieutenant Jackson Walsh. Tears of relief filled her eyes. "Jack! Is that you?"

"Beth? What's going on?"

Her hands trembled as she removed the chair, but hesitated after checking the time on her wristwatch. "I thought you worked the midnight shift."

"I'm working a double tonight."

"How do I know it's you!"

"Come on Lizzie, stop playing games."

"Oh, how I love that name," she cried and unlocked the door. Jack threw the door open and she fell into his arms. He wrapped his arms around her and waited until she regained her composure. When she relaxed against him, he held her away.

"Are you hurt?" His expression was pained as he searched her face.

"How did you know to come?" she asked, not yet convinced she was safe.

"I was a few miles away when an anonymous call came into the station regarding a break in." Jack guided her onto a chair, knelt down, handed her a tissue and held her hand. "It's time to level with me."

She dabbed at the tears and blew her nose. "I won't tell you anything."

"Come on! I know you're in trouble. Let me help!"

She stood, reached for her suitcase and ignored his question.

He grabbed the suitcase from her and blocked the doorway. "I'll haul your ass down to the station and. . ."

"And what? Torture me until I tell you everything?" Beth questioned, defiantly. "I hardly think so. You don't have a legal reason to detain me."

Jack stepped aside and followed her to the motel office where he wrote a police report for the clerk from Beth's statement and waited hile she checked out.

At her car, Jack watched suspiciously. "You know who tried to break in, don't you?"

She wouldn't look at him. "No, I don't."

"Bull shit!" He followed her back to Lena McCray's house, stepped out of his patrol car and escorted her to the door. "I'll be watching the house all night. My shift ends at seven tomorrow morning."

Beth stretched on her tiptoes and planted a kiss on his cheek. "Jack, you are my guardian angel."

He gently caressed her cheek. "If you change your mind and want to talk, I'll be out front."

She placed her hand over his, deeply touched by his gesture of affection.

* * *

Beth tossed and turned the entire night. Several times she tiptoed to the window to make sure Jack still stood guard. Each time, she was relieved to find his unmarked sedan positioned in the same spot.

In the kitchen, she warmed a glass of milk and pressed a hand against her stomach, hoping to calm the churning, painful bundle of nerves that tore at her insides. Only one more day and she could leave this nightmare behind. The grandfather clock bonged three times. She resumed the restless pacing and wondered if her sanity would remain intact for the duration of the long, lonely night.

She must've dozed off, because she woke with a start sometime later. She brewed a pot of coffee and found a pair of boots and a heavy winter parka by the back door. She poured two cups of coffee and opened the door to a blast of frigid air. The wind drove the snow sideways, which temporarily blinded her as she trudged to Jack's parked car.

She tapped lightly on the foggy window and peeked inside when the door opened. "I thought you could use some fresh coffee."

Jack patted the seat next to him. "Thanks, Beth. Come in and close the door."

"Thanks for watching out for me, Jack," she said as she slid into the passenger seat.

Jack brushed the damp hair from her face. "I wish you would let me do more."

She sipped her coffee while he studied her. "I know you do."

"Well, damn it! Tell me who you're afraid of?" Beth continued to say nothing, but could see the frustration in his eyes. "You're just as stubborn as you were when we were kids!" he growled. "Except, when you were little you protected your mother. She's gone, Beth. Who are you protecting now?"

His words struck a painful chord. She opened the door and turned to brush a quick kiss on his cheek. "I wanted you to know how much I appreciate what you've done for me."

He handed her the empty cup and felt powerless as he watched her disappear into the house.

* * *

Jack took a last look around to make sure the house was secure before driving to the station to check in before his shift ended. He parked his patrol car in the back lot, entered through the side door, and kicked the snow from his boots. Before he filed the reports from the previous night, he stopped at the dispatcher's desk and leaned on the counter. He smiled and waited while she finished her phone conversation.

"Hi, beautiful," he said when she disconnected the call. "How are things with you?"

Sandy looked at him warily. "What do you need now, Walsh?"

His deep grin betrayed his attempt to sound innocent.

"A call came in around nine last night. Can you play it back for me?" Jack tapped his fingers on the counter while Sandy scanned through excerpts of incoming calls. He stood up straight and pointed to the recorder. "Stop there. Rewind it a bit."

The caller spoke softly. "I'm at the Motor Lodge on Highway 52. There's a man trying to break into one of the rooms. He woke me up pounding on the door! Sounds like he's making threats to the person inside."

"What's your name, Sir?" The caller hung up. Sandy looked at Jack. "That's all there is."

He smiled. "Thanks a million, Sandy. I owe you."

As he neared the end of the report, his thoughts were interrupted.

"Hey, Walsh, how's the graveyard shift these days?"

Jack looked up from his computer to find Andy Thompson, one of the veteran detectives, lean against the corner of his desk. "It never changes much. How are things with you?"

"About the same." Andy strained his neck to glance at the report. "Heard there was a bit of excitement over at the Motor Lodge last night."

"There was an attempted break in. The perp got away before I arrived at the scene." Jack continued to type and shifted to shield Andy's view of the report. He scanned the document for accuracy before he printed out the pages. After he locked the papers in his desk drawer, he stood to leave. "Have a good one, Andy." Jack headed toward the door. Andy nodded, but said nothing as he stared at the locked desk.

* * *

Jack arrived home in time to join his family at the breakfast table before Brad left for school.

"Hi, Honey," Suzy smiled and stretched on her tiptoes to kiss him.

"Good morning," he said and reached for Suzy's hand. Her smile faded. "Is everything all right? You look worried."

"I'm just tired." How are the two of you feeling?" He beamed as he patted their unborn child.

"We're just great, although the living quarters are a bit cramped."

Jack leaned forward to kiss her again.

Brad entered the kitchen and slumped into a chair. Jack reached to smooth a chronic cowlick in his son's hair. "Good morning, partner."

Brad rubbed his eyes. "Hi, Dad."

Jack poured a glass of orange juice and set it down for Brad. "Did you get all of your homework done?"

Brad shook his head. "Mom even checked it for me didn't you?" he asked Suzy.

"Yes. You did a great job, too." She smiled and poured milk on his cereal.

Jack studied his son proudly while Brad gulped down his breakfast. "Do you want me to drive you to school, Pal?"

"No thanks, Dad. Jason's mom is picking me up." Bradley grabbed his book bag.

"Well then, come here and give your old man a hug before you rush off," said Jack.

Brad quickly threw his arms around Jack's neck. "Bye, Dad. I love you."

"I love you too, Son."

He rushed out the door when the sound of a car horn beeped.

"Are you going into the store this morning?" he asked Suzy.

"No, I don't start until this afternoon." She peered at him over her glass of juice. "What's the matter? I can tell something's on your mind."

Jack stared into his coffee. "I'm concerned about Beth. Last night someone tried to break into her motel room."

Suzy's shocked expression met his gaze. "Is she all right?"

"She's not hurt, but she's terrified." He squeezed her hand. "She's hiding something, but as usual, won't talk. I followed her back to her aunt's and watched the house all night."

"Do you know who tried to break in?" Suzy asked.

"I don't know, but I intend to toss a few questions around today." He gulped down the last of his coffee and loaded the dishes in the dishwasher.

Suzy joined him at the sink and wrapped her arms around him. "It gives me the creeps." Jack held her close, sensing her uncertainty.

"You'll be careful, won't you?"

He tenderly placed a kiss on the top of her head. "I'm always careful," he whispered as he tried to calm her fears.

At the door he turned to Suzy. "I'm going to the hardware store to talk to Sam."

Suzy walked him to the door and buttoned his coat. "When are you going to sleep? You worked a double last night."

Jack grinned at her scowling expression. "I won't be long."

* * *

The hardware store didn't open until ten o'clock, but Sam always arrived early to enjoy the quiet. He would drink his coffee uninterrupted and contemplate his future plans.

This morning he found Jack huddled up by the back door to shield him against the driving wind. No one knew Sam's routine better than Jack.

Sam greeted him with surprise. "What are you doing here this time of the morning?" he asked as he unlocked and pushed the heavy door open.

Jack stepped into the store. "I need to ask you a few questions."

Sam raised his eyebrows at his good friend. "Come back to the office." Jack waited while Sam made a pot of coffee, turned on the computer and heat to warm up the store.

Sam set two cups on the desk and sat in the chair.

"Thanks," Jack said. He reached for the coffee and cleared his throat. "I know you don't like to talk about Beth, but I need to ask you a few questions about last night."

Sam felt his patience stretch thin, he could tell Jack was in full cop mode. The last person he cared to talk about was Beth. "What about last night?" he asked.

"I responded to a report of a break in at the Motor Lodge outside of town. Someone tried to force their way into Beth's room." Jack paused as Sam sprung from the chair.

"Is she hurt?" Sam balled his fists tightly as he faced Jack.

"She's all right physically."

Sam relaxed his fists. "What does this have to do with me? The only time I saw Beth was at the funeral home." Sam sat down once more and returned Jack's intense cop stare.

"I'm asking because you were closest to Beth. You may know something that could help me try to figure out what happened to make her leave in the first place."

Sam began to leave the office. "Look, we've been over this before. There was a time I cared. It was a long time ago, it's over." Sam felt the fire in his eyes as he glared at Jack.

"Sam, listen to me for a minute. I've discovered information that might make you feel differently about what happened to her."

Sam cursed as he stormed from the office. "I wish she never came back here! First Suzy, then Carrie and now you. Can't you get it through your thick head, I'm no longer interested in knowing why she left?" Jack watched Sam's face soften. "I'm not going through this again. I wish everyone would stop bothering me with questions about her. I don't care anymore!" Sam opened the cash register.

Jack sat on the counter. "If you didn't care, you wouldn't get so dammed emotional every time Beth's name is mentioned."

Sam attempted to bury himself in the task of counting money as he placed it in the register. "I've got work to do."

Jack looked out the front display window, and quickly headed for the door. "I'll be back in a bit."

"I'm sure I can count on it," said Sam as he counted the money for the second time.

* * *

Jack paused in the doorway out of sight and observed Lena McCray's car parked in front of the lawyer's office across the street. He continued to watch while Lena stepped out to deposit change into the parking meter. Then a gust of wind blew the scarf away and exposed Beth's face as she rushed inside the building. He wondered why she was dressed like her aunt.

Beth paced nervously at the back door. She expected the appointment with the lawyer to last much longer. Gram wasn't due to meet her for another half-hour. So, she waited, worried and paced some more.

At last Gram rushed toward her. "How did everything go?" asked Rose as she removed her coat.

"It was quick and easy. I signed everything over to you and Aunt Lena. I'll call you when you get home to give you all the details."

Silently, they exchanged outer clothing. Beth turned around and modeled Gram's coat, hat, and boots she wore. "How do I look?"

"You look like me, simply ravishing!" Rose smiled and attempted to close Beth's much smaller coat around her. She tucked her white hair under the hat Beth had worn into the building. "I don't know, honey, do you think this will work?" she asked, skeptically.

Beth shrugged, somberly. "I hope so."

"With all this caution you're taking to leave town, I'm reluctant to let you drive home alone. You be careful. I'll return on Saturday, so call me then."

"I will, Gram." Beth hugged her grandmother. "Now, remember, wait until I'm gone for ten minutes before leaving through the front door."

Beth rushed toward the back door. Her heart rate accelerated when she discovered Jack walking toward her. Beth smiled as she attempted to pass him, but he turned to address her.

"What's with the disguise?" he asked.

She avoided eye contact with him. "I'd love to stay and chat with you, but I'm in a rush."

He grabbed her arm and she turned to him, jerking her arm free. "Beth, just tell me one thing. I need to know if you're running from Sam." He stared at her sternly, clearly intent on getting an answer.

Beth closed her eyes and realized for the first-time what Jack must be going through, wondering if his best friend was responsible for her distress. She gently reached to touch his hand. "Sam would never hurt me. You most of all should know that."

He sighed and felt his shoulders relax. "You don't know how relieved I am, Lizzie."

Tears stung her eyes when she saw the profound support on Jack's face and when he reached out to her she gave him a quick hug. "I have to go." She glanced one more time at Jack and waved goodbye.

Beth started the engine of the rental car Gram had parked by the back door and said a silent prayer the person who followed her would be fooled by this flimsy diversion. Slowly, she drove to the end of the back alley, turned toward the highway and hoped like hell her worries were left behind.

* * *

As Jack walked back to the hardware store, he watched Beth's car pull out of sight and wondered if he'd ever see her again.

Sam looked up from the paperwork and rolled his eyes as Jack stepped in from the cold. "Are you back to harass me some more?"

"As a matter of fact, I am," Jack said with a grin.

"I think you're taking this cop thing a little too serious. You might consider moving to a big city so you can find some real bad asses to bother!"

Jack laughed good-naturedly. "What could be more fun than bothering you?"

He leaned against the counter, pulled a folded paper out of his jacket, and passed it to Sam.

Sam was slow to unfold the paper, shocked to discover his high school senior picture, destroyed almost beyond recognition. He frowned. "Where did you find this?"

"Come with me and I'll show you."

"I can't right now." Sam checked the time. "Suzy isn't due in until this afternoon, and Dad has a doctor's appointment."

Jack walked to the front window and turned the open sign over to read closed. "It won't take long."

Sam shook his head as he pulled his keys out of his pocket and threw on his coat. "My car is parked in back. This better be worth catching Suzy's wrath for closing the shop."

"I'll take full responsibility." Jack winked and followed Sam.

* * *

When Jack asked him to stop the car in front of Beth's old house, Sam looked at his friend, perplexed. "What are we doing here?" Jack stepped out of the car but said nothing. Sam blocked his path to the house. "Answer me, Jack."

Jack lowered his voice. "Let's go out back. I'll explain everything once we're inside."

Sam followed, but was doubtful anything Jack had to say would change his feelings. "If you dragged me over here because of one of your crazy hunches, I'll have to hurt you." He muttered as he helped Jack set a ladder against the back of the house.

"Stop whining and lower your voice," Jack growled.

Jack climbed and opened the window he had unlocked the previous day. Sam scowled impatiently while Jack pried the screen loose. He followed Jack and grumbled,

"What the hell's so important we have to break. . ." his words trailed off when he joined Jack in Beth's bedroom and saw the bullet-riddled walls and furniture. He felt shaky and sat on the edge of the bed to observe the disturbing scene. "What happened in here?" He turned to Jack.

"I don't know. Yesterday, I was passing by on my way home and saw Beth sitting alone in her car. I decided to ask her a few questions, but she wasn't talking. She was too frightened to go inside her own house. While Beth waited in the car, I helped her grandmother search for the house deed and other papers," said Jack.

"Beth was always secretive about what went on with her mother," Sam said quietly. "It looks like her mother went ballistic in this room." Sam pointed to the bullet holes and broken mirror. "This probably happened the night Beth left town." Sam gathered a cloth doll from the shelf next to the bed and recalled the time he got it for her at the Ann Harbor Art Fair. They had just begun dating. Beth was eighteen and he was twenty-one. Some fancy artist from out of state crafted it as a limited edition. It cost him a lot more than he should have spent, but it was worth the price to see how much Beth loved it.

He tossed the doll onto the bed. "Is this all you wanted to show me? I should get back to the store." Sam took a step toward the window.

"I'm not convinced Beth would leave town because her mom went crazy. It wasn't her mother who tried to break into her motel room and threaten her last night." Jack paused when Sam hesitated. "Tell me why she was scared to death to come into this house, or why she was disguised as her grandmother today when she left town?

Sam turned back to Jack, his irritation apparent. "I don't have an explanation and I don't want to think about it any longer!"

"When did you turn into such a bitter, uncaring jerk?" Jack moved closer to confront him.

Sam's mouth dropped open. "What are you talking about?"

"I'm talking about the way you are blowing off the realization Beth is in some kind of trouble, yet you can't see how much she's hurting because you're wallowing in your own self-pity."

Sam felt his temper flair as he stepped toward Jack. "You have no idea what I'm feeling."

"Get off it, Andrews. If you'd open your eyes, you might understand Beth left town because she didn't have a choice. I'll bet the same person who scared her away two years ago also threatened her last night."

Sam relaxed his clenched fists and felt confused, but no longer irate. He needed to stop this right now. The last thing he wanted was to get involved. "I haven't time to listen to this nonsense. I'm going back to the store."

Jack grabbed Sam's arm. "I know why you're so afraid to discuss this."

Sam shoved his friend. "You don't have a clue what you're talking about."

"It was so obvious at the funeral home." Jack shoved him back. "You still love Beth, don't you?"

Sam reached for the doorknob. "I'm leaving before we both say things we'll regret." When he found the door jammed, he tugged on the knob harder. It wouldn't budge. "Damn it, Walsh," he yelled as he kicked the door and splintered the molding. Sam faced Jack. "You're so full of it. Why don't you leave me out of this?"

"I know Beth still loves you, as well." Jack's voice was no longer accusing. "I'm telling you Sam, she needs our help."

Sam sat on the edge of the bed and felt the crack in his protective armor leave a gap around his heart. Hell, the moment he saw Beth at the funeral home, he realized his anger and indifference toward her had only been a façade to cover the hurt and betrayal. "Who did this to her?" he wondered out loud, feeling the agony of losing her all over again. Turning his anger on the person responsible for Beth's fear.

Jack sat next to Sam and placed a reassuring arm across his shoulders. "That's exactly what you and I are going to find out."

* * *

The afternoon dragged while Sam waited for Suzy to arrive at the store to relieve him. He couldn't deny he still loved Beth. The desire to find her invaded his only thought. He was anxious to speak with Jack to see if there were any further developments.

Before Jack went home to get some sleep, he planned to stop at the station to run a check on Beth's license plates and a trace on her driver's license to see if she has a current address on file.

Finally, Suzanne rushed into the store, her arms filled with packages and gift-wrap. She smiled brightly as Sam helped her with the packages. "There's more in the van. I want to wrap Bradley's Christmas gifts and hide them here at the store. He's already snooping around the house."

"You're spoiling that kid rotten!" commented Sam when he looked at all the bags stuffed full of toys and other goodies.

Suzy smiled gently. "You know how much I love to shop. Besides," she paused and surveyed her purchases, "some of these gifts are for Jack. Bradley isn't the only one who likes to snoop!"

Sam laughed. "Don't tell me Officer Walsh peeks into hidden places for his presents."

Suzy laughed with him. "Oh yes he does. Where do you think Bradley gets his inquisitive nature?"

Sam's smile faded when he thought of how empty the holidays had been since Beth left. Hopefully, this year would be different.

Sam returned with the remainder of the gifts. "I need to run a few errands, Suz. I'll try to get back here as soon as I can."

She studied him for a moment. "You rarely leave the store in the middle of the day. What's up?" she asked.

"I'll tell you all about it later, Miss Nosy."

"Take your time, Sam. Dad's going to stop by after his doctor's appointment. We'll be fine."

* * *

Lena McCray greeted Sam at her door and smiled brightly. "Sam! Come in. Beth has already left town, if that's why you're here," she stated.

""Hello Ms. McCray, I wanted to ask you a few questions about Beth."

Lena frowned. "Like what?"

"I'd like to know where I can reach her." He watched Lena's expression grow leery.

"I can take a message for you, but I don't know where she lives."

He searched her face and found no apparent reason not to believe her. "How about her grandmother, can you tell me where she lives?"

"No, Sam. I'm sorry. Beth has her reasons for her secrecy, she wouldn't be happy if I were to. . ." Lena stopped when Rose entered the living room.

"Hello. I'm Beth's grandmother, Rose Brockton." She extended her hand. "And you're the young man who upset Beth at the funeral home." The quick frown Rose glared in Lena's direction didn't go unnoticed by Sam.

"Rose, this is Sam Andrews. He and Beth were practically engaged before Beth left town." Lena scurried from the room.

"What is it you wish to find out?" Rose asked.

"I was hoping you would tell me how I can get in touch with her." Lena returned with a pencil and paper to hand to Sam.

"If you write down your number I will give it to Beth the next time she calls."

While Sam drove back to the hardware store, his thoughts returned to Beth and the reason she left. The gnawing sensation in his chest grew heavy as he dwelled on the time he'd wasted blaming her for hurting him. She was in trouble and needed his help. His eyes burned as he recalled her frightened, fragile face when he first saw her at the funeral home. He gritted his teeth and berated himself for ceasing to believe in her. The gap around his heart opened further and he inhaled deeply. He'd closed his heart to Beth in order to try and forget her. Now he felt the burn of letting her down, when she needed him the most.

* * *

Later in the evening at the Apple Orchard Inn, a waitress named Cindy smiled when she saw Sam take a seat in one of the empty booths.

Her heart gave a little flutter, which it normally did, whenever she saw an available guy, especially one who fit the ultimate definition of a hunk, like Sam Andrews. She fussed with her hair and checked her make-up in the mirror behind the counter. She frowned as she walked to his table, sighed to herself, and wished he'd study her as intently as he did the menu.

He briefly glanced up from the menu when she placed a cup of coffee in front of him. "Thanks," he commented.

"You're welcome, Sam." She flashed him a bright smile. "What can I do for you tonight?"

Sam ignored the double meaning of her words. "I'm waiting for Jack to join me, so I'll stick with coffee for now."

Cindy lingered at the table as he continued to read the menu. "I guess you've seen Beth Brockton since she's been back in town, haven't you?"

"Yes, I saw her." He frowned.

"Did she act crazy? Did you find out why she left town?" Cindy was all ears and bright eyed.

Sam was irritated by the small-town attitude that everybody's business was open for public discussion. "I didn't really talk to her much," he stated, without a hint of emotion.

Cindy didn't bother to hide a triumphant smile as she turned away from the table after her silent beeper went off for the second time. She batted her thick eyelashes, heavily laden with mascara. "I'll be with you in a moment."

Sam impatiently checked his watch, anxious for Jack to arrive with some news of Beth's whereabouts. He regretted they hadn't selected another place to meet.

When Jack entered the restaurant, Sam was ready to bolt from his seat. "What did you find out?" he asked Jack before he had a chance to be seated.

Jack laughed. "And to think, just this morning you didn't even want to hear Beth's name mentioned."

Sam paused when Cindy approached the booth with an easy smile for Jack. She leaned over to flirt with Jack and smiled provocatively. "Hi Jack! How are you?"

"I'm just great, Cindy. How about you?"

She pouted her lips. "It's real slow in here tonight. I thought the snow would bring everyone out for dinner. You know how people love to talk about the weather. What can I get for you guys?"

"I've already had dinner at home, Sam. Do you need to order?"

Sam ordered a hamburger for the sole purpose of giving Cindy something to do so he and Jack could talk privately. After Cindy disappeared into the kitchen, Sam leaned across the table toward Jack. "Come on, Walsh. What did you find out?"

"The car checked out to be a rental registered in Florida. Her driver's license is expired and still listed her mom's address. She doesn't have any current license plates on file, and the last plates issued in her name were from the car she drove in college." Jack rubbed the stubble on his chin.

"What about her social security number?" Sam asked, clearly disappointed.

"The last source of income lists the Aidan Theater as her employer from two years ago."

Sam's scowl deepened. "How the hell are we going to find her?" Cindy returned to refill Sam's coffee, but he waved her off. "I've had enough, thanks."

As soon as she was out of hearing range, Jack continued in a quiet voice. "I have a friend at a precinct in Detroit. I gave him all the information on Beth I could think of, including her grandmother's name and possible location. You did say Beth spent summers at her grandmother's home in the Tri County area, didn't you?"

Sam studied Jack and nodded. "Somewhere close to Saginaw Bay, I forgot the name of the town. Do you think she changed her name?"

Jack shrugged. "It's a strong possibility. I gave my friend her mom's maiden name. He has access to much more sophisticated computers than I do. Hopefully, he'll come up with something. In the meantime, maybe I can work on her grandma. She's staying at Lena McCray's."

Sam rolled his eyes. "I tried to get information from her earlier, but she looked at me like I was a carrier of the black plague."

Jack chuckled. "Grandma Rose likes me." He punched Sam on the arm. "You just have to learn the art of charming older women." His smile brightened when he nodded toward Cindy. "Check it out."

Sam followed Jack's gaze and met Cindy's yearning expression as she watched Sam from across the room. He cringed when she smiled at him suggestively.

"For that matter," Jack continued, "you could use a little finesse with the younger ladies, too!

CHAPTER FIVE

When Beth finally opened the door to her apartment, she was disappointed a feeling of relief didn't come immediately. She brewed a cup of hot tea to soothe her taunt nerves. Between the hazardous driving conditions and the necessity to be constantly on the alert, she barely had the strength to stand upright. She tried to relax and let the herbal tea perform its magic, but her mind wandered to all the events that happened the past few days. Knowing it was unavoidable to run into Sam sometime on her visit home didn't make the impact of seeing him any less traumatic. Just thinking of the contempt she saw in his eyes made her shudder. She knew how much he must despise her, but seeing it only made the reality much harder to endure, and it hurt. She inhaled deeply and felt a stabbing sensation, as if the pain were physical.

She tended her few houseplants and sorted through junk mail, but the diversion wasn't enough to block away thoughts of him.

She'd left him without a word of explanation. He had every right to hate her. She anguished over what he must have gone through when he found her gone. She covered her face with her hands. What would Sam do if he found out she was pregnant with his child when she left town? Didn't he have a right to know he was a father? It was wrong not to tell him, but she couldn't risk anyone finding out about Samantha. Those who wanted her silenced would stop at nothing to get to her. Beth knew Sam would not sit by quietly and let that happen. He'd want a full-blown confrontation and it would only put them all at risk. No, she was convinced to leave things the way they were.

She couldn't allow herself the luxury of dreaming about him for even an instant. But, oh how she loved him. It was ludicrous to deny she cared about him as much as she had the day she left Aidan. She buried herself in paperwork, knowing from past experience how useless it was to dwell on hopeless dreams.

* * *

While Jack waited for information from his Detroit precinct source, he re-examined the events which had occurred around the time of Beth's departure. Perhaps he missed something when he'd searched for clues over two years ago. He was training at the police academy then and didn't have access to sophisticated information systems. Besides, he had to keep at it. Sam and Suzy were driving him nuts with questions regarding new information.

He visited the Aidan Cinema but found nothing helpful there. Most of Beth's co-workers were no longer employed at the theater. He'd make a trip back to the theater later in the evening to question the night manager.

* * *

Suzy looked out the living room picture window to watch Bradley trudge through the snow on his way to his friend's house. She chuckled to herself when a snowball sailed through the air and smacked Bradley on the back. Brad turned and saw his Uncle Sam crouched behind Jack's parked car. Brad ran over to the opposite side, ducked down to grab a hand full of snow and packed it into a snowball.

Jack stepped up beside Suzy and placed his arm around her shoulder. "What's so funny?" he asked and followed the direction she pointed to.

"Sam is on the other side of the car."

They both laughed as Sam charged around the car and sprayed an arsenal of snowballs at Bradley, who didn't stand a chance, but fought back valiantly. When Brad was sitting on top of Sam, washing his face with snow, Sam called out, "Okay, I give up! You win."

Brad giggled uncontrollably as he rolled to the ground.

Sam laughed heartily and pulled Brad to his feet. "Where're you off to partner?"

"I'm going to Jason's. We're making a snow fort. Wanna come see it, Uncle Sam?"

Sam brushed the snow from Brad's collar and smiled at his nephew's innocent face. "I need to talk to your mom and dad first, but I'll stop by before I leave."

Brad flashed a semi-toothless smile. "Awesome! I'll see you later."

He paused at the curb before crossing and waved to Sam.

Sam watched Bradley cross and then turned to enter the house. Suzy poured Sam a cup of coffee, while he hung his wet outer clothing on the hooks by the back door. He stepped onto the rug in front of the stove and shivered, rubbing his hands together.

Suzy brought him a towel as melted snow ran down his face. "Sure doesn't look like you were dressed for a snowball fight."

Sam sipped the coffee. "One must always be prepared when spontaneous battle strikes." He grinned as the warm liquid traveled through him and she smiled in return.

Jack joined them with a pad of paper and a state map in hand. He opened the Michigan map, spreading it on the kitchen table while Sam and Suzy observed. "Well, just as I suspected, there's no available information on Beth's location," he said.

Sam shuddered as a wave of disappointment ripped through his gut.

Jack continued, "This is Rose Brockton's address." He tore the top sheet of paper from the notebook. "My source found the address listed under James Brockton, Rose's late husband.

Sam read the address: 267 Elmwood Avenue, Pineville and entered the information into his cell phone. "Where the hell is Pineville?" He followed Jack's pointed finger to a town just south of Saginaw Bay Lake Huron about mid-state. "Do you think we'll be lucky enough to find Beth living there?" he questioned.

Jack shrugged and tipped back in his chair. "I hope so, it's the only lead we have."

Suzy gently patted the back of Sam's hand. "I'm sure the two of you will locate Beth. I feel so bad for her! Imagine having to leave everything behind, including your identity." Suzy looked at Jack, then to Sam.

Sam didn't take his eyes from the map, disturbed by the reminder of Suzy's words. "I'm worried we won't locate her before something happens." He refilled his coffee and turned back to them. The questions he'd blocked away were back in full force. "How much danger is she in?" He faced Jack. "How do I begin to look for her, Jack? You're the investigator, not me."

"I'd start looking in Pineville. You know she teaches third grade and you know where her grandmother lives. I believe her grandma's the closest person in her life right now. Beth might not live in the same town, but I'd bet anything she lives close by." Again, Sam's gaze followed closely as Jack indicated various points on the map. "Concentrate on the Tri-County area here. Start with the library and the Board of Education, the local newspapers. If they give you a list of third grade teacher's maybe you'll be lucky enough to find a name similar to Beth's. You can also get the names of elementary schools."

Sam listened with intense interest while he wrote down the information.

"Beth's grandfather, James Brockton, was a college administrator at Central Michigan University and a prominent figure in the region. I have a hunch Rose Brockton used her connections to provide Beth with a safe identity." Jack paused. "It's going to take a lot of time and leg work, but if you want to find her, then you're going to have to dig deep."

Sam looked directly into Jack's eyes and stated with determination, "I'll find her." For her sake, as well as his own, he had to discover the reasons behind the tortured look he saw in her eyes at the funeral home.

"I went back to the theater to question the night manager about Beth's last night at work, he remembered when Beth left for the night, she was on her way to pick up her mom from the bar. I'll visit Max's Tavern to see what information I can get there."

Sam heard a tone of regret in Jack's voice. "I wish I had done a better job of investigating when Beth first disappeared. Two years is a long time to expect people to remember crucial information to the case."

Sam felt the weight of Jack's words. "I'm the one responsible for giving up on her so easy. I'll never forgive myself if something. . . " His words trailed off and he forced himself to stop these thoughts before they drove him insane. He turned to Suzanne and questioned, "Do you think you can work extra for me at the store?"

She smiled warmly and gave him a hug. "Of course I will. Dad's ready to come back to work full time, anyway."

"I might as well get started." He shook the melted snow from his coat and smiled. "Right after I check out Bradley's snow fort."

* * *

Beth hid in the darkness while someone tried to force his way into her room. She helplessly watched in horror while an ax crashed through the door and rendered a gap expanding larger with each blow. A hand appeared through the splintered hole. It stretched and groped for the doorknob. When the door crashed open, she screamed and bolted upright in bed.

Her heart pounded, she was frozen with fear. She struggled to free herself from the nightmare that engulfed her. In her panicked state, she couldn't distinguish between reality and her dream.

She switched on the lamp next to her bed. It took some time for her rapid breathing and racing heartbeat to return to normal. Angry tears sprang to her eyes. Why couldn't she escape from her fears during sleep?

Several hours later Beth was surprised to see the sunlight filter between the window blinds. At the window, she searched the street below. What she expected to find, she wasn't certain, but she was sure her life would never seem safe again. It had been three long days since she returned from down state, the same amount of time she'd been a recluse in the apartment. She'd force herself to go back to work and school, afraid if she continued to hide, she'd never have the courage to step foot outside again.

She'd become Alisa Rose again and leave Beth Brockton behind. Would hiding behind a name be sufficient security for her to feel safe again?

Safe! When was the last time she felt safe?

The night hours were the most difficult. It was impossible to find solace in sleep without being awakened by fragments of the past which stalked her. But as painful as the nightmares were, the peaceful dreams of living happily with Sam were far worse. It was less painful to wake in horror than endure the pain of waking from a dream about Sam to find he wasn't there.

* * *

One afternoon in the teacher's lounge, Ann Woroczyk, a fourth-grade teacher, touched Alisa's arm. Alisa nearly jumped a foot and splashed coffee everywhere. "I'm sorry, Ann," she said as she wiped up the spill. "I'm a little jumpy these days."

"You look pale, are you ill?" asked Ann. "What's going on?"

"I'll be all right once I get back into a routine."

Ann stared at Alisa, deep furrows marred her forehead. "Do you think you came back to work too soon? Maybe you need more time to deal with everything."

"Really, Ann, I'll be fine." She smiled slightly and placed a reassuring hand on Ann's shoulder. Ann was in her early fifties, outgoing and easy to talk to. They'd hit it off the first day Alisa began teaching last fall.

Since then, Ann had taken the younger peer under her wing to help smooth the adjustments to the rigors of the job.

Ann continued, "Since I lost my mom, it seems like all security I had is gone.."

Alisa looked at her coworker, having no clue what it would be like to have similar feelings for her mother.

They sat on the sofa together. Ann unwrapped her sandwich and passed half to Alisa. "Here, eat this. You look like you're half-starved!" She paused and peered over her glasses at Alisa. "You aren't suffering from an eating disorder, are you?"

"No!" Alisa took a small bite of the sandwich to escape further interrogation.

Ann passed over a handful of grapes. "Well, I just want you to know if you need a friend to talk to, I hope you'll come to me."

Alisa felt warmness wash over her. "Thanks, I will."

* * *

Sam checked into a small motel near the Interstate highway somewhere in the middle of the Tri-County region. He had no clue how long he'd be staying in the area so he booked a cheap, but clean room at weekly rates. Over dinner at a small coffee shop in town, he opened a map of the area and a local phone book to plot out his next course of action.

Earlier, a trip to the Pineview Board of Education only provided him with a list of elementary schools, nothing more. The picture of Beth he showed to the desk clerk was of no value. Afterward, she looked at him accusingly, like he was some horrible, abusive ex-husband who stalked his wife. Then she refused to give him any more information.

He searched the lengthy list of primary schools and felt a bit hopeless. He needed a break. It wasn't like he was searching for Beth in a big metropolitan area, but it still seemed impossible.

In the small motel room, he studied the picture of Beth. Her dark eyes sparkled and her smile was so bright it appeared as if she didn't have a care in the world. He took the photo when she'd graduated from college, not long before she left town. It seemed like a lifetime ago, but he remembered it well. The day was warm and sunny, as late spring days in Michigan often are. They sat on the campus lawn between classes and shared the hopes and dreams of their future. They talked about getting married in a year. Talked about everything couples in love share.

He placed the picture back on the night table and closed his eyes. He wondered if she was safe. Was she happy? Was she thinking about him? Sam opened his eyes as he considered new angles. What if she had a new life with someone else? Maybe she was married and had started a family. He sat upright and switched on the light. What if she wasn't in trouble after all? If Jack let his cop imagination run wild and dragged

Sam into some far-fetched scheme, then there'd be hell to pay. "Damn it, Walsh," he cursed out loud.

But, when the vivid image of Beth's sad, fearful eyes flashed before him, his heart confirmed she guarded some terrible secret. Again, he switched off the light and pulled the blankets up around his shoulders.

Somehow he'd find her. She probably wouldn't be happy about it, but he wasn't going to leave her alone until he convinced her they belong together. Or she convinced him they were better off apart.

Unwillingly, he thought about the time after she left town. Sam and Jack repeatedly talked to relatives and friends, but no one knew why she disappeared. He badgered Beth's mother and aunt with questions. Linda Brockton was sauced half the time and didn't seem to have a grip on reality. It was Lena McCray who finally convinced Sam to move on without Beth. He recalled her exact words.

"You may think you know Beth, but inside she's deeply troubled." Lena had told him. "I'm afraid the problems from her past have driven her away." Lena patted his arm in an effort to reduce the shock from the effects of her words. "I'm only telling you this because I can't bear to see you remain hopeful she'll return."

Afterwards, when Jack said there could be some truth to Lena's story, Sam seemed to give up hope of ever seeing Beth again. He gradually began to come to terms she'd left on her own terms without caring enough to say goodbye.

Sam wasn't proud of the way he handled the situation afterwards. He folded up his feelings into a neat little package and sealed it tight. He started to drink heavily and date anyone willing and able. He didn't care who he hurt in the process, including himself. He wasted a good deal of time blaming Beth for his actions.

Eventually, he cleaned up his act when he met a fellow intern on an environmental job in Chicago. Her name was Kara and what they had together was the closest thing to what Sam thought he needed. But there was one flaw, Kara wasn't Beth. As much as Sam tried to entertain illusions of he and Kara having a lasting relationship, he discovered he was only fooling himself and broke Kara's heart in the process.

No, he wasn't proud of the way he behaved.

Restlessly, he turned onto his side, suddenly aware of the stale air. He threw off the covers and opened the window. It was suffocating in the damn room! What the hell was he doing? Searching for a lost cause? Then images of Beth's face slipped back into his mind. By damn, he'd find her and let her convince him she no longer cared! Only then would he walk away and try to forget her once and for all. Good luck with that!

When he opened his eyes early the next morning, Sam decided how useless it was to make further attempts at falling back to sleep. He wasn't sure if the lumpy mattress or visions of Beth in someone else's arms were the reason for his sleeplessness, but he didn't care to struggle with the culprit any longer.

At the Coffee Café in town, he read the local paper for anything of interest. His attention was drawn to a small article announcing holiday programs and concerts in the school districts. Gulping down the remainder of his coffee, he tossed a few bucks on the table for a tip and made the decision to start his quest at the library researching newspaper articles and other school related information.

It turned out to be a long, uneventful day at the library. Sam was weary as he propped his head on his hand and stared blankly at three years-worth of newspaper articles he reviewed. He carried the stack of folders to the research desk.

The librarian who assisted him earlier smiled. "Judging from your expression, I gather you didn't have any luck with your project."

Sam shook his head and glanced at the nameplate on the desk. "Mrs. Nelson, could you help me find a particular teacher? I don't recall her name, but she is highly recommended by a friend of mine as a math tutor for my son."

The librarian looked at him puzzled. "I don't know how I can help if you don't know her name." She turned to her computer ready to enter data. "Do you know which school she teaches at?"

"To tell you the truth, I don't even know what city, but I think she teaches in the Tri-County area."

Mrs. Nelson continued to click away at the keyboard and he felt his spirits lift when he heard the hum of the computer printer.

Mrs. Nelson stood and retrieved the print out. "Here's a list of elementary teachers from the Tri-County area. I don't know if it will help, but it's the best I can offer."

Sam thanked her for her assistance. He didn't have a clue how it would help either, but it was one more piece of information he didn't have yesterday.

After a full week of searching for clues, Sam wasn't any further ahead than when he first arrived. It turned out the list of teachers was of little value. After he'd eliminated the men's names from the list, there were still so many names left. None of the names resembled, "Brockton" or "McCray", although, there were several "Elizabeth's" who taught the third grade, which might prove helpful.

Sam spent the weekend sitting in his car staking out Rose Brockton's home. His thoughts were constantly centered on Beth. He knew it wasn't smart to get his hopes up, anticipating an appearance from her, but it sure beat hanging around each elementary school in all three counties with the remote possibility of running into Beth. So far, he was amazed no one had reported him for hanging around elementary schools looking suspicious. It was already the weekend before Thanksgiving, and Sam debated whether to go home for the holiday if he didn't find her at Rose Brockton's house.

Each night around midnight, he returned to his motel room feeling more discouraged than the night before. If only he had a better lead to help him locate her. He was frustrated, but if it took weeks or months, he was determined to continue. He knew he was stuck and couldn't move forward with his life until he found her.

* * *

"What do you mean you're not coming over for Thanksgiving dinner?"

Alisa detected the hurt in Gram's voice. "I think it's a good idea if I stay away from your house for bit, Gram. I'm sorry."

Rose sighed. "Then I'll come to your place to cook. I really don't want you to be alone on a holiday."

Alisa felt ashamed for disappointing Gram. "You'd better not come here either."

Rose paused. "What in the world is going on? Is someone bothering you?"

"No one is bothering me. I just need some time to adjust from the trip back home." Alisa didn't want to worry her grandmother. She closed her eyes and attempted to settle her racing mind. Maybe she'd feel better if she could share the irrational thoughts she had about someone always watching.

"Well, that's all the more reason for you to come over. It'll do you good to get out of your apartment and enjoy a traditional holiday celebration. Besides, we haven't talked since I returned. I have some things of your father's you might like to have."

A tug of emotion traveled through Alisa. She never met her dad, but he seemed closer to her than her mother ever was. He was always in the back of her mind when she grew up. Knowing how much he would have loved her helped her through some difficult times. "I promise we'll get together as soon as my life seems more settled. I don't mean to disappoint you, Gram."

"You just relax and do what you need to do, honey. Don't worry, I'll have dinner with my neighbors." Rose's voice sounded convincing. "They've already invited me over."

This was little consolation for Alisa knowing she would miss the reassurance and security of Gram's company. "Maybe we can get together after Thanksgiving." Alisa sighed.

"That'll be fine. By the way, it's almost time to go shopping together for gifts to send to Aunt Lily. Or have you forgotten?"

Alisa pinched the bridge of her nose to fend off unwanted tears. "No, how could I forget?" Her voice faltered and she felt her heart sink a bit more. This holiday season was always the most difficult time of the year. "I'll call you next week, Gram. We'll choose a date then."

Alisa felt depression sink lower as she walked home. She entered her empty apartment and felt worse. She placed her hands on her chest. It ached with the heaviness of depression. Like an elevator being pulled down..down.. until it crashed at the bottom. Other than a few gifts from her students, scattered around, her apartment was literally void of any personal touches. It appeared as if nobody lived in this space at all. It was proof Alissa merely existed. She didn't have a life.

Her thoughts drifted to Aunt Lily in Maine. It had been so long since she'd heard any news. Would Samantha be talking?. How could she be seventeen months already? Were her eyes as blue as her father's?

She stopped herself from further thoughts, sank down on the couch and wrapped herself with the quilt Gram made. She closed her eyes and was desperate to think of solutions to mend her bleak existence. For the millionth time, she broke into sobs of despair.

* * *

Jack entered Max's Tavern, located about five miles north of Aidan. He hoped to beat the happy hour crowd, but marveled the bar was so busy on a weekday afternoon. Then he remembered the next day was Thanksgiving. He surveyed the patrons seated by the bar and at small tables scattered around the darkened lounge. The scent was always the same at these places, a combination of old, stale cigarette smoke and cheap liquor. He approached the bar and sat at the stool on the end.. He didn't have to wait long before the bartender was near. He was a big, burly guy who would've looked more at home in the wilderness chopping wood than working in a dingy bar located in a small, blue-collar town. Jack read the initials "USMC" from the tattoo inscribed on his massive forearm.

"What can I get for you, buddy?" The voice was as gruff as his appearance.

"I'll take whatever local brew you have on tap." Jack studied the bartender while he drew a cold one from the tapper and set a frosted mug on the worn, wooden bar. He nodded at Jack, but never uttered a word. The bartender turned to refill a beer for a customer wearing a flannel shirt and well-worn blue jeans who made eyes at a pretty lady seated in a booth.

A petite, brunette waitress shifted her weight from foot to foot and waited for a drink order at the opposite end of the bar and flashed an impatient look at the bartender.

"Come on Charlie, I've got tables waiting!" Her tone was whiny and annoying. Charlie took his time to approach the waitress to fill the order.

Jack sipped his beer and gazed into the hazy mirror lined against the wall behind the bar, where he could inconspicuously assess almost everyone in the bar without turning around to do so. A few of the faces he recognized, but most were strangers.

From across the bar, Sally Cantrell's eyes narrowed when she observed Jack in the mirror. His gaze met hers for only a split second before she looked away, too quickly. "What's Jack Walsh doing in this neck of the woods?" she asked the bartender as she lined dirty glasses on the bar.

Charlie shrugged. "Never saw him before."

"I saw him last summer when he gave me a speeding ticket." Jack never made her list of favorite people, even in high school, she never disliked him personally. Jack was always friendly, and not bad looking either, if you happened to go for the athletic boy-next-door type which was definitely not her style. She silently debated whether to pretend she didn't recognize him, but involuntarily, her eyes again met his in the mirror. Jack raised his mug in a silent salutation. "Shit!" she said to herself.

Jack watched Sally deliver a round of drinks to four middle aged men who appeared to have had enough already. She joked heartily with the customers and threw her head back with laughter. Her over-frizzed hairstyle appeared so teased and lacquered with hair spray, it didn't even move. Her hair was bleached until it was almost white. Sally always had a severe look, even so, the years of hard living had not been favorable on her prematurely aged face. She was only a few years older than Jack, making her thirty-five or so, but she looked at least fifteen years his senior.

He watched her sway her generous curves as she sauntered over to join him at the bar. Jack couldn't shake the feeling he was a defenseless prey ready to be toyed with by a large jungle cat.

"Hey, Jack. What brings you in here?" Her sly smile only enhanced the lines around her eyes.

She nodded at Charlie then turned to speak to Jack and pointed to the side door. "Come outside while I take a smoke break."

"I thought I'd check out this side of town for a change," he said, casually and followed her outside.

"Well, there sure as hell isn't any more action here than what you see in Aidan, so what gives?"

Jack smiled slightly at her blunt words. "Actually, I'm interested in finding out if anyone knows what happened the night Beth Brockton left town over two years ago."

Sally snorted. "You've got to be kidding! That's ancient history. Why would anyone care?" Jack noted her expression had changed from one of cocky self-assurance to contempt.

They turned to face the door when it opened. "Hey, Sal! How 'bout another round on table three?" Charlie noted and closed the door.

She opened the door and said to Charlie. "I need a screwdriver, a whiskey and water and a bottle of North Woods." She turned her attention back to Jack.

Jack chose his words cautiously. "I'm following up on a lead Beth was on her way here to pick up her mother the night she disappeared."

Sally slowly walked over to hand a bar tab to Charlie, who proceeded to ring up the order. Suspiciously, her eyes continued to watch Jack while she placed the drinks on a tray. "Charlie, get my friend Jack here a beer, on the house." She delivered her order and stopped to pick up empty bottles and glasses at another table.

Jack gulped the last of his beer while Charlie placed the fresh one in front of him. "Thanks, Charlie."

The bartender scrutinized Jack before he grunted something in reply. Sally returned to Jack at the opened back door picked up the lit cigarette, taking another long drag. "What makes you think Beth ever made it here? Maybe she stopped somewhere else, or decided not to come here at all."

Jack watched her closely. "I'm just trying to reconstruct the events as they occurred that night."

Sally motioned toward the mousy brunette waitress. "Barb has been here forever, but her old man only lets her work the day shift and Charlie was still in the Marine's back then."

Jack listened and observed her body language. "How about you, Sally? Do you recall anything unusual about that night?"

She moved next to him and stared into his eyes with defiance. "If you think I was involved with her disappearance, you're on the wrong track, Officer Walsh!" She enunciated the words with sarcasm.

"Don't get excited. I'm not accusing anyone of anything."

She nervously played with her ring. "Well, like I said, I don't think you'll find out a thing."

Jack looked around the room once more. "Who worked the night shift back then?"

Sally followed his glance. "No one here now, except me. I work whatever shift I can make the most money at!" She paused and looked around the room to make sure her customers were content. "Of course, Linda Brockton worked that shift, but she won't tell you nothin'." She smiled at her own tasteless joke. Jack disregarded her comment without reacting. From the other end of the room, the customers were growing impatient. "I have to get back to work. You're going to have to talk to someone else. I can't help you."

"Or won't help," he added, in a quiet, controlled voice and watched her temper flare. "What do you have against Beth?"

Sally examined her nail polish. "She came by the bar often to give Linda a lift home." Sally narrowed her eyes at Jack. "I didn't care for her, that's all."

Jack wondered what there was about Beth to dislike. "Why not?" he asked.

"The way she pranced around this place and had every man drooling after her made me sick!"

"That doesn't sound like Beth," Jack stated.

"Ha!" Sally snorted. "Then you don't know her as well as you thought."

Jack cooled his thoughts and tried to think objectively. "So, you didn't like her because she attracted attention ?"

"Yeah, especially when she flirted with my boyfriend." She glared at him once more. "Go to hell, Walsh! I have nothing more to tell you." Flippantly, she plastered a phony smile on her face and swayed over to a nearby table. Again, her offensive laughter was heard over the noisy hum in the dreary tavern.

Jack looked at Charlie and held out a ten-dollar bill. Charlie took the money, rang the total on the register and placed the change on the bar. "Who's the owner of this bar?" Jack hoped the big ape could speak.

Charlie looked down at the money Jack was sliding toward him. "Name's Bill Tanner, usually comes in at night. No special time."

Jack passed the bills over. "Thanks, Charlie."

* * *

Near the end of her shift, Sally sighed impatiently and rolled her eyes at the middle-aged couple who wouldn't take the hint it was closing time fifteen minutes ago. She already cashed out her tabs for the night and rolled her loose change in exchange for bills. Charlie had placed the money in the safe and was putting on his coat. Sally tapped her fingers impatiently on the bar, her feet ached like a bad tooth and she was bone weary.

The bar was closed for Thanksgiving, but it was just another day off as far as she was concerned. Her folks moved to Tennessee four years ago, so she'd spend another holiday alone. What was the big deal? Holidays were just one big hassle. She checked out the progress of the poky couple seated in the booth. They appeared to be in a world of their own, totally oblivious to their surroundings. "They must be meeting on the sly," she mumbled to Charlie, "why else would they be sitting in this bar, looking into each other's faces, as if they can't bear to say good bye? If they were married, they certainly would have left by now." Charlie turned on the overhead lights to illuminate the bar brightly.

The couple finally got the message and stood to leave.

In the parking lot of Max's, Sally waved to Charlie as she pulled her car onto the road to head for home. She worked a double shift to allow one of the other girls the day off to travel home for the holiday.

Again, Sally thought about her plans for tomorrow, which included doing her nails and touching up the dark roots in her hair. Big whoopee!

She entered her apartment, kicked off her boots and tossed her keys on the coffee table. She looked around the room with disgust. She hated her dump of a place. Her boyfriend promised to marry a year ago. She hoped to have a house of her own by now. First, he needed to find the right time to divorce his wife. Sally felt her blood pressure rise as she wondered how long he'd use the lame line to keep her off his back. Sally poured herself a healthy swig of bourbon on the rocks and lit a cigarette. Her stomach churned when she thought about how much time she'd wasted. Not that she had many options left open to her. The guys certainly weren't lined up at her doorstep like they used to be. She turned the radio on low, the silence in the apartment added to her feelings of loneliness.

If only her boyfriend could sneak away from his family for a few hours tomorrow, it would help make the day seem brighter and it would also take her mind off the homemade pumpkin pie she'd be missing. Oh, and to have one little taste of Mom's roasted turkey with sausage stuffing. With a far-off gaze, Sally swirled the ice cubes in her glass around distractedly. Shit! She must be getting soft in her old age. She hated the holidays. She turned up the volume on the radio and hoped to drown out the harsh reality her life was a pitiful contradiction to the plans she'd designed for herself years ago.

CHAPTER SIX

Sam lifted another forkful of instant mashed potatoes to his mouth. He longed to be home with his family instead of eating a generic version of Thanksgiving dinner in a greasy twenty-four-hour truck stop. It was the only place he found open on the holiday evening. The entire day was spent watching for any trace of Beth at her grandmother's home. He called Jack to report the only activity he noted was Rose Brockton crossing the street to spend the afternoon and early evening with her neighbors. Afterwards, she returned to her own home to retire for the night. To his disappointment there was no sign of Beth.

Sam studied the other lone patrons scattered around the diner. He wondered, as he watched each of them consuming their meals, if this was their usual routine. It certainly wasn't the life style for him. He needed the satisfaction and security of coming home to a family each night, especially on holidays. He and Beth had talked about having a house full of kids.

Suddenly, the urge to find her was overwhelming. He picked up the tab as the waitress approached him with a piece of pie which closely resembled pumpkin. "Your dinner includes a piece of pie, Sir."

Sam waved off the pie. "No thanks, I'm full. Give it to another customer."

She looked at him curiously. "Most customers in this place don't turn down food, especially when it's free." Sam handed her a generous tip.

"Thanks!" she smiled, gratefully, "Happy Thanksgiving."

On the drive back to the motel room, Sam fought the sinking feeling he might never find Beth. She could be anywhere, and the odds of finding her seemed more remote as each day passed.

* * *

"Shit!" muttered Sally, as she attempted to pick up the ringing phone without messing up her second coat of nail polish. "Yeah. Hello!" She frowned and held up her hand to inspect the damage done to two nails.

"Hi Sal, it's me."

Sally's frown was replaced by a sly smile. "Oh hi, Hon. What's goin' on?" She made an effort to mask the eagerness in her voice. A gal must never let her guy know how much she wanted to see him, especially if he was the one who kept her dangling with the promise of leaving his wife when the time was right.

His voice sounded nervous as he spoke softly. "I need to come by."

Sally drummed her nails on the phone impatiently. It didn't take a Rhodes Scholar to determine he was sneaking the call from somewhere at home with his wife close by. Sally noted the messy state of her apartment. She cradled the phone against her shoulder as she picked up dirty dishes and personal items around the room. She had long ago given up hope he might get away to see her. "When?" She glanced at the time.

"I'll be by in an hour or so."

Sally hated to be at his beck and call. It really went against her grain, but what choice did she have? For the time being they had to steal whatever time they were able to piece together.

She flew around the apartment to straighten the place and quickly showered. While she sprayed her hair with another layer of hair spray, she heard the front door open. She popped her head out of the bathroom and smiled. "Hi, Sugar," she cooed, "I'll be right with you." She hummed to herself while she purposely kept him waiting.

"Come on, Sal. I don't have all night, for Christ's sake!"

"All right! What's the big hurry?" she asked as she entered the living room. She held his large hand and curled up beside him. "Anxious to see me?" She smiled and snuggled closer as he slipped his arm around her. He wasn't the most handsome man in the world, but he was big and macho which she liked about him, especially when she could use her feminine wiles to get him to do almost anything for her. He was her big teddy bear.

"I wish it could always be like this," she murmured. She knew how edgy he got when she brought up the subject regarding a more permanent arrangement, but she couldn't resist getting her digs in.

When he turned her to face him, she noted his ruddy complexion was more flushed than usual.

"What have you been up to?" he asked. The impatience in his voice was obvious.

"Oh, you know, pampering myself on my day off work." She noticed a menacing darkness in his steel gray eyes and frowned slightly. "What's wrong, baby? You look like you're mad at me."

He set his drink on the table, but didn't bother to use one of the floral coasters. She knew how to lighten his brooding scowl. As she wrapped her arm around the back of his neck and gently pulled him toward her, kissed him eagerly, but stopped when she he didn't reciprocate. She studied his face once more, irritated by the frequency of his mood swings of late. She stood to light a cigarette.

"What is it?" She placed her hands on her hips, annoyed she'd dropped everything at his insistence.

When he walked toward her, his stocky build seemed threatening. "I understand Jack Walsh was at the bar yesterday asking you questions about Beth Brockton."

Sally glared at him. "Yeah, so what? Who cares about her or why she left town?"

He grabbed her by the arm and roughly pulled her toward him. "What did you tell him?"

"Ouch, you're hurting me! What's gotten into you?"

He shook her, hard. "I asked you a question. Answer me!"

"I didn't tell him anything!" Her anger jumped into defense mode. He smacked her across the face. She pulled away and swung back her arm to retaliate, as anger and hurt surged through her, but he grabbed her wrists to block her attempted shot.

"I take it personal when the people I trust lie to me." His eyes were glassy, but didn't hide the rage he couldn't control. She'd seen the look before. She also knew he was high on cocaine and it wasn't the time to argue. He pulled her to him when she didn't answer.

"Why would I lie to you? I don't know anything about Beth Brockton, exactly what I told Walsh. Ask him yourself if you don't believe me."

He pushed her away and stepped to the door. "The next time something like this happens, I expect you to tell me about it right away. Do you understand?"

She nodded her head as if she understood, but all she felt was anger that seethed inside of her. He opened the door and ducked when Sally picked up her drink. He slammed the door shut and heard glass shatter.

"Stupid bitch!" She heard him yell.

Sally picked up the pieces of broken glass. What's gotten into him? He'd never hit her before. This was all because of Beth Brockton. She surveyed the damage to her face. Already her lip was swollen and her nose was bleeding. "Bastard!" she grumbled out loud and delicately pressed ice to her tender face.

It didn't take Sally long to switch gears from being the helpless victim to wanting full-fledged retaliation. She grabbed her car keys and stormed out the door. She knew exactly how to get even with someone in his position.

* * *

After Jack completed the incident reports at the end of his shift, he leaned back in his chair and placed his feet on the desk. His shoulders were tense and he felt as if he could sleep for a week. His regular sleeping routine was cut short while he spent his off-duty time searching for clues surrounding the mystery of Beth's disappearance. He sorted through the stack of mail he'd ignored all week and tossed the junk mail into the wastebasket under his desk.

Suddenly, he sat upright in his chair when he opened a letter addressed to him. He read the typed words: *Back off the Brockton case, or else!* He read the note again and thought the words gave credibility he was onto something worthy of investigation. He'd been acting on a hunch, but this proved there was a much larger mystery to solve than what he'd originally suspected. He refolded the note, then examined the envelope postmarked two days earlier from Detroit.

During the drive home, the impact of the words hit him, *Back off. . . or else*. Or else what?

He lingered in the driveway of his house and debated whether or not to share the contents of the letter with Suzanne. She had every right to be informed of the threat which could affect the entire family. He had no choice but to discuss this with her.

* * *

Suzy stared at the note for several seconds before she searched Jack's face. He held her hand when he saw fear in her eyes. "I don't want Bradley to hear," she whispered. "What do you think this means?"

"There's a lot more to the story. I seem to be scratching the surface, and upsetting someone in the process."

Suzy folded the note and slipped it under the place mat when she heard Bradley's footsteps descending the stairs two at a time. He entered the kitchen all smiles and hurried over to greet Jack.

"Hi, Dad." Jack held Brad close, but his gaze met Suzy's worried expression.

Bradley grabbed a blueberry muffin on his way to the door. "Bye Mom, Dad."

When the door slammed behind him, Suzy looked at Jack. "I'll do whatever you think is right, honey," she said.

Jack studied her sweet, troubled face, momentarily marred by a deep frown.

"Don't put the burden of this decision on me, Jack. You tell me what we should do."

"It's now a matter of police business when a threat like this occurs. I should turn this whole case over to another officer." He frowned, torn between this options.

Suzy reached to squeeze his hand. "I love my brother and I know Beth has always been like a sister to you." She looked at him with tenderness in her striking blue eyes. "I trust you more than anyone in the world. I know you'll do what's right." Jack held her hand tightly when he saw her eyes mist with tears. "Who do you think sent this note?" she asked.

Jack shrugged his shoulders. "I talked to a few people at the theater where Beth worked. I also questioned several people at Max's Tavern. No one remembers anything about her disappearance. Something happened to Beth between the time she left the theater and arrived at the tavern. Somebody knows exactly what, but evidently wants it to remain a secret." He felt the need to protect her as he embraced her against him. "I promise I won't let anyone harm you or Brad."

Suzy stretched to kiss him. "I'm more worried about your safety. I can't bear to think what life would be like if. . ."

He placed a finger on her lips to hush her fears and bent to kiss her.

* * *

Jack sat in his regular seat at Max's Tavern. Charlie automatically set a local draft beer in front of him and nodded a greeting. Jack felt honored to have received such special treatment; Charlie was warming up to him.

"Is Bill Tanner in tonight, Charlie?" inquired Jack. Charlie nodded toward the back room.

While Jack waited for Tanner, he looked around the room. Several of the faces he recognized from his previous visits. He spotted Sally who was seated at a table with a group of women. She smiled in response to the conversation, but he saw her nervously glance at him.

He saw how she rubbed the palms of her hands on her apron as she stood to take an order from a couple seated at a booth. At the bar, she avoided eye contact with Jack as she arranged glasses on her tray for Charlie.

Charlie scowled while he poured booze and mix to fill the order. "The cop wants to talk to you, Sal." He nodded his head toward Jack.

Sally nervously looked at Charlie, then glared at Jack who heard her say, "You can tell him to kiss my ass! I have nothing to say to him." She turned away in a huff and delivered the drinks then rejoined the ladies from her bowling team.

Jack frowned when he noted the shiner Sally had attempted to conceal with make-up. On closer inspection he saw her swollen lip. His thoughts were distracted when the owner of the bar entered the main lounge.

Sally jumped to her feet and grabbed a cloth to wipe the bar. Bill stepped over to Jack while he motioned for Charlie to fix a couple of drinks. "I'm Bill Tanner." He extended his hand to Jack. "You must be the cop who wants to talk to me."

Jack nodded his head. "Yeah, I'm Jack Walsh."

Charlie placed the fresh drinks in front of the two men and turned to wash the dirty glasses lined on the bar .

Jack studied Bill Tanner in detail. He appeared to be in his mid-forties. Somehow, he didn't look like a small bar owner. Jack recognized him from last year's election when Tanner won the race for councilman. From his finely tailored sports jacket to his leather Italian loafers, he appeared to dress like the successful business man he was.

"So what do you want to talk to me about?" asked Tanner as he took another sip from his drink.

Jack scrutinized his face before he continued. "I'm looking for any information about a night two years ago when Beth Brockton was on her way here to pick up her mother. I need to know if anyone saw her or anything suspicious about that night." Jack calmly crossed his leg and focused on Tanner.

Tanner's forehead knotted in a slight frown. "Such a long time ago. I sure don't recall anything out of the ordinary."

Jack dug deeper. "Do you remember seeing Beth Brockton on other occasions?"

Bill swirled the ice in his glass and narrowed his dark eyes. "Sure! She often came here to pick Linda up after her shift. Linda usually stayed after work to get sauced. She was always in need of a ride home." Jack considered this information for a moment before he continued. "Could you get me a list of the people who worked here then?" Bill's expression remained unchanged, but his eyes darkened further.

"I'll see what I can do." He waved to a customer seated at a table. "If you'll excuse me, I have to get back work."

Jack nodded. "If you think of anything, I'd appreciate a call." Jack handed him a card with his pager number.

Bill took the card. "I'll do that," he said and turned to join his friends at a booth.

* * *

Later in the evening, Jack stopped at the Aidan Theater to talk to the manager. He found Rick Williams behind the concession stand repairing a pop dispenser.

"Looks like the pop machine is winning," quipped Jack.

Rick shot Jack a look of disdain, set the screwdriver down and wiped his greasy hands on a towel. "What do you need now, Jack?" He didn't bother to hide his irritation.

"I'm just checking to see if you have the names of employees who worked with Beth Brockton." Jack smiled.

"No! I really haven't had time to look the information up." Jack noticed how Rick's face flushed as the line at the counter grew longer, along with their impatience. "I've got to fix this pop machine. We're between shows."

Jack stepped aside and leaned on the counter. "Go ahead. I'll wait."

* * *

Sleepily, Sally fumbled around on the nightstand in search of the snooze button on the clock radio. She slowly opened one eye to check the time. It was only five-thirty in the morning! That was the middle of the night for her. She gently nudged her lover. "Babe, it's time to get up," she mumbled.

He groaned and threw his arm across her. She snuggled closer and was reminded of last night when he appeared at her door to apologize and beg her forgiveness for acting like such a jerk. He blamed his anger on his jealous response to Jack Walsh getting friendly with her. He promised he'd never hurt her again, gave her a beautiful pair of sapphire earrings, and told her how they matched the color of her eyes. Then he spent the entire night with her.

He must really feel bad! She smiled to herself with satisfaction as she slipped out of bed. At least he cared enough to feel guilty. Sally threw on a red, silk robe and said, "I'll make a pot of coffee while you shower."

He stirred and mumbled a gruff, "Yeah. Whatever." He stumbled toward the bathroom and turned on the shower. As he checked out his overnight stubble in the mirror, he wondered what he'd tell Doris tonight when he got home from work. She was going to read him the riot act for not coming home last night. He smiled as he stepped into the shower. Whatever hell Doris had in store for him would be worth the romp in the sack with Sally. What a wildcat she could be, especially when he bought her some trinket and fed her a few crap lines.

While he shaved the shrill sound of his pager made him jump.

He retrieved the pager from his pants pocket, noted the number and quickly dressed. He made the call from the phone in Sally's bedroom. "Yeah, what's up?" he asked.

"You know the little problem I asked you to take care of?" The voice on the other end of the phone was calm, yet serious.

"I sent the note last week, he must've got it by now." He listened to the sound of a lengthy sigh and felt certain uneasiness.

"Evidently the note wasn't enough to back him off. Perhaps you need to be a little more aggressive."

He swallowed hard, his mouth suddenly dry. "How aggressive?"

"Just enough for him to realize we mean business."

He sighed and hung up the phone. It was times like this he wished he never got involved in this mess. Yet, when he considered the perks that came with the territory, he never regretted his involvement for long. He searched the medicine cabinet and found some antacids, then joined Sally for a fast cup of coffee before heading off to work.

* * *

Sam's thoughts were a million miles away as he stared at the food on his plate. Another late-night dinner, alone at a small bar and grill, had done a number on his appetite. He decided a few creature comforts like a home cooked meal, a comfortable bed and a good night's sleep would go a long way to lift his sagging spirits. He pushed his half eaten, tasteless sandwich aside and made room to spread the evening edition of the Tri-Star Newspaper on the table. He read each word carefully as not to miss something of importance.

When he examined the local news section, his eyes rested on a picture of a group of kids who had collected canned goods for the needy. He scanned the caption under the picture about a third-grade class who collected more canned goods than all other classrooms at Richard R. Smith Elementary School in Cabot's Cove. Sam took note of the happy, proud faces of the students.

He glanced to the next article, but stopped and examined the photo once more. Something about the teacher in the picture caught his attention. Half of her face was hidden behind one of the students in the back row so he couldn't make out enough of the face to tell if the teacher was Beth. He read the small blip under the photo more carefully . . . _Third grade students with their teacher, Alisa Rose._ Sam scrutinized Alisa Rose's face. It sure was a long shot. Maybe he was so desperate for this person to be Beth he was reading into things. . He folded the paper and tucked it under his arm. At least it was something to investigate. Hell, it was Friday night, he couldn't do anything about it until Monday, anyway. He stood to pay the bill and felt a bit more optimistic.

* * *

Jack stepped out of his patrol car and cautiously approached the rusted blue compact he pulled over for speeding past him on one of the country roads outside of town. As he stepped to the window, he frowned when he recognized the passenger in the vehicle as one of the Wilson kids, Patty, who lived on his street. She couldn't be old enough to be on a date this late.

He waited while the driver, a young man not much older than Patty, lowered the window and then pointed his flashlight toward the passenger. "Do your parents know you're out driving around at this time of night, Patty?"

Patty's eyes were as round as saucers as she shook her head. "Yes, Officer Walsh. They were expecting me home twenty minutes ago. That's why David was driving so fast. We're late!"

Jack directed his attention to the driver, whose face appeared flushed with anxiety. "Let me see your driver's license and registration, young man." Jack examined the birth date, relieved when he discovered David was old enough to drive.

"You know speeding can get you in a lot more trouble than bringing a young lady home past her curfew, don't you?"

David shook his head in agreement. "Yes, Sir."

Jack studied both the kids' faces, they looked as if they were going to pass out. He handed the license and registration to David. "I'm only going to give you a warning this time, but I want your word you'll be careful to obey the posted speed limits." He hid a smile when they both looked at him gratefully.

"I promise. Thanks, Officer Walsh."

Jack watched the car slowly merge onto the road and travel just under the speed limit toward town.

He eased his car onto the road and drove the opposite direction and hoped Rick Williams finally had the names of the employees Beth worked with at the theater.

* * *

A perky young lady who worked behind the concession stand informed Jack that Rick Williams was off work for the evening. "He left this for you, though." She handed him a sealed envelope and turned her attention to a customer.

Jack stepped away from the counter, opened the envelope and read the names of nine former employees with the dates they were employed. He tucked the list in his coat pocket. Hopefully, someone was on the list knew the secrets Beth so cautiously guarded.

As he drove back to town, he wondered if Sam had made any progress. He sure sounded discouraged the last time they talked. Jack wished something promising would break soon. He was deep in thought when his attention was drawn to his rearview mirror. He noted headlights from an approaching car were rapidly gaining speed. Jack couldn't make out the type of car; the idiot had his high beams on. He maintained his current speed and patiently waited for the car to catch up. It was only moments later when the car passed him in a blur. Jack switched on his siren and flashing lights and stepped on the gas pedal in hot pursuit. "What's your big hurry, buddy?" he mumbled, as he watched his speedometer pass eighty.

Jack turned a corner and caught a glimpse of the car, but it was too far ahead to get a make on the license plate. He continued to follow and half expected the car to come to a stop when the driver realized a cop followed. Jack rounded another corner. Again, he lost sight of the car as he followed through the winding country roads outside town. His tires screeched as he rounded a tight turn. Jack grasped the steering wheel firmly and fought to keep the car on the road.

He reached for the radio hand control and spoke clearly into the mouthpiece. "This is car twenty-four in pursuit of a dark sports car, license unknown, headed east at a high rate of speed on Ridgeway Road, near Holliman. Requesting back up."

"Ten four, Walsh. Officer Hutchins is in your vicinity. I'll radio him for assistance."

"Roger that." Jack set the mic down and tried to gain enough speed to read the license number. By having the advantage of knowing each and every turn in the roads he had traveled his entire life, he was able to anticipate the sharp turn in the road around the next bend. Before he rounded the corner, he decreased his speed to keep his car in control. The back of the car fishtailed, but he expertly maneuvered to avoid a spin out. As he punched the gas pedal, he was suddenly aware of something in the road several yards in front of his car.

"What the. . ." he yelled and quickly turned the wheel to avoid hitting a tire in the center of the road. This time Jack was powerless to control the spinning car as the surrounding trees and road rushed by the windows in a flash. "Son of a bitch!" he shouted, as he swerved the car to avoid a tree in his path. The car veered off the road down an embankment and flipped over once before it came to a stop in a field.

Jack felt a blast of pain before darkness engulfed him.

* * *

Sam flopped down on the bed in his motel room and opened the newspaper. Once again, he studied the photo of Alisa Rose with her third-grade class. He squinted in an attempt to create Beth's face out of the hidden facial features of Alisa Rose.

He tossed the paper aside and sighed. Would this be the clue he'd been searching for? By Monday, he could be out of this shabby, lonely motel room, and with any luck at all, Beth would be safely in his arms.

He switched off the light and when he stared into the darkness he pictured Beth's face. He tried to remember the sound of her voice, the softness of her touch. He flipped the light back on and opened the latest novel from his favorite author. He lost himself deep in the midst of Middle Eastern terrorism, which was much more conducive to sleep than images of Beth's soft lips against his.

* * *

Sometime later, Sam sat upright to the sound of loud ringing. He grabbed the phone, his heart already raced from the abrupt awakening. "Hello!" he grumbled.

"Sam, its Mom!" Her voice was noticeably shaken.

Sam turned on the light, searched for his watch and noted the time. Suddenly alert, he couldn't shake the feeling something was wrong. "What is it? Is Dad all right?" He dreaded the answer as he felt his heart sink from the anticipation another heart attack could be the reason for this call in the middle of the night.

"Your father is fine, dear."

Sam paused, relieved. "What then?" Could it be Suzy or the baby?

"It's Jack. His patrol car ran off the road tonight." Her voice shuddered. "He's in the hospital, unconscious."

Sam pinched the bridge of his nose. His head already throbbed from lack of sleep and the tension mounted at a fast clip. "What's his condition?" The words sounded strange as he spoke.

"Right now he's in critical condition. Can you come home? Suzanne could use your support right now."

Sam was already on his feet throwing his belongings into his duffel bag. "I'm on my way right now, Mom. Tell Suzy to hang in there."

It wasn't until he was halfway home he made the connection between the threatening letter Jack received and the coincidence of the accident. He forced his foot on the gas pedal. Something was terribly wrong with this picture.

When he entered the waiting room on the third floor of the hospital, he rushed to his mom's open arms. She looked tired and beside herself with worry. "How is he?" he asked and made a clumsy attempt to steady his voice.

"There's no change. Suzanne is with him now. She won't leave his side for a moment. Perhaps you can convince her to get some rest."

"Where's Bradley?" Sam searched the waiting room, only to discover he and his mom were alone.

"Your dad is with him tonight. Suzy didn't want to wake him with the news. She'll tell him in the morning."

Sam walked down the hall corridor, found the room and paused in the doorway to observe. He heard the hum, whirl and clicks of the tubes and machines which were vital to Jack's survival. His eyes stung with tears when Suzy turned to face him. She was usually the strong one whom everyone turned to for support. But now she appeared lost and frightened.

"Oh Sam!" she cried and rushed to him.

Sam held her tight but wasn't able to form words past the lump in his throat. "Shh. . ." was all he could manage. She looked up and led him over to the bed where Jack was lying pale and lifeless, except for the steady ventilation from the respirator that filled his lungs. Sam placed his arm around Suzy's small shoulder and drew her to him for support.

Suzy wiped her eyes with a tissue. "I can't believe I still have any tears left."

Sam pulled a chair over and gently guided her into the seat. "You need to get some sleep. Go home with Mom. I'll sit here for the rest of the night."

Suzy's blue eyes were bright with anticipation. "No! I wouldn't sleep if I were at home. I need to be here with him. . . "

Sam knelt in front of her and took her cold hands into his. "What happened?"

"Everything is still under investigation. I guess Jack radioed the station last night around twelve-thirty to request back up during a car chase. When Tom Hutchins arrived at the scene, he found Jack's car in a ravine flipped upside-down. That's all anyone is telling me."

Sam turned to look at Jack once more and saw that his arm was in a cast and his head bandaged. "What are the doctors telling you?" A small part of him didn't want to know the answer.

"He's suffered a head trauma. They don't know the extent yet." She held Jack's limp hand. "They took him to surgery to repair a fractured arm. There doesn't appear to be any other internal injuries." She paused and sighed deeply. "The doctors said that Jack is lucky to be alive. You know how determined he is when it comes to a challenge."

Sam sat next to the bed, but didn't quite know what to do. He recalled when his dad was in Intensive Care after open-heart surgery and the nurses encouraged Sam to talk, even though Dad appeared to be unconscious. "He can hear you," they assured him.

Sam closely studied Jack's face, disappointed when he didn't see his lopsided, goofy grin. "You need to get better, do you hear me?" He watched closely, but the only reaction was the hum of the instruments. "That sound is enough to drive anyone out of their mind," he said softly. "Tomorrow I'll bring a radio so Jack can listen to his favorite country station." Sam smiled and recalled their many battles over Jack's country or Sam's rock station. This was one time he'd gladly concede to Jack's poor taste in music.

* * *

The news of Jack's accident traveled fast through the small town and the surrounding communities. It wasn't often a local cop was hurt in the line of duty around these parts. Along with the shock and excitement the accident generated, speculation and rumors ran rampant. It was the talk of the town.

Before the stores opened in town each morning, it was customary for several of the merchants to meet at Dobson's Drug Store for coffee and gossip. Now, the men didn't consider it gossip as much as catching up on current events, but the wives smiled knowingly. It was just plain old gossip no matter what words they choose to call it.

"They say Jack swerved to avoid hitting a deer," Jim Fitch stated while he took a sip of his coffee.

"Where did you hear that, Jim? The newspaper says the accident is still under investigation." Bob tossed the paper across the counter in Jim's direction.

Jim frowned and stared at a picture of Jack's smashed patrol car. "That's what I heard at Sid's when I filled up the truck."

Cal Ritter picked up the newspaper. "It sure is a shame. Jack's a good kid. I hope he's going to be all right. How's Suzy handling everything, John?"

John Andrews lifted his eyes from the front page of the newspaper. There was concern for his son-in-law etched in the lines on his forehead. "She's a little better this morning. Jack has shown definite signs of improvement overnight."

"I wonder if it was more than just an accident." The men turned to look curiously at Mike Angelino, owner of the local pizzeria.

"What do you mean?" asked John. "Have you heard something to indicate it was intentional?"

"I don't know. I suppose I'm letting my imagination get away from me, but it seems odd Jack would lose control of his car without something causing him to do so." The men grew quiet while they contemplated this information.

"Maybe I can get some information from Tom, he was the officer who first arrived at the scene," stated Tom's dad, Marv Hutchins.

John Andrews looked at his watch and stood to leave for the hardware store. "Let me know what you find out from your boy, Marv."

* * *

That evening at Max's Tavern, Sally Cantrell glanced at the newspaper Charlie tossed on the bar in front of her and looked at him as if to say she wasn't the least bit interested in the boring news. "Yeah, so what?" she shrugged and looked around the bar. It was a slow night. She pulled her tips out of her apron pocket and made a disgusted face.

Charlie pointed to the local column on the front page. "Check out the article on your friend, Jack Walsh." He tapped on the paper.

Sally stuffed the money back into her pocket and grabbed the paper out from under Charlie's massive hand. Quickly, she read the article about the accident and frowned. "Wow! I wished he'd drop dead when he was here bothering me, but I didn't mean it." She narrowed her eyes and remembered how her boyfriend reacted when Jack asked her questions about Beth Brockton. She leaned toward the bartender and lowered her voice so no one else could hear.

"Do you think someone did this to him on purpose, Charlie?" Charlie shrugged, backed away and continued to polish the bar.

"I don't know anything except to keep my nose out of everyone's business but my own."

CHAPTER SEVEN

Alisa Rose clasped her hands together and watched from the wings of the stage as her students sang the final song of the holiday pageant. She gazed at the polished faces of the children. They looked so innocent, dressed in their holiday best. Their faces were bright with eager anticipation as they sang to their family and friends seated in the auditorium. Alisa peered around the curtain and caught a glimpse of the audience. She was delighted to find the same enthusiastic expressions smile back at the students. The kids loved this time of the year. They were so excited and happy. She couldn't share the same feelings of joy. For her, the holidays were another painful reminder of shattered dreams.

For just an instant she felt a flutter of alarm wash over her as she searched the audience more carefully. Who was out there watching her? She felt an eerie sensation inch up her body as the hair on her arms stood straight up. She ducked behind the curtain and tried to catch her breath. She inhaled slowly to calm herself before a full-blown panic attack ensued. Why this feeling of vulnerability slithered into her thoughts so easily was beyond reasoning. Grateful when the song came to an end, she smiled as the audience stood and loudly applauded the children's efforts. She stepped from behind the curtain to escort the students from the stage to the classroom where refreshments were served for the kids and their families.

When everyone had departed, Alisa sat at her desk to rest for a moment. She wasn't ready to go out into the frigid night and then home to her empty apartment. She picked up a gold paper star one of the kids made for her and turned it over to read the words, Love, Mandy White. As Alisa stared at the star, she imagined the star Sam placed on the top of the Christmas tree at his parent's house on Christmas Eve. Mrs. Andrews made all the holiday traditions come to life. Alisa closed her eyes and vividly recalled the smell of mulled cider that simmered on the stove, holiday music played softly in the background and a fire crackled in the fireplace. After Sam set the star at the top of the tree, he would turn to her with a smile and pull her to her feet to help him hang the mistletoe.

Why did everything remind her of Sam? Quickly she gathered the papers she had to catch up on that weekend, but knew all of the diversion she attempted would not rid her mind of Sam.

"Hey, Alisa. If you're ready to leave, we can walk out with you." Startled, Alisa looked up to find Ann Woroczyk at the doorway.

"Great, Ann. Let me grab my things."

Together they walked outside to the parking lot. "You did a great job organizing the program, Alisa. It was lovely."

Alisa smiled. "Thanks, Ann. I really enjoyed it." Ann turned toward her car. "See you on Monday."

Alisa started the ignition and stepped outside to scrape ice from her windows. She nervously searched the parking lot for anything out of the ordinary. Luckily there was a steady flow of cars exiting, so she wasn't alone.

She despised this feeling of uncertainty. Could she remember a time when she didn't jump at every shadow or noise? How long could she live like this, wondering when someone might appear out of nowhere to harm her?

Again, she surveyed the parking lot before she jumped into the car to drive home. She was too tired to think about the papers she had to grade and the lesson plans to be completed, not to mention the final exam in her lit class she hadn't studied for.

She parked her car in the assigned spot behind the apartment building and grabbed the stack of papers. Her arms were full and she struggled to maintain her balance on the icy ground as she locked the car door. This was the most unsettling part of her day, when she had to enter the apartment alone. She arrived home later than usual which made her feel exceptionally vulnerable.

She rushed to her second-floor apartment, uneasiness crept over her as she quickly climbed the stairs. While she reached into her coat pocket for keys, a noise from below alerted her. She turned to see if someone climbed the stairway, her heart raced instantly. She wanted to cry out when footsteps sounded on the metal stairs. Her hands were numb as she fumbled and attempted to fit the key into the lock. Hurry!! The deafening command echoed in her brain.

She turned toward the stairs and cried out when a dark figure advanced toward her. She dropped the books and papers as he grabbed her by the arms and spun her around to face him. She hit at him with her fists. "Leave me alone!" she screamed.

He attempted to grab her flailing arms. "Beth! Stop it!"

She looked at him, but her panicked thoughts didn't allow her to focus. He ducked when she swung her fisted hand at his chin. "It's me.
. .Ouch!" he yelled when she kicked him.

Although she missed her intended target, she could tell the impact of her foot on his knee caused just as much damage. Frantically, she pushed him away and retrieved her keys.

"Damn it, Beth! It's me. . . Sam!"

For an instant his words didn't penetrate her jumbled thoughts. SAM! Finally the word registered in the far reaches of her mind. She blinked. It couldn't be Sam.

He held her firmly and forced her to look at him, but she struggled to free herself. "I won't hurt you." His voice was filled with tenderness as he drew her close and gently touched his lips to her forehead.

She closed her eyes and wondered if this was another cruel dream. The rugged smell of his leather coat and the spiced scent of after-shave assaulted her senses and stirred up memories. It wasn't a dream. She felt as if she were in a fog and gently brushed his cheek with her leather-gloved fingertips. "Sam!" Her words were barely audible. "How did. . ."

Sam held her close and buried his face between her coat and her cheek. "I thought I'd never find you," he whispered against her, his words choked with emotion.

Beth jerked away, searched the street below and expected to find someone else climb the stairs. She covered her mouth with her hand, this was far worse than any nightmare.

"Why are you here?" she asked, but turned away before he could answer and unlocked the door. She had to get him inside before someone discovered them together.

Her books were scattered on the cement landing and the student's assignments blew about from the slight wind while several floated down the steps. She rushed to retrieve the wayward papers, as Sam gathered the books. Again, Beth searched the street below. She hesitated in the open door and dreaded the thought of being alone with him.

He pulled her into the apartment, closed the door and locked it securely. He switched on the light and stared at her intensely. His blue eyes were filled with question, or was it confusion? His strong jaw was set for confrontation. His sensuous lips, fixed in a thin line, revealed no emotion. He shoved both hands into the pocket of his jeans. "We need to talk."

Beth stubbornly marched across the room into the kitchen to set the kettle onto the flame to boil water for tea. Why this sounded like it was the answer to her problems, she hadn't a clue. She only knew she needed time to think, time to clear her thoughts.

Sam followed and watched as she placed tea bags into a pottery pot. She refused to look at him as awkward silence loomed over them. Sam continued his position from the doorway. It was obvious he looked as uncomfortable as she felt. Her cheeks burned and her hands trembled as she offered him a cup of tea.

When he moved closer, she turned, afraid her true feelings would be revealed if she met his gaze, afraid he'd discover she was lying when she asked him to leave. She was certain her body would betray her thoughts when she attempted to push him away. If he touched her, she wouldn't be able to hide the reality she wanted him to hold her forever. She clutched her fist to her chest and tried in vain to still her aching heart.

"How did you find me?" she asked. She had to know how easy it was for him to locate her and wondered when others would follow.

"I've been staying in the area for over three weeks, searching for you. I discovered a picture in the paper of Alisa Rose with her students. Most of your face was covered, but I had a hunch it was you. At first I missed the connection with the names. I'd forgotten your middle name is Rose." He reached for her hand. "Why did you change your name?" he asked.

She pulled her hand free. "You have to go!" The anxiety in her voice escalated.

"Tell me what's going on." He stepped closer

"There's nothing to talk about." She brushed past him and removed her coat. She saw his tortured expression. He didn't move and it drove her crazy. "I mean it, you have to go." She tossed his coat at him.

He set his coat down and was at her side before she could react. "Not until you tell me what I want to know." His expression, intensity and strength had her reeling.

"I have nothing to tell you." Tears filled her eyes as he brushed a stray lock of hair from her face. She closed her eyes when he moved closer and spoke in deep, hypnotic tones.

"I'm not leaving."

Beth searched his face for only a second, but averted her gaze so he wouldn't read what she was desperate to hide. How easy it would have been to fall into his arms to seek the warmth and protection she craved.

She moved away and clenched her hands into tight fists against her sides. She had to stop these treacherous thoughts. "I have so much work to do this evening. It's already late."

He didn't move. His arms were crossed across his chest, his stance unwavering.

She opened the door and felt the panic rise when he sank down into the worn cushions of the couch, stretched his long, muscular legs and set his boots on the coffee table. He smiled at her smugly and rested his head on the couch. "Go ahead and work. I said I'm not going anywhere." He closed his eyes. "I'll just get a little shut-eye until you're finished."

Powerless to gather her wits, Beth gritted her teeth, aggravated by his lack of cooperation. "Fine!" she sniped at him, "but it's going to be a long wait!"

Beth stormed into her bedroom and shut the door with a bang. She sat on her bed and folded her arms across her chest as frustrated tears sprang to her eyes. She jumped to her feet, unable to sit still and began to pace. She was desperate to think of a plan to convince him to leave. But how was she going to get rid of him before he broke down the vulnerable barrier she had struggled so hard to build? He couldn't stay! She grew weary of pacing. She couldn't hide in her room forever. She had to confront him. "Damn!" she cursed as she opened the door.

Sam opened his eyes and she tried to ignore the sad smile pull at the corners of his mouth.

She sat at her desk and organized the papers, all the while she fought to concentrate on her task instead of Sam's beautiful eyes. She had forgotten the breathtaking effect of his eyes. He watched every move as she graded the papers, but she wasn't able to give the students' homework her full attention.

After several moments, Sam stepped behind her and looked over her shoulder. "Do you enjoy teaching?"

She nodded her head positively in reply and felt the skin on the back of her neck tingle. Her body stiffened as he knelt behind her and moved close.

"Do you ever think of what we shared together?" he asked.

His question caught her off guard and her fragile reserve slipped another notch. Still, she said nothing as she attempted to correct the papers. When his lips brushed the nape of her neck, she set down the pen that shook uncontrollably in her hand.

"I know you still care about me, Beth." He wrapped his arms around her and tenderly caressed her arms.

She didn't possess the discipline to move. "Please, Sam."

"Please what?" he whispered against her ear.

"Please stop," she whispered in return.

He swiveled the chair around until she faced him. "You don't want me to stop." He leaned closer still, his lips touched hers gently at first, then became insistent. The kiss deepened as she enfolded her arms around him. His body was hard against hers, he was the only solid thing in her life. He felt real and wonderful.

Suddenly, an image so frightful flashed across her mind. Her body braced as she opened her eyes with a start and pushed him away. "You must go!" she pleaded. "Please go!"

He looked at her, the confusion in his eyes quickly turned to anger. "No."

"There's nothing to tell you." She tried to move away, but he jerked her back to face him.

"I'm done playing games, Beth." His resolute gaze held hers. She was powerless to look away. "I need you to tell me why you left without a word." His eyes narrowed and burned bright. "I tried to hate you for leaving me. Then Jack convinced me you were in trouble. I realized I would do anything to find you, to protect you."

"I'm not in any trouble. I just. . ."

"Jack took me to your house. I saw the bullet holes in your bedroom, I saw my picture blown to pieces." Beth closed her eyes to block out the painful images. "Why didn't you come to me if you needed help? Why did you leave without saying good-bye?" He was shaking her.

"I can't tell you anything." Her stance became determined as her eyes searched his.

"Tell me why Jack received a threatening letter after he asked questions about you."

A wave of panic traveled through her, unraveled what was left of her determination in an instant. "Make him stop!"

Sam relaxed the grip on her arms. "Someone ran him off the road.

He's been in the hospital for over a week."

Beth opened her eyes to stop the spinning sensation and sobbed as she stumbled toward the bathroom. Sam found her splashing cold water onto her face. She turned and held onto the sink for balance. "Is he all right?" Her voice trembled.

"He was unconscious for a few days, but he's coming around. I had to threaten him with bodily harm until he agreed to stop further investigation."

Beth sighed. "Are Suzy and Bradley all right?"

He stepped toward her, but he stopped when she backed away. "They're both fine now that Jack is conscious, and ornery as hell. They're staying with my parents."

"Thank God." She turned away, afraid her fears would be transparent.

"I told him I would find out who is responsible for doing this to you. To us!"

Beth grabbed his arms. "No! You can't get involved, Sam. Tell me you'll stop. Please." Her voice broke as she pleaded.

"I'll stop when you tell me everything. When I know you're safe."

Beth stormed past him. He roughly spun her to confront him.

Beth was desperate for him to end this dangerous inquiry. His safety was at stake and the more he knew, the more dangerous it would become. She had no choice but to hurt him once more. "What happened is in the past, Sam. It doesn't involve you."

"What do you mean?" he shouted at her furiously. "It has everything to do with me, and I intend to find out exactly what it is."

Beth looked into the reflected rage and passion in his dark blue eyes. She longed to hold him, she wanted to tell him exactly what he wanted to hear, but realized she was left with no alternative. She had to send him away hating her even more than he did before. She ignored the burning nausea in her stomach.

"Sam," She couldn't bear to watch him. "I'm engaged to someone else." The words formed, but left a bitter taste in her mouth.

Sam roughly slammed her against the wall. She cringed from the look of betrayal in his eyes. "I don't believe you!" he yelled and pushed her away.

"It's true," she cried, "we teach at the same school."

He glared at her with contempt, picked up his coat and stopped at the door as if he wanted to say more, but instead stepped outside and slammed the door shut.

The sound reverberated through her and she numbly sank to the floor and reeled from his unspoken words.

* * *

When Sam walked into the hospital room, he was pleased to find Jack laughing with two fellow officers, Tom Hutchins and Andy Thompson.

"Hello, Sam." Tom extended his hand. "Hi, Tom, Andy."

"Where have you been keeping yourself, Sam?" Andy questioned. "I haven't seen you around town lately."

Sam glanced at Jack, then back to Andy. "I'm working on a temporary consultant job out of state to filter toxins from Lake Erie."

Sam saw Jack lift an eyebrow. "How are you feeling, Big Guy?" Sam leaned over to get a closer look at Jack. The color in his cheeks had returned to normal and his eyes were clear.

Jack sneered. "I'll feel a hell of a lot better when they let me out of this prison so I can eat a decent meal." Sam sighed. What a relief it was to know Jack was back to normal.

"When are they going to let you go home?" asked Andy.

"After every single cell in my body is thoroughly inspected, I guess." When Tom and Andy left the room, Sam checked to make sure they were gone before he spoke.

"Well? Did you talk to her?" Jack asked in a low tone. Sam nodded his head yes as he watched the television. "What did she say?" Jack asked impatiently.

"She wouldn't give me any information about what happened. She doesn't want me to come back." The constant ache in the pit of his stomach thundered unmercifully. "She's engaged to some guy she teaches with."

"What are you talking about?" Jack frowned.

Sam picked up the remote control from Jack's bed and flipped through the channels. He didn't want to discuss it.

"There's no way Beth is engaged!" Jack stated. "She told you that so you'd stop asking questions. You backed her into a corner. She was desperate."

Sam appeared distant as he changed the television programs. Jack pressed the button on his hospital bed and raised his head so he could look into Sam's eyes. He pulled the cord attached to the remote control and yanked it from Sam. "Your reactions are totally emotional. I told you to stay objective." Jack lectured.

"How in the hell am I supposed to stay objective?" Sam closed his eyes and tried to collect his thoughts. "You got me into this mess, Jack. Now I'm worse off than I was before. I never should have listened to you." Sam stood to leave.

"Stop acting like a first class idiot! Think about what she said and read between the lines."

Sam's patience was worn thin. "That's all I've been thinking about since I left!" Sam restlessly paced the room. He replayed the conversation with Beth over and over in his mind and tried to remain objective. But each time he got to the part about being engaged to someone else, he lost all objectivity. Yet, when he recalled the haunted look in her eyes, he knew if she was engaged to someone else, she wasn't happy about it. Jack's words echoed, she was trying to protect him. From what? He was frustrated there were no answers to the nagging endless questions. "Damn! I'm an idiot," he groaned as he sat at the edge of Jack's bed.

"I'm glad you've come to your senses." Jack chuckled.

Running his fingers thorough his hair, Sam blurted out, "She wouldn't have kissed me like she did if she were engaged to someone else!"

* * *

Alisa didn't know how she was able to get through the days which followed Sam's departure without falling completely to pieces. She went through the motions in a daze and managed to turn off all thoughts of him. She crammed her hours with all the things she needed to do. She took the final exam in her lit class, worked on the lesson plans for next semester and the student evaluations due in Mr. Gordon's office before school closed for Christmas vacation.

With all the distractions, she found herself with the monumental task of digging out from under a mountain of paperwork. Each night she worked well past midnight and only rested when she nodded off to sleep from sheer exhaustion. She dragged herself through the days with barely enough energy to stand, let alone maintain control of a room full of overexcited third graders.

* * *

Alisa smiled at one of her students while she untied the ribbon on the gift he'd placed in her hands. His little face looked like it was ready to burst as he watched eagerly as she carefully removed the wrap from the package. She lifted a small star shaped ornament with an angel sitting on top and watched it spin in the air. She fought back tears and hugged the little boy. "Thank you, Robbie. This is beautiful."

He grinned proudly. "I picked it out myself."

"I'll always think of you when I look at it. I promise."

He beamed. "Cool!" He zipped his coat and rushed through the door to join the rest of the students who poured out of the building to freedom from school for the next two weeks.

"Have a safe holiday," she called out after him.

The students only had a half-session and she intended to use the remainder of the afternoon to complete her assignments. Deep in thought she labored over her work.

"Hey Alisa, are you going to spend the entire vacation working?" Alisa looked up to find Steve Mason, a fellow teacher, at the doorway. "I'll be done in a few hours, Steve." His worried expression touched her.

"You need to get away to some warm, tropical paradise. Why don't you and I sneak away to Jamaica?"

She smiled. "I don't think your wife would approve, but thanks for the offer."

Steve grinned also. "Well, you can't blame a guy for trying." He looked at the papers on her desk. "Seriously, why don't you ask Mr. Gordon if you can turn this assignment in after the holidays?"

Alisa shrugged. "I'd just as soon get it out of the way so I don't have to think about it all vacation."

"Suit yourself, but try to enjoy the break."

"Thanks, I will."

Later, in the teacher's lounge, she was surprised to find so many teachers still at school. She thought she was the only person without a life.

"Alisa, I'm on the decorating committee for the charity New Year's Eve dinner-dance at Cabot's Cove Country Club. Do you think you'll attend?"

Alisa poured herself a cup of coffee and turned to Jane Summers, a kindergarten teacher. "I don't know what my plans are just yet, Jane."

Jane held out an envelope. "Here's a list of all the information and ticket price. You're welcome to bring a date if you want."

Alisa noted the slight question in Jane's voice. "I'll let you know, Jane. Have a happy holiday."

"I hope you can make it. It's always a great party."

* * *

Sam located the classroom, stood in the doorway and observed Beth as she erased the chalkboard. She appeared deep in thought and oblivious to her surroundings. He couldn't help but smile at her obvious attempt to dress the part of a schoolteacher, with her black pencil skirt and pale pink knit sweater. Her chestnut hair was swept into a French twist and glasses perched on the bridge of her nose. Yet, nothing could disguise her long legs, the gentle curves of her slender body and the wayward curls of hair that rebelled against the restraints of her pinned hair. He smirked to himself and imagined all the young boys in her class had to have a gigantic crush on her.

She backed away from the board and jotted a few words in the notebook she held. When she turned, her startled expression met his smiling gaze. The surprise in her eyes turned quickly to distress. "Sam!" She placed her glasses on the desk and nervously rubbed her hands together to rid them of chalk residue. When he walked toward her, she grabbed the chair for support as what little color drained from her face and she bit her lower lip. His heart filled with love, he wanted to protect her from whatever thoughts forced her to react so to his presence.

He leaned on her desk. "I came to apologize for my behavior last week. I lost my temper, Beth. I'm sorry." Her gaze darted nervously to search the doorway. "Or should I call you Alisa?"

She looked at him tensely and placed her finger to her lips in a silent, pleading gesture for him to keep quiet.

He lowered his voice. "We need to talk." She brushed past him then shut the door.

"Are you afraid your betrothed will hear us?"

When she whirled around to confront him, her cheeks were no longer pale, but flushed. "Do you think this is a joke? I have nothing to tell you." Her whiskey- colored eyes glared at him as she jutted out her chin.

Sam almost laughed and recalled how obstinate she could be when she was annoyed. "You have plenty to say to me." He was much more stubborn than she could ever hope to be. They faced each other, but neither spoke. Sam wanted to kiss away the ridiculous smudge of chalk dust on her upper lip. He wanted to take her into his arms and hold her so close she'd understand he was strong enough to protect her. She'd understand he'd never let her be alone again.

Beth was the first to look away and he could see how much it bothered her to do so. He casually sat on the corner of her desk and crossed his arms upon his chest. The longer he watched her, the more frazzled she appeared. Finally, she looked up with tears clinging to the tips of her dark, thick lashes. His chest hurt as he longed to kiss away her fears.

"You can't stay here and interfere with my life any longer, Sam. You have to go."

"Look, if I didn't feel so bad about the way you are struggling to keep your voice steady, and the fact you are the most beautiful women I've ever seen, then I'd really lose my temper." He cleared his throat. "What do you mean interfere with your life? What about our life?" His voice strained to remain calm.

"We've been over this already, Sam. There's nothing to talk about." He leaned across the desk and studied her with determination.

"This time I'm not going to leave until you tell me everything." He pointed his finger at her accusingly. "Don't think you can fool me again by concocting another ridiculous story about being engaged to someone else." He could tell she was ready to jump into defense mode, but instead she sat down and looked defeated.

"We can't talk here." She glanced at the time. "I have less than an hour to complete this work." She pointed to the papers on her desk and Sam detected her desperation.

"All right," he conceded. "I'll be back at five o'clock." At the door he turned to her. "Promise you won't disappear again?" He held his sadness in check.

"I promise," she whispered as he left the room.

* * *

"Damn!" she swore under her breath and pounded the desk with her clenched fist. Was it too much to ask to be left alone to live her miserable, lonely, pathetic life without interference? She covered her face with her hands. She hadn't the strength to face another confrontation with Sam. She forced her attention to her work.

Finally, she stretched to ease her tense muscles and sighed with relief as she sorted the completed papers into a neat stack. She had just enough time to meet with Mr. Gordon and freshen up a bit.

Mr. Gordon wasn't in his office, so Beth placed her assignment on his desk and wrote a quick note to wish him a happy holiday. In the teacher's restroom she examined herself in the mirror. Her face appeared drawn from nerves and her eyes were bloodshot with visible dark circles which were accented by her pale complexation. She applied a dab of color to her cheeks and rubbed the smudged mascara away with a tissue. She attempted to straighten her hair, but the curls refused to behave. She turned to review the overall picture and sadly thought she was definitely not the same carefree woman Sam was engaged to. "Oh well. It doesn't matter." She held her head up with confidence. "He'll be gone after tonight. There's no reason to fret over what he thinks of my appearance." Suddenly, the false sense of confidence was replaced with a stabbing pain of loss.

In the classroom, she found Sam reading the holiday poems on the bulletin board and she unlocked the closet to gather her belongings.

Sam held her coat while she slipped her arms into the sleeves. "Thank you," she murmured.

He followed and at the door she turned to make sure everything was in order before she switched off the lights. She rushed back to her desk and retrieved the ornament Robbie had given to her.

Sam looked at the box and questioned, "Is that a gift from a secret admirer?"

"You could say that," she smiled, coyly. "He's eight years old."

"If you're trying to make me jealous, you need to come up with a more believable story."

Her gentle laugh rippled through the room, but stopped when she noticed Sam's peculiar expression. "What's wrong?" she asked.

His gaze met hers and she could read the conflict and rage under the surface. "I'd forgotten how musical your laughter is," he said. She pivoted away from him, the lightness of the moment vanished.

Both were silent as they walked to the parking lot and Sam stopped by her car. "Do you want to stop somewhere for dinner, Beth? I'm starving." When she fretted, he quickly continued. "Tell you what, I've had my fill of restaurant food. Let's eat at your place."

Unable to make eye contact with him, she turned away and her mind screamed, "You shouldn't be here!" Out loud she said, "I don't have a thing to cook at my apartment."

"Let's stop at a grocery store. I'll be glad to cook," he volunteered.

Beth sneered. "Since when do you like to cook?"

"There are many things you don't know about me." His expression was still intense which added to her unease. He lightly skimmed his fingers on the side of her face. "You can't stand the thought of us getting close again, can you?" he asked.

She brushed his hand away and unlocked her car. "Follow me," she instructed.

* * *

At the meat counter, Sam turned to Beth. "Pick something out, but keep it simple. I didn't say I was a great cook."

"I'm not really hungry." Subconsciously, she reached to quiet the war zone in her stomach.

Which Sam didn't miss as he frowned. "How about grilled chicken?" He reached over to take her hand. "No wonder you look like a twig.

Your stomach is probably a mess from nerves. All the more reason for you to tell me what's bothering you."

Beth pulled her hand away. She wasn't sure how much she would endure of this pretense.

At the checkout stand, Sam placed the food on the counter as the teen-aged cashier scanned the items. Beth noticed the way she flirted with Sam, and had no clue why this affected her. She wanted to put the little blonde hormone in her place, but chided herself instead. What was the matter with her? She studied Sam while he retrieved the groceries from the cart. She really couldn't blame the cashier for flirting. His brown leather jacket accented his broad shoulders and his blue jeans fit him perfectly and gave just a hint of his strong, muscular legs. His dark brown hair needed a trim, and his five o'clock shadow only added to his brawny appearance. He faced her and his dark blue eyes searched hers for meaning. Embarrassed, she was quick to look away.

The cashier rang up the final item and smiled at Sam provocatively. "Your total comes to thirty-eight, sixty-two, Sir."

Beth reached into her wallet for the money.

"I got it," said Sam.

Beth held the money out to the cashier. "No, I'll pay."

The cashier looked at Beth blankly and took the money from Sam. "He offered first." She punched the amount into the register. "He's not only cute, but a gentleman too!" She winked at Beth, who felt her cheeks flush hotly.

Sam continued to grin as they walked to their cars. "You're enjoying this, aren't you?" she demanded.

He opened the car door for her, his smile faded. "Yeah, I'm getting a real kick out of watching you squirm from the battles raging inside you."

Beth couldn't think of a quick retort.

At her apartment door, Beth automatically searched the street below for suspicious looking cars.

Sam followed her gaze. "What are you looking for?"

"For things that go bump in the night."

She unlocked the door and ushered him inside quickly, then set the dead bolt. He walked past with the groceries as she hung coats in the closet.

When she entered the kitchen, a jolt of panic traveled through her. Sam unpacked the groceries as if he'd performed the task before. His flannel shirt sleeves were folded to below his elbows. His hair was a bit wayward which only added to his handsome allure and his dark stubble sent her over the edge. He appeared so comfortable, as if he belonged in her apartment. What was she doing? This was insane. He wasn't going to stay, she mustn't forget that.

He searched the empty cupboards. "Where are your pans?" Beth pulled her one and only pan from the dish rack. "This is all I have," she said.

"How do you cook with this?" He questioned.

She could feel the tension build between them, and she had a dreadful feeling it wasn't because she had only one pan. "There's a lot you can do with only one pan." She stated, much too defensively.

Sam placed the chicken onto the broiler tray and stepped to her. "Where do you keep your seasonings?"

Beth blushed and passed him a bowl filled with packets of assorted condiments that accompanied carry out orders. He shook his head clearly appalled.

"Since when did you become such a gourmet?" she stated.

He selected a lone packet of soy sauce and sprinkled it over the chicken. Then he opened a package of wild rice mix. "Do I dare ask for a measuring cup?"

"Just guess, makes it more interesting." She tried to remain light, but sensed his presence acutely as she prepared a tossed salad. She chopped at the vegetables blindly, as if the aggression helped soothe her taunt nerves. "Ouch!" She dropped the knife and quickly ran water over her finger.

Sam attempted to examine her cut, but she pulled away. "Let me see," he demanded.

"It's nothing," she said, but her voice shook.

He forced her to face him and he touched the tears on her cheek. "Then why are you crying?"

"I'm not crying because it hurts!"

He examined her finger. "Where are the bandages?"

She wrapped a paper towel around the cut. "I'm all right!"

Sam backed away. "Don't you have any bandages?" She didn't answer. "How do you manage, Beth? This is pathetic."

She whirled around to face him, angrily. "Do you mean pathetic like my life?"

"I didn't say that, but since you mention it, your life is. . ."

"I do just fine, thank you," she interjected. Beth continued to toss the salad while Sam turned the chicken under the flame. She set the table and made an attempt to piece together enough silverware and dishes to complete two sets.

She stared at the hodgepodge when she was finished and decided the results were pathetic, indeed. Thank goodness for plastic silverware. "It will have to do," she stated. He watched her curiously, as she looked around her apartment and turned to him. "It's not much, but I don't have time to cook or decorate. I teach and then go to school at night to complete my graduate degree. I usually eat on the run," she said defensively, hoping to avoid further commentary from him.

"Do you have time to date anyone special?" he asked, his voice forced with nonchalance.

Much too quickly she stated, "No. . .I don't."

He lifted her chin with his fingertips as her gaze met his. "Then I'm glad your life is so pathetic." She smiled weakly and her skin tingled from his slightest touch.

When dinner was ready, Sam pulled out a chair for her to be seated. He poured wine into paper cups, lifted his and tapped it against hers. "To us."

She lowered her eyes as sadness settled around her like light snowflakes. She lifted her gaze when he reached for her hand.

"Are you all right?" he asked, gently. She nodded and picked up the plastic utensils to cut her chicken. The fork promptly broke and a plastic fork tine with a chuck of chicken attached sailed across the table and hit Sam on the cheek. For a moment, Beth covered her mouth and didn't know whether to laugh or cry.

"Is it tough? I warned you at the store that I'm not the greatest cook," he said quietly.

When she looked up at him, her face lightened into a bright smile and she was instantly overcome with a fit of nervous giggles. He laughed, also, as he reached to cut her chicken into bite-size pieces with the only real silverware on the table.

She took a bite. "This is delicious, Sam." She searched his eyes. "How is Jack?"

"He's doing fine. He's out of the hospital in Suzy's clutches." She tried not to smile as she rearranged most of her dinner. Sam had no problem with his appetite as he reached for a second serving. Beth drank her wine and wondered when the confrontation would begin and when the thudding in her chest would calm to a roar.

"Tell me what you've been doing," she asked lightly, but could hardly breathe.

"I completed my master's degree in chemical environmental engineering, and worked for a company that manufactured paint products for about six months. I didn't like being cooped up in a plant facility. I missed working outdoors."

She wasn't surprised. The entire time he attended college, he interned for wildlife agencies specialized in the preservation of the Great Lakes and Michigan Forestry. She remembered his campaign to start a recycling program in Aidan when he was in high school.

"I have a side business testing well water for chemicals and bacteria. I do the work out of my parent's basement. Much to my surprise, it has turned out to be quite lucrative. I have just started to send out resumes`. My dad's recovering from bypass surgery."

Beth felt a stab of guilt. "Oh, I didn't know he was sick." She lowered her gaze and bit her lip.

"How could you have known?" Sam said softly. "He's almost back to work full time, so I can get serious about my job search." He stopped when he noticed the faraway look in her eyes. "I don't know where the future will take me," he said. "How about you?"

She abruptly stood to clear the table while Sam tried to make coffee. He searched for a can opener and found an old manual relic which only worked every fourth turn. Beth tried to steady her voice. "I don't have a coffee maker."

He slammed the coffee can on the counter. "This is a hell of a way to live," he yelled as he tossed the can opener back into the drawer.

"I'm trying to survive here. I told you I manage as best I can," she said as she reached for a jar of instant coffee from her sparse pantry.

"Fine?" he shouted. "You call starving yourself fine? Or being afraid of your own shadow fine? Look at you, you're a wreck." His eyes were on fire as he glared at her.

She tossed the jar of coffee at him and yelled back, "I didn't invite you here. You have no right to talk to me this way." She stormed from the room and he stalked after her. "You need to leave this instant. I don't want you to come back here again. It's over between us." She angrily brushed past him and shut herself in the bathroom. Angry tears filled her eyes as she buried her face in her hands. The truth of his words stung. She was well aware how empty her life was, but it was all the more painful to have him point it out. She tensely brushed out her hair.

After several minutes, she heard a light tap on the door. "I'm sorry I keep losing my temper, Beth. It's because I don't understand how you could choose this life over the one we planned together." He turned the knob, but the door was locked.

His words struck her wounded heart. She opened the door and found him holding a lump of clay shaped into an animal of uncertain species. "That's a gift from one of my students. A little boy made it for a Mother's Day project. He gave it to me because he doesn't have a mother." A lone tear trickled down her cheek.

"You must be special to your students." Sam set the sculpture back on her desk.

"I hope so, they're special to me."

"You keep saying this is your life, but it should be our life!" She turned away to block out his painful expression. "What happened to our dreams?" he whispered.

Beth stared out the window. "Those were dream, this is reality. I never confuse the two any longer." When he reached to take her into his arms, she backed away. "Damn you, Sam! You have to go!"

He stood behind her and she knew he waited for her resistance to break. "I won't leave. Not anymore," he stated softly, but firmly. He knew her resolve had melted away when he reached to hold her, she crumbled against him.

He was so strong, he felt so right and she knew for this instant her life depended on his strength.

"You can't hide from me any longer, Beth. I swear, I'll talk to every person in Aidan until I get answers."

She cried against him. "Promise me you won't," she pleaded. "Promise me!" she insisted.

"Then tell me what happened. I can't help you if you won't talk to me." She saw tears in his eyes. "Maybe we can both move on with our lives," he whispered against her hair. "Together."

"I. . .I can't," she choked in reply.

"Tell me who hurt you." The more she struggled to push him away, the tighter he held her. "Was it your mother?"

"No!" she cried.

"Who then?" He held her so close she felt his heart pound.

"Sam, please. . .You're making this so hard!"

He glared at her with contempt. She'd never been afraid of Sam before, but the fire in his glower frightened her.

"Hard!" he choked on the word. "Let me tell you what hard feels like!" She tried to move away, to cover her ears with her hands, but his fingers dug into the flesh of her arms and held her in place.

"The day after you left was hard." She turned, but he shook her until she glared back at him.

"I don't want to hear this," she sobbed.

"I thought you were abducted or your mother beat the crap out of you. That was hard, damn it!" His grip relaxed on her arms, but she didn't dare move. "I searched for you, I asked questions, but never found answers. I never stopped waiting for a frigging phone call. The thought tormented me you took off with someone." His gaze was distant. "But the hardest thing of all was you broke my heart."

"Sam. . ." She placed her hands on his chest.

He held her face between his hands and forced her to look at him. "Tell me why you crushed my dreams." His anguish tormented her.

"What happened before I left Adain nearly destroyed me."

He continued to firmly hold her against him. "All right, Beth. I'll leave and never come back if you tell me you don't love me anymore."

She covered her face with her hands. "I don't," she cried.

"Say it," he demanded.

"I. . .don't. . . I can't love you."

"Say you don't love me. Damn it!"

"I don't love you," she shouted at him.

When he pulled her limp body against his, she was powerless to fight him any longer. "Not so convincing," he whispered as he gently smoothed her hair and kissed her forehead. Her sobs torn at his heart. "No. No, baby, don't cry." He pulled her even closer. "Shhh," was all he could manage as tears glazed his eyes.

When he lifted her into his arms, she clung to him as if nothing could separate them again. On the couch, he gathered her against him and for several moments, she struggled with the decision to tell him or not. He was determined to find the answers; she knew he would keep his promise and contact every person in town. She closed her eyes and allowed his strength to comfort her. She discovered questions, anger and hurt in his questioning eyes and knew what she had to do.

"I worked late at the theatre the night I left town. Then I picked up my Mother from the bar." Her voice shuttered, and she inhaled deep to calm her words. "I found mom passed out in one of the booths. The owner usually allowed her to sleep it off." She closed her eyes to remember every detail. "So I left her there." Beth sank into the warmth Sam offered.

"When I arrived home, it was after one o'clock in the morning. My mother often forgot to lock the doors, so I wasn't concerned when I entered the house and the front door was open."

She watched Sam's eyes search for answers and felt him grip her tightly as if to prepare for the impact of her words.

"Someone was in the house." She buried her face against his chest to block the frightful images. "He lunged at me. When I tried to fight, it only enraged him more. He started hitting me as he dragged me up the stairs to my bedroom where he. . .he raped me."

Sam sighed deeply and held her tight.

"I'll never forget the madness in his eyes," she shuddered. "He pulled out a gun, he pointed it at me. I thought he was going to shoot, but then he started blasting everything in the room. When he saw your picture, he told me he would kill you if I ever saw you again. He threatened to kill me if I told anyone what happened. He said he would hurt me again if I didn't leave town. After he left, I went to my aunt's house. She wanted to take me to Aidan County Hospital but I made her drive me to my grandmother's."

Beth stopped when she saw the reflection of pain in his eyes. "I had to get as far away from you as I could. I know this is hard to understand, but I did what I felt was right. I didn't leave to hurt you, I left to protect you." She touched his face as he took her hand into his and kissed her palm. "I told my grandmother to leave me at the hospital here. I pretended I didn't know what happened or who I was." She looked away as she recalled the painful memories. "I was in the hospital for three weeks to recover from surgery to repair my broken jaw. They made me stay because of my so-called amnesia." She paused to catch her breath. "It gave Gram enough time to provide me with a false identity. I never asked her how she came up with Alisa Rose, but suddenly I had a social security number, a birth certificate with a bank account and all of my college credits changed to Alisa's name."

"Who did this to you, Beth?" he asked.

"I won't tell you."

Sam couldn't sit still; he held her away from him. "I have to know."

"No! In order to protect you, there are things you must never know."

He stood and paced, deep in thought. "It doesn't make sense. Why would he threaten you? What are you hiding?" Sam clenched his fists together as he knelt in front of her. "What if we go back and tell Jack everything? If you press charges, then whoever you're afraid of will be sent to prison. You'll be safe." He ran his fingers through his hair.

Beth stood and tried to catch her breath. "For how long? A few years maybe? It's not worth the risk, Sam."

Sam followed her into the kitchen. "Do I know him?" he asked.

"I don't know. It doesn't matter."

"Like hell it doesn't matter. I want to kill the son of a bitch," he shouted.

Beth cringed from his angry words and gently placed her arms around his neck. "That's exactly why I can't tell you. There's no doubt in my mind he'll kill you first." Tears fell down her face. "You have to go home and never come back here."

"I won't leave you alone again, and I won't live my life without you!" The conviction of his words drove through her like an arrow.

"Haven't you listened to what I've said? You can't stay. He'll follow you. He'll find us, and I won't be able to live through the horror again!" She confronted him with terror in her eyes.

"I'll tell my family I got a job somewhere out of state. I won't even tell Jack where I am," he answered quickly.

She adamantly shook her head. "It won't be enough to keep him away. He'll find me just like you did. There are too many innocent people involved."

Sam studied her for a moment and grabbed her hands tightly. "I won't walk away to let you deal with this alone. You're going to have to get used to the idea I'm here to stay." He guided her chin so he could see directly into her eyes. "You should have come to me when it first happened. We could have dealt with it then. Why didn't you trust me?"

She closed her eyes. "I wanted to tell you, but I couldn't. Try to understand I've only told you a part of the story. If something were to happen to you or anyone else because of this, I could never live with myself." She rested against him and felt drained of all energy. "I'm so tired," she sighed.

He pulled her tightly against him to lead her to the couch and covered them both with the quilt.

Beth listened while the rhythm of his heartbeat soothed her shattered nerves. "I love you, Beth. I always have, I always will." He kissed her tenderly.

Again she closed her eyes. For the moment, the only thing she cared about was sleeping in his arms. "Sam?" she whispered as her eyes fluttered open.

He looked at her, questioning. "Hmm?"

"If you stay tonight, I don't know if I'll be able to live without you again."

His heart filled with love as he held her tightly. "Go to sleep. I'll be here."

"Promise?" she whispered. "You won't leave?

"Never." He gently kissed away the worry lines on her forehead. Soon her soft breathing was slow and regular as she relaxed against him. Yet, he couldn't sleep. As much as he tried, he couldn't block out the images of the pain she'd endured. He knew she was holding back part of the story, but for now he'd respect her wishes and wouldn't press for more information.

He kissed the top of her head, as the scent of wildflowers filled his mind. He longed to soothe away her fears as she slept soundly in his arms. Every now and then a faint sigh escaped her lips as she breathed softly against his neck.

In the early hours, Beth opened her eyes to find Sam watching her. From the street lamp outside, enough light filtered through the curtains and allowed her to see a slight smile on his lips. "Are you really here?" she asked softly as she lightly touched his cheek. "Or am I going to wake to find you gone?"

He held her fingertips to his lips and kissed them softly. "I told you, I'm here to stay."

CHAPTER EIGHT

Sally added ice to her drink and topped it off with more bourbon. She lounged on the couch, turned down the volume on the television and tried to listen to the conversation her boyfriend was having behind the closed door of her bedroom. She strained her ears, but couldn't clearly make out his words. Must be something to do with work. He got paged all the time, even when he was off duty. If his wife wasn't interfering with their time together, than it was his stupid job. No wonder he was so touchy all the time. She picked up the remote control to increase the volume.

"Yeah, I know Sam Andrews left town again," Andy stated defensively. "He said he has a temporary job out of state."

"Why the hell didn't you follow him to find out where he was going?" boomed the voice into the receiver.

Andy held the phone away from his ear. "Look, I'm not the one who's obsessed with Beth Brockton. I say she's too terrified to talk. I don't think she's a threat."

"The trouble is you don't think at all. You'd better start considering Beth Brockton a threat. Unless you become more concerned about finding her, my friend, we're going down together."

Andy cringed from the thud of the phone in his ear. He sat on the edge of the bed for a moment and allowed the foreboding warning to digest. Hell, how much of a risk could one frightened girl be? She was much too intimidated to say anything to anyone.

"What was that all about, Andy?" Sally asked.

"It was work!" He paced and lit a cigarette.

Sally patted the couch cushion beside her. "Sit down, baby. I'll fix you something to eat."

She started to rise, but he stopped her. "Don't bother. I'm not hungry." He brooded and thought about the phone conversation. His mind was distracted with thoughts of how to locate Beth Brockton. She probably had a fake identity or else something would have turned up on her by now. He placed an arm around Sally. "How well do you know Lena McCray?" he asked.

"Why?" She frowned.

"I need you to get some information for me." He watched as her expression change from curious to skeptical.

"We don't exactly attend the same tea parties, if you know what I mean," she sneered.

"Maybe you could go to McCauley's where she works to ask her advice about redecorating your apartment," he baited her.

Sally still frowned. "Who's paying?"

"Damn it! You sound more like my wife all the time," he shouted.

Sally tensed and crossed her arms. "Yeah, well let me remind you, I'm not your wife."

He sensed her irritation and fought to keep his temper under control. He scooted toward her and playfully nuzzled her neck. "Come on, Sal. I'll pay for whatever you want done to this place."

"What do you want me to do?" She smiled slyly and surveyed the room.

Andy chuckled knowing if he opened his wallet wide enough, he could get Sally to do just about anything. "Find out where Beth Brockton is."

When Sally abruptly turned to face him, her smile faded instantly. "What's the big deal with her all of a sudden? First Jack Walsh, and now you!" She peered at him, suspiciously. "You got a thing for her, or what?" she demanded.

"It's confidential police business," he snapped and felt his tolerance level stretch to the limit.

Sally's gaze continued to question. "What happened to Jack Walsh, anyway? Is it a coincidence you got all bent out of shape when he asked questions about Beth Brockton, and then he mysteriously ended up in the hospital?" Her eyes opened wide when he sharply pulled her to face him.

"You need to know when to shut your trap about certain things." He glared at her.

She tried to shake his hands away. "Let go!" she said and glared back at him. He relaxed his grip and she moved to light a smoke. "What's gotten into you, Andy? Why the sudden interest in Beth Brockton?"

When he discovered a rare look of vulnerability in Sally's eyes, his anger only increased. He rubbed his face and groaned, "I'm under a lot of pressure at work."

She sat next to him. "You don't need to take it out on me," she said, her tone wary.

He pulled her against him and she critically studied the dingy furnishings in her apartment, as if she were already calculating the cost. She smiled up at him coyly. "So, tell me again what you what me to find out from Lena McCray?"

* * *

When Sam entered the apartment with bagels and coffee, Beth rushed to greet him. "I haven't slept so soundly in years," she snuggled close as he held her tight.

"I can't believe I'm standing here, holding you like this," he whispered against her hair. He inhaled the scent of early morning rain and his throat tightened.

Knowing the brief reunion they had shared couldn't continue, Beth felt a sharp pang of remorse. She stepped away and stared into her coffee in silence. All the while, Sam never stopped watching her and took her hand. "What's going on in that head of yours?" he asked, as he handed her a coffee.

"I wish you'd never found me." She rushed from the room.

He found her weeping softly into the pillows on her bed, wanting desperately to ease her pain. "You have to go back home and forget you saw me."

Sam gently ran his hand along the soft curves of her back. "I'm not leaving you. We went over this last night."

"It's no use pretending our lives will be the same as before." She sat up, held his hand and pleaded with him. "If you go home again, you can never come back here. Someone will follow you," she cried, softly.

"I won't go home until you tell me it's all right," he said gently and reached to catch a falling tear.

"You can't get a job where your name can be traced through social security." She studied his face for a reaction, but couldn't read his thoughts.

"There are ways to work around that," he assured her.

Beth felt bewildered. "We'll have to hide your truck right away. It can be traced."

He pulled her close. "What happened that makes it necessary for you to worry about all these things?" he asked. "I'll do whatever you think is necessary to make this work." He held her away, "but I'm not leaving. Do you understand?" His face reflected the determination in his voice. Finally she slowly nodded her head in agreement.

"I don't know if I can. . ." she stopped.

"What is it, Beth?"

She turned her head away, ashamed to look at him. "What if I can't. . ."

"Can't what?" he asked and tipped her head so she looked at him. His puzzled expression revealed he was clueless as to what she was trying to say.

"I haven't been with anyone since..." She watched his confused expression soften to one of concern.

"What happened to you has nothing to do with what we shared. In your heart, you know that, don't you?" She was unable to speak. "We'll work it out. We won't do anything until you're ready." The gentleness of his words reached her shattered soul and she held onto him tightly. "You know I'll never hurt you," he whispered.

"Yes." She wished she could make her voice sound more convincing. She felt him shudder as his muscles tensed.

"I want to kill the bastard who did this to you." He led her back to the kitchen and sat her down at the table. He placed a bagel and a container of yogurt in front of her. "Now it's my turn to set some ground rules." She watched him, curiously. "Each morning we're going to work out." She opened her mouth to protest, but he held up his hand to stop her. "And you're going to eat three solid meals which I am going to personally prepare." She smiled and felt an overwhelming sense of love for him. "Deal?" he asked as he extended his hand to finalize the agreement.

"Yes," she answered and shook his warm hand.

He pushed the food toward her. "So what are you waiting for?" he demanded as he pointed to the food. "Don't make me force feed you."

* * *

Deep in thought, Beth wondered how to relax and feel secure when each day had been a struggle to merely survive with her wits intact. How could she let Sam back into her chaotic life? He didn't understand the demons that still lurked, ready to harm them without warning. How could she prevent herself from becoming dangerously complacent with the false security Sam had to offer?

Her thoughts were interrupted when she suddenly realized Sam stood before her, wrapped in a towel. The fresh scent of soap and shaving cream had floated into the room behind him and hovered long enough to dull her senses.

"Hum?" she muttered, not aware of what he was saying to her.

"I said, what are you worrying about now?" He grinned at her as if he was pleased with the knowledge that his presence in a skimpy towel was the cause of her distraction.

She frowned and felt her cheeks flush. "I was thinking about what we need to do first." She watched while he sorted through his sports bag and wished he would be less casual about standing around half- naked while she tried to think of important matters.

"I know the first thing I need to do is find a laundry mat." He held up a pair of crumbled, limp jeans. "These will have to make it through one more day."

She laughed. "There's a washing machine and dryer in the basement."

"Then I need to get in touch with Suzy." Her smile faded quickly, replaced by a deep frown. "I have to inform my family I won't be home for Christmas, Beth. Otherwise they'll send out a search party to locate me." He paused. "I would never do anything careless to risk your safety. I'll stick with the same story about working on a secret government clean up job I told a couple of cops who were visiting Jack at the hospital." Beth jumped to her feet and her senses came to full panic.. "When?

Which cops?" Her heart lunged in her chest when he answered,

"Tom Hutchins and Andy Thompson. I told them I'm working on a temporary job out of state." He stepped to her. "What's wrong?" he questioned. "You're shaking."

Beth closed her eyes tightly but didn't answer. How long would it take before they were found? What an idiot she was to think Sam could stay. It only placed him in danger. She opened her eyes. "Did you talk about me?" she asked, biting her lip nervously.

"No, they were just leaving the hospital when I arrived. We didn't talk about anything other than where I've been lately." A slight frown grazed his forehead as he touched her lip. "Are you okay?"

She composed herself. "You get dressed while I figure out what to do with your truck." She quickly dried her damp hair and dialed Sam's phone. "Gram, do you have room in your garage to store a truck?"

"Sure I do. What are you up to now?"

"I'll explain when I get there. Are you going to be home this morning?"

"Yes, dear. I'll be home all day."

Beth turned to see Sam's concerned face as he tucked his tee shirt into his jeans. She stepped over and wiped a trace of shaving cream from his chin. He took her by the arms. "Tell me why you reacted so strongly when I told you about Tom and Andy?"

Beth pulled away. "It makes me uncomfortable when I think about home." She could tell he wasn't convinced by her vague response, but he remained silent and didn't confront her with the questions he obviously held back.

"You can follow me to my grandmother's house. We can store your truck there."

* * *

As they stepped out of their vehicles, Rose Brockton joined them in the driveway and warily watched Sam.

"Gram, this is Sam Andrews."

Rose observed him. "I know who he is!" she said as she opened the garage door. "You can use the spot there." She pointed to the empty space and turned to face Sam and Beth. "What's this all about?" Her voice was sharp and demanding.

"Have I done something to upset you? If you don't want us to use the garage, just tell me," said Beth.

"No, it's him I'm not real keen on." Gram talked about Sam as if he didn't exist.

Beth looked at Sam and shrugged. "What do you have against Sam?"

Rose continued to glare. "Park your truck, young man. You come with me." Gram pulled Beth toward the house.

Inside the warm kitchen, Beth looked at Gram and questioned, "Tell me what's bothering you."

Gram faced her with crossed arms. "I don't trust him one bit." As if to emphasize her meaning, she wagged her finger with each word. "Anyone that good looking is up to no good in my book."

Beth bit her lip to hide a smile. "Is that the only reason you don't like him?"

"How can I trust anyone from your past? You won't tell me anything, but I know something terrible happened."

When Beth saw the tears in Gram's eyes, she placed an arm across her shoulder. "I love Sam with all my heart." She studied Gram's eyes.

"You're sure he never hurt you?" she questioned with a doubtful frown.

"Never."

"Is he the father. . ." She stopped mid-sentence when the back door opened and Sam stepped onto the rug.

Reluctantly, he looked around the corner. "Is it safe to enter?" he asked, tentatively.

Beth took his hand. "It's perfectly safe, Sam. Gram is like a mother hen. She won't bite." Rose continued to scrutinize him.

Sitting at the table across from Sam, Beth smiled into his eyes sympathetically and reached to hold his outstretched hand. He appeared to be holding up rather well under Gram's watchful eye.

Rose's face softened for the first time since he entered the kitchen. "Tell me why you're in this area."

"To be with Beth." He squeezed Beth's hand.

"What took you so long?" Rose narrowed her eyes suspiciously. "If you care about her then why did it take almost two years to start searching for her?"

"Until Beth came home for the funeral, my only concern was trying to get her out of my mind." He faced Beth for a moment, then turned his attention back to Rose. "We were engaged when she disappeared. I was devastated when she left." He looked away, as if ashamed.

Rose set a plate of raspberry tarts and a pot of hot tea, in the middle of the table.

Beth smiled brightly. "Oh, Gram, you are such a sweetheart. I haven't had one of these in years!" She eagerly reached for a tart. "Oh Sam! You must try one! They're heavenly." She exchanged smiles with Gram.

"When I was a little girl, Gram and I made tarts from leftover scraps of pie pastry," she managed to explain during mouthfuls. "Whenever I visited Gram, I'd go home with five extra pounds.

Rose passed the plate to Sam. "Believe me, she needed the meat on her bones. Still does."

* * *

Sam jogged to the pay phone at the corner and pulled up his collar in a futile attempt to shield the gusts of wind that blew in from the bay and whipped sharply against his bare face. Dialing the hardware store, he was relieved to hear Suzy's voice. "Hi, Suz. It's me."

"Sam! Your voice sounds too good for words."

"Keep it low. I don't want anyone to know I'm calling."

"Why? Is there a problem?" she asked, lowering her voice.

"Beth is terrified someone from town is going to come looking for us."

"I don't blame her. After what happened to Jack, I think there are plenty of reasons for concern." She paused. "You'll be careful, won't you?"

Sam smiled into the phone. "I'll be fine. How's Jack?"

"He's home now and grumpier than an old bear. He's anxious to talk to you."

"Let him know I'll contact him soon. I can't give you a phone number or address. In fact, if anyone asks, stick with the story I told

Mom and Dad about working on a government clean-up job. No one can contact me." Sam felt uneasy as he surveyed the area around the phone booth. He felt like an agent on a mission, except he didn't have a clue who the enemies were or if they even existed.

"When can you come home?" she asked.

He felt the reality of the situation begin to sink in. "I don't know. Probably not for some time."

"You're not coming home for Christmas?" The surprise in her voice echoed the disappointment he attempted to conceal.

"I'm afraid not. I need to stay here."

* * *

Sam returned to the apartment to find Beth wrapped in a quilt. The uncertain look on her face transformed into a relieved smile. He sat beside her. "Are you okay? Is something wrong?"

She curled against him. "Having you walk through the door on a regular basis will take some getting used to."

He smiled in return and kissed her lightly. "We have the rest of our lives to adjust." He smoothed her hair.

"I'm sorry, Sam. I've turned into a neurotic mess, haven't I?"

"We'll change that, too." He winked at her and smiled broadly then opened the door. Beth watched curiously and sprang to her feet as he struggled to push a huge, cut pine tree through the doorway. Once inside, Sam held the tree upright while she gingerly touched the needles.

She examined the evergreen and covered her mouth with the tips of her fingers, much too surprised to speak. The wide base of the tree filled over half the room, while the top was bent at an angle against the ceiling. She closed her eyes and breathed in the fresh scent of pine. "It's beautiful," she whispered and circled the tree.

Sam continued to display the tree while she stared in wonder. He propped the tree against the wall as Beth turned to him with tears in her eyes. "I've never had a Christmas tree of my own."

His heart sank knowing more each day about her past. "Never?" he asked softly.

"My mother never celebrated the holidays," she stated.

"From now on you can select any tree you want."

She searched his kind, loving face. "I don't have any lights or ornaments for decorations," she stated.

Sam smiled and pulled her to him to rub the worry line creased along her forehead. "I figured as much. We'll have fun shopping for everything together."

* * *

Long past midnight, Sam set a bright star on top of the tree while Beth gazed in awe at the twinkling lights, ornaments and tinsel that cast magical colors around the room. In only two days, Sam had transformed her drab existence into an enchanted fantasy filled with bright colors, scents and sounds. Her heart filled with joy as he climbed down from the chair and they stood side by side to admire their first Christmas tree together. He wrapped his arm around her and she rested her head on his shoulder. "It's magical, Sam."

"Christmas is magical." He kissed her sweetly. "Especially with you,"

How wonderful it would be to share one's life with someone so thoughtful, so caring. Beth continued to gaze upon the tree, her thoughts drifting to images of a life she had long ago forsaken. She recalled an existence she never dreamed would be possible for her to attain, one she and Sam had just begun to make a reality before her dreams were cruelly shattered.

Grinning, he reached into his pocket and pulled out a sprig of mistletoe to dangle over her head. "I almost forgot this."

When he kissed her, Beth felt the room reel about her. Although she was powerless to stop her body from reacting to his touch, her mind wasn't ready. How could this be happening so quickly? Was it love in his eyes or passion? She stepped away.

Sam took her hand and brought her fingertips to his lips. "It will take time, but it's going to be all right." He held a box out for her.

"What's this?" Surprise laced her words.

"Something we both can use."

She slowly opened the box to find a phone and looked puzzled.

"It's a burner phone." He opened the screen on the phone. "It can't be traced so you can give the number to only the folks you want to be in contact with."

He pressed a button. "I've already entered your Gram's and my numbers." He showed her how to add numbers and makes calls. "Keep your calls to a minimum. You need to keep it charged," He held out the charger surprised to find tears in her eyes. He placed a hand on her cheek. "No more facing the elements to make a call. It's right here at your fingertips."

She leaned into him and buried her face against his chest. "You've thought of everything. Thank you, Sam."

* * *

When something startled Sam awake, he discovered Beth huddled against the headboard, shaking uncontrollably. He reached to offer comfort, but she frantically pushed his arm away. "No!" she screamed and struck him again when he tried to hold her. He rubbed the sting on his arm and stated calmly, "Nothing is going to hurt you." She sobbed and babbled in a language only she understood in her nightmare. It broke his heart to see her this way. When he touched her again, she fell into his arms. "Shh. . . you're safe." His eyes blurred with tears. How long would she be punished for something she had no control over?

"The baby. . .," she mumbled.

Sam whispered soothing words as he stroked her hair. "It's all right."

"She's crying. . .please. . ." Her words trailed off and patiently he rocked her until she relaxed against him. She wiped the tears from her face. "I'm sssorry I. . .I. . ." She spoke with a shudder. Sam lifted a corner of the blankets to cover them. He lay beside her shivering body and pulled her close until the warmth from his body eventually calmed her.

"I'm sorry I disturbed your sleep," she said.

"You don't need to apologize."

She shivered once more. "I hope you remain this understanding when I wake you every time I have a bad dream."

"Does this happen often?" he asked.

"Practically every night."

Sam shut his eyes, frustrated. "How can you live like this?"

She sighed while she traced the pocket of his tee shirt with her finger. "It's the way my life has been since I left Aidan. I don't have a clue how it feels to sleep through the night."

"You were talking about a baby crying." As he spoke the words, he felt her body tense.

"Was I?"

He felt his face flush with anger. "Don't you think the nightmares would disappear if you were to prosecute the bastard who did this to you?"

Beth closed her eyes and held him tightly. "Then the real nightmares would begin."

* * *

McCauley's Decor bustled with holiday shoppers when Sally Cantrell entered the store. She paused to admire the huge decorated wreath placed in the entranceway and was greeted by the scent of bayberry candles lined along the fireplace mantel. Soft harpsichord music added to the festive mood, along with boughs of pine garland hung everywhere. Casually, she strolled around the shop and browsed at the tasteful displays of wallpaper, matching borders and color- coordinated paint. She admired the contrasting fabrics draped over antique accent pieces. She picked up a porcelain vase and when she noted the price, she felt a wave of pleasure as she gingerly set the vase down. "Oh, Thompson, this is going to hurt you much more than it will me," she chuckled.

"Hello, Sally."

Sally looked up to see Lena McCray approaching her. "Lena, how are you?"

"As you can see, extremely busy! What can I do for you?"

"I want to redecorate my apartment, but I don't have a clue where to begin."

Lena motioned for her to follow. "Let's look at the decorator's schedule. I know he's booked until late January."

Sally frowned. "I'd rather work with you." She noticed Lena's surprise. "Scott is the expert, Sally. I think you would be happier with his advice."

"Lena, the reason I came to this shop is to give you my business, but I can go somewhere else if you'd like."

Lena poured a cup of gourmet coffee. "Oh, no! I'd be more than happy to assist you. I'm just not accustomed to having a customer request my help."

Sally gladly accepted the coffee. "You shouldn't sell yourself short. I noticed how lovely your home was decorated when I visited the day of Linda's funeral." She saw Lena blush. "So, when can we get started?" Sally asked.

Lena laughed. "We can start right away. My schedule is not nearly as busy as Scott's."

* * *

Suzy stopped the car in front of Dobson's Drug Store and frowned when Jack leaned to give her a quick kiss. "Stop worrying so much. I'm feeling fine," he said.

"You've only been home for a few days, Jack. I wish you'd just take it easy."

He awkwardly maneuvered the cumbersome cast on his arm and stepped out of the car. "I hardly think the good doctor would classify having coffee with the guys as overexerting myself."

Suzy narrowed her eyes. "The good doctor doesn't realize how worked up you guys get at these coffee cliques."

"Come on, Suzanne. It's not like we're doing anything stressful like watching a Lion's football game or playing poker." He winked at her playfully.

He was about to close the door, but Suzy stopped him. "Jack, don't forget what we talked about."

He leaned against the open-door frame and bent to tap the end of her nose. "I promise not to ask any questions about Beth."

Suzy reached to squeeze his hand. "Sam will figure out the mystery. You need to let it go."

Jack closed the door and considered her words as he entered the drug store.

"Hey! It's the walking wounded!" called out Jim Fitch. All eyes focused on Jack as he walked to the small café attached to the drug store.

"How are you feeling?" asked Bob Dobson as he set a mug of coffee in front of Jack.

"Not bad." He studied the guarded faces of the men who watched him. "Lighten up, guys! I'm okay."

Cal Ritter nudged John Andrews. "Jack, I was reviewing your life insurance policy the other day, and I'd say you're overdue for an update." The men burst out laughing and Jack joined in.

"I'd probably get rated high risk, don't you think?"

By the time Tom Hutchins, a fellow cop, entered the drug store, most of the group had departed. Tom waved as he approached the counter and patted Jack on the back. "It's good to see you up and around."

"Believe me, I'm happy to be home. It was especially hard on Bradley, wondering if I was going to be home for Christmas or not." Jack studied his friend.

Tom rubbed his eyes. "I'll be really glad when you come back to work. It's hectic when we work short-staffed."

Jack held up his cast. "Won't be for another six weeks or so, according to the doctor. I'm already driving Suzy crazy. I'd much rather be at work." He turned to Tom. "Any new developments regarding the tire in the road?"

"According to the final report, no tire was mentioned. Nothing was found in the road to support your theory," said Tom.

Jack slammed his fist on the counter and felt the ever-present ache in his head intensify. "That's bullshit! I had to swerve to avoid hitting the damn thing! I saw it right in the middle of the road! What other reason would make me lose control of my car?"

"Hey, I believe you, Jack. Whoever you were chasing must have stopped to remove the tire before I arrived at the scene."

Jack forced himself to calm down. "I get a little crazy when I think someone deliberately forced me to crash. I wish I had a clue who's responsible."

* * *

Beth slowly opened her eyes to the touch of Sam's lips gently brushing her cheek. "Time to get up!" He smiled when she hid under the pillow. "Come on, Baby. Time to start our workout program." He gently nudged her.

"It's the middle of the night! I'm supposed to be on vacation." Sam snatched the pillow away and rolled her near to face him. "It's the best time of the day to work out."

She pulled the covers over her head. Sam sat next to her and waited patiently for her to move. He ran his hand lightly up and down her soft, bare leg rested on top of the blanket. She uncovered her face and stared at him impatiently. He grinned, slyly. "If you'd rather stay in bed, I'm sure we could get creative with other forms of exercise."

He noted the failed effort she made to hide her smile.

"That's not fair!" She jumped out of bed and leisurely stretched.

His smile faded when he looked at the scant tee shirt she wore and noticed the way her hair curled wildly in every direction imaginable and fell softly down her shoulders, and the faint tint of color on her cheeks and the sassiness of her pouted lips. He resisted the urge to toss her back onto the bed. He could control himself within reason, but a saint he wasn't. "Dress for the outdoors," he barked, definitely feeling the need for a good workout himself. He stormed out of the room.

Sam handed her a glass of orange juice when she joined him in the kitchen. "What are you wearing?" he questioned.

She looked at her clothing and held her down jacket open to show him. "Two sweatshirts, a turtle-neck and two pair of wind pants."

"And a partridge and a pear tree." He laughed, "You're going to roast." She laughed too and looked out of the window. "I hardly think that's a possibility." She added insulated mittens, a scarf and earmuffs to her attire. "Do you think the muscle mania babes at the gym would be jealous of this get up?"

"You defiantly make a strong fashion statement." He laughed as he slipped on a light windbreaker.

"You'll catch pneumonia, Sam."

"This is all I need. You'll see." He performed a few stretching exercises. "It's important to stretch your muscles before exerting yourself."

Beth scowled and made an effort to copy his movements. "I won't be able to exert myself long enough to need my muscles stretched," she mumbled. "I'm not the exercise type, Sam. Really." She fretted as he kissed her on the nose.

"This won't hurt too much."

She walked behind him at a warm up pace. "How far are we walking?"

Sam picked up the pace. "A couple of miles should be a good start."

Beth increased her speed until she walked beside him. "A couple of miles, you mean like two?"

Sam started to jog and grinned. "You continue to walk at this pace. I'm going to jog ahead and then circle back to see how you're doing." She opened her mouth to protest, but he already jogged away and ran to the next corner, then back to her. He chuckled when he saw her jacket and one of the sweatshirts tied around her waist. She carried the scarf, mittens and ear muffs.

"Is it getting a little warm out here now, babe?" He grinned while he jogged around her.

"Damn show-off!" she grumbled.

Sam threw his head back and laughed. "This is going to be more entertaining than I thought." He felt her burning glare as he jogged away.

* * *

They sat on the bottom step of the apartment building and Sam watched while she caught her breath. "Now was that as bad as you thought it would be?"

She opened one eye and shot him a look of disgust. "It was worse!"

Sam picked up a hand full of snow, packed it lightly into a snowball and tossed it at her. Her eyes shot open and she lunged at him, knocking them both into the snow bank. Beth fought wildly as she covered his face with snow. He turned her over and returned the deed.

As she laughed, a thrill went through him as the worry and apprehension disappeared from her face. "How long has it been since you laughed like this?" he asked.

She stopped struggling and his heart performed a crazy dance when her lips met his. He sensed her defenses relax and he forced the kiss to stop before it led beyond the boundaries of his control. He reminded himself to let things progress slowly as he pulled Beth to her feet.

Her dark eyes sparkled. "I feel like I'm beginning to wake from a dark slumber. I love you," she whispered.

Sam threw back his head and inhaled deeply as he lifted her into his arms and twirled her around. His heart soared with exhilaration as the words he had stopped longing for filled him with pleasure. "I love you," he whispered and brushed the wet snow from her face and kissed her once more.

* * *

Early Christmas morning, Bradley tiptoed down the stairway in the dark. His parents were still asleep, so he was careful not to make any noise. He waited at the bottom of the steps and let his eyes grow accustomed to the dark. His heart pounded rapidly from the anticipation of what he might find under the tree. Last week the only gift he wanted was for his dad to come home safely from the hospital. Since that wish already came true, he asked for a set of snow skis. He searched under the tree. His mom was really good at disguising gifts, but a pair of skis and poles would be a real challenge, even for her.

After he was sure none of the packages fit the description he hoped for, he decided there wasn't anything to do except wait for his parents to wake up. He sat on the couch, rested his head and intended to close his eyes for a few minutes.

* * *

Beth opened her eyes to discover she was alone in bed. She jumped to her feet, threw on her robe and rushed into the living room. She sighed with relief when she discovered Sam on the couch. Quietly, she knelt on the floor and watched him sleep. Did she wake him with another nightmare? When would he grow tired of her secretive, troubled lifestyle? She didn't want to wake him, but she missed the shelter of his protective arms. She brushed aside a lock of hair from his forehead and felt a surge of love stronger than she ever dreamed possible. How miserable her life had been without him. The glistening lights from the tree distracted her attention and she inhaled deeply to let the pungent odor of pine clear her mind. She rested her head on the couch beside Sam for a moment longer.

* * *

Jack tried to turn over in his sleep, but the cast on his arm caught in the blanket and woke him. He opened his eyes and realized it was Christmas morning. Bradley never let them sleep late, especially on Christmas Morning. Surely he must be up by now. He slowly rose from bed, but his body suddenly reminded him how sore he was from the bumps and bruises he sustained in the accident. When Suzy stirred next to him, he turned to her. "Merry Christmas, honey." He bent to kiss her, but groaned. Suzy smiled and sat half way to meet him.

Together they looked into Brad's bedroom and found it empty. Jack's heart pounded for a split second as he hurried down the stairs to discover Bradley curled up on the couch, fast asleep. Jack gathered his son in his arms.

Suzy studied Jack curiously. "Are you all right?"

He took her hand. "I'm fine." Brad rubbed the sleep from his eyes and his smile brightened the room.

"Merry Christmas, kiddo!" Jack kissed the top of Brad's head as tears blurred his vision.

Brad looked at his dad. "Can we open our presents now? I've been waiting for hours."

"Go for it!" Suzy and Jack laughed as they watched Bradley dive toward the presents.

* * *

Sam opened his eyes and his heart filled with love when he discovered Beth asleep, her head resting awkwardly on the couch beside him. When he stirred, her eyes fluttered open to meet his. "Did I keep you awake last night?" she asked, her sleepy eyes filled with concern.

Sam placed his hand behind her neck and drew her close so their lips meet.

Indeed, she was the cause of his restless tossing and turning. He wasn't able to keep his body and mind from thoughts she wasn't ready to deal with. "I was the one who couldn't sleep. You were sleeping so soundly, I didn't want to disturb you." His smile deepened. "I was too excited about Christmas to sleep."

Beth laughed. "You're kidding!"

Sam pulled her to her feet and searched under the huge branches of the tree. He placed a small package in her hand. Beth looked at the gift, then at Sam. "Open it!" he prompted.

Slowly, she untied the gold ribbon and carefully peeled the tape from the red metallic paper covered with gold stars. Sam shifted his weight impatiently from one foot to the other.

Beth stopped to question him. "What's the matter?"

He wasn't able to control his excitement any longer. "Will you hurry?" Smiling, she peeled the tape carefully. Finally, she opened the box and her eyes opened wide with surprise when she discovered the gift inside. Sam slid a diamond ring onto her finger, the same ring they'd picked out together three years before. "I hope the answer is still yes," he murmured.

A strangled cry escaped her as she threw her arms around him. "Oh, Sam!" He lifted her off the ground as she cried against him. A slight frown marred her beautiful face as he set her back on the floor. "So much has happened since then. I can't believe you still want us to be together."

"What are you saying?" he asked when he saw doubt cloud her face. "I've never stopped loving you or wanting us to be together forever."

"The reasons I left Aidan still exist. I can't possibly marry you with this much turmoil in my life. It wouldn't be fair to you." She began to remove the ring, but Sam stopped her and held her hand tightly.

"We'll wait to get married once all this mystery is settled. There's no one in the world I want to spend the rest of my life with, except you."

She held him close as tears fell down her checks. "There's no one else for me, either." She held up her hand and they watched sparkles burst from the diamond as it caught lights from the tree. "When did you get this?" she asked.

He smiled sheepishly. "I put it in layaway after we looked at rings together. It was obvious you had your heart set on this one, remember?"

Beth smiled through her tears. "How could I forget? I didn't think you'd buy it, though. We were only dreaming."

His smile faded. "It wasn't a dream for me. I still owed money on the ring when you left town. I purchased it anyway, hoping to give it to you when you returned."

"I can't believe you waited," she cried.

He kissed the ring and then her wet cheek. "Don't you know by now that I'd wait forever?"

CHAPTER NINE

Lena walked from room to room in Sally's apartment measuring dimensions and jotting notes onto a pad of graph paper. Sally hovered over her, anxious for feedback about what changes to the apartment Lena anticipated. Lena opened a book of wallpaper samples and pointed to a floral print. "This would look great in the bedroom, Sally. What do you think?"

Sally studied the pattern and imagined Andy's reaction. He was a meat-and-potato kind of guy, not the tea-and-crumpet sort at all. "I was thinking of something a little less fussy."

Lena turned the pages and pointed to a bold, geometric design. "Maybe we can settle on something between the two." While Lena continued, Sally contemplated how to initiate the subject regarding Beth Brockton. "Has Linda's house sold yet?"

"There have been a few interested parties," said Lena.

"I'm sure Beth will be relieved when the place finally sells." Sally looked at Lena hopefully.

"Beth left me in charge. She wants nothing to do with the sale of the house."

Sally frowned. "That seems odd. She lived there all her life."

Lena sighed. "We were never close. I haven't the faintest idea what goes through her mind."

Sally casually turned to question Lena. "Do you have Beth's address? I'd like to send her a sympathy card."

"No, I don't know where she lives." Lena opened another decorating book.

"What about this print?" Sally sensed the subject off limits for the time being so she turned her attention to the rich colored floral and striped pattern.

* * *

Sam raced Beth back to the apartment after their morning jog. Although he had given her half of a block lead, he passed her easily.

She found him waiting for her at the apartment door and laughed. "You cheated."

He pulled her to him and kissed her on the tip of her nose. "At least you were able to jog this far."

"I have to make a call from the pay phone." Sam ran with her and waited while she dialed. "Hi Jane." She placed her hand over the mouth piece and whispered to Sam, "Do you want to go to a New Year's Eve dinner dance?"

Sam smiled. "Sure."

"Yes, I'd like two tickets for the dance. I'll be bringing someone with me." She rolled her eyes. "No, Jane. You don't know him." After setting the phone down, she stepped over to Sam.

"I'll need something to wear other than jeans," he said. Beth hugged him.

"We'll go shopping. I can't wait to show you off to my co-workers. They are constantly trying to match me up." She laughed. "I've been a recluse for so long, they think I'm not interested in men."

Sam bent to kiss her. "We'll have to convince them otherwise, won't we?" When he kissed her, Beth felt the center of her universe tilt. Her gaze met his and for the first time, she answered his kiss without fear.

The night of the party, Beth nervously prepared for the evening. It had been so long since she had attended a social event. She studied her image in the full-length mirror and wished she had picked out something more conservative to wear. The black crepe mini-dress clung to her. Why did she let Sam talk her into purchasing it? Perhaps the way he looked at her when she modeled it for him at the store had something to do with the final decision. She felt sexy and confident then, but now she felt exposed as she futilely pulled on the hem to cover her legs.

While she applied the final touches of make-up, she heard a knock at the door. She stepped out from the bedroom and thought Sam was still in the shower. She wasn't used to anyone visiting her apartment, so she nervously looked through the peephole in the door. She laughed and opened the door when she discovered Sam standing outside.

They stared at one another, but neither spoke. Sam looked as if he stepped directly from the pages of a gentleman's magazine. He was dashing, dressed in a black suit and crisp white dress shirt. The midnight blue tie made the shade of his eyes appear darker, more mysterious. From behind his back, he offered a bouquet of pink tea roses to her. "I've imagined this date in my mind for a long time," he said.

She couldn't take her eyes from him. She accepted the flowers and felt the breath catch in her throat. "Thank you." Her voice was soft, as she brushed a light kiss on his cheek. "I'll be ready in a minute," she said and backed away toward the bedroom.

* * *

Sam closed his eyes and took in measured breaths as the fragrance of her exotic perfume lingered in the room. It filled his senses and her beauty rendered him helpless. He was afraid if he moved, he'd give in to the overpowering urge to sweep her off her feet and make passionate love to her all night long. He watched while she arranged the flowers in a vase and when she smiled at him shyly, his heart lurched in his chest. She didn't a have a clue the bewildering effect she had on him.

As they entered the dining room at the country club, Sam paused in the entrance when he sensed her reluctance to enter.

"You'll remember to call me Alisa, won't you Sam?" Her eyes searched his as if she needed reassurance.

Sam placed his hand at the small of her back. "Don't worry, I won't blow your cover," he whispered as he pulled out a chair for her at an empty table. "What can I get for you from the bar?"

"I'll take a glass of red wine, thanks."

When he returned with their drinks, several couples were seated at the table.

"Alisa!" Jane Somers approached the table and smiled brightly. "I want you to meet my husband, Gregory. Greg this is Alisa Rose, the newest member of our faculty." Greg smiled and took her hand. "It's nice to meet you."

Sam noticed the flicker of interest in Gregory's eyes as he studied Alisa. He also noted her blush when she introduced him. "This is my fiancé, Sam."

Jane was obviously surprised. "I didn't know you were engaged!" Jane smiled at Sam. "Congratulations."

All eyes focused on the couple as Sam led Alisa to the dance floor.

Alisa giggled when Jane said to Ann Halsted, "Isn't he yummy?"

Sam held her as she floated in his arms. There was no one around as he closed his eyes and wondered if there was anything sweeter than being this close to the one who held your heart in the palm of her hand. He detected her heart beat against him. Was it possible she felt as wonderful? When she nuzzled against his neck, he inhaled slowly. He was in agony.

Was he destined to only hold her like this for the rest of his life? He stiffly grasped her in his arms and hoped to distract his thoughts away from the brutal truth her soft body swaying against his was pure torture. His mind spun as a faint scent of perfume invaded his flustered brain. He closed his eyes and surrendered to the fact it was pointless to fight this feeling of desire when she was so alluring. So beautiful. So near.

When the song ended, she looked at him and questioned, "Are you all right, Sam?"

He opened his eyes, surprised the music had stopped. He stiffly backed away and felt like an idiotic schoolboy with a case of overactive hormones. "Why do you ask?" he forced a reply. He continued to hold her, not able to trust his hands if he moved.

When another song began, she smiled innocently. "I never realized how much you like to dance. I used to have to drag you to the dance floor." She pressed against him once more, but he abruptly held her at arm's length. He couldn't continue to hold her without reacting to his basic instincts. He'd just have to keep his distance from her. It was his only defense. "Actually, I'd like to sit this one out if you don't mind." He detected her puzzled expression as he escorted her back to the table.

After dinner, Jane enlisted Ann and Alisa's assistance to arrange the centerpieces at the dessert table.

Sam watched Alisa's every move, but his thoughts were distracted as Steve Mason sat next to him. "Man, you are one lucky guy." Steve smiled and nodded his head in Alisa's direction. "We all think the world of Alisa. It's great to see her looking happy for a change."

Sam acknowledged Steve's words. "Believe me, I know how lucky I am." Across the room Sam watched her laugh with Ann. Steve continued to talk, but Sam couldn't take his eyes from her. He was drawn to everything about her.

Ann glanced in Sam's direction. "Look at the way he watches you." Alisa's heart caught in her throat when his gaze met hers from across the room. "You are hopelessly in love with each other, aren't you?"

Alisa forced her attention away from the intensity in Sam's eyes and felt a flutter of desire in the pit of her stomach. She nodded her head as she arranged some white roses in a vase.

"There's nothing more exciting than to be so desperately in love with someone, that to be apart for more than a moment feels like an eternity." Ann sighed.

Alisa attempted to listen to Ann's conversation but her attention was clearly on Sam as a tall brunette dragged him to the dance floor. He was no sooner seated when someone approached him again. He meekly turned to Alisa. "Do you mind?" he asked.

She shook her head. "Why would I mind?" When she was left alone, her heart sank.

"My, your fiancé is certainly a hit with all the women," Jane commented sometime later.

Alisa felt the nasty sting of jealousy slither into her thoughts. Why was he acting like this? It wasn't like him to flirt so boldly. He had avoided her most of the evening. Was he already weary of her? Did he regret finding her again? These unwelcome thoughts inched their way into her mind.

Sam returned, set down a glass of wine and pulled up the chair next to her. He reached for her hand and smiled into her eyes. She turned away, not wanting him to read her childish thoughts.

When a romantic song began, several couples headed for the dance floor. Sam turned to her and asked, "Would you like to dance?"

"No, thank you." She faced him. "Are you having a good time?"

He completely missed the intended icicles hung from every word. "Yes, I am." He turned to her. "And you?"

She was about to answer when they were interrupted. "Alisa, how are you?" She turned to find Mark Clements slide into the chair beside to her.

"Hi, Mark," she smiled. "Sam, this is Mark Clements. His son is one of my students. Mark, this is Sam Andrews."

"Nice to meet you." Sam frowned.

"Do you mind if I borrow your date for this dance?" Mark smiled at Alisa. She began to shake her head no.

Sam reached for this drink. "Go ahead Bet. . .ah. . Alisa. Enjoy yourself."

Alisa made a half-hearted attempt to concentrate on Mark's conversation, but her attention was focused on Sam. When Sam's gaze met hers, she felt a rush of heat travel through her from the intoxicating spell cast upon her.

Finally, the song ended and Mark took her hand. "Thanks for the dance, Alisa. I hope to see you soon."

Alisa felt herself being drawn toward Sam. She stood before him and it was impossible to look away. Were they suddenly the only two people in the room? Her breath was rapid and shallow. Just being near him was suffocating. Sam stood to pull out her chair.

He leaned toward her, his breath warm as he whispered, "Was he holding you close enough?"

Alisa jerked her head around and felt her anger rush to the surface. "Look, Romeo, you're the one who danced with everyone wearing a dress tonight!"

He faced her. "A few minutes ago you didn't want to dance with me! Yet you jumped at the chance to dance with him. Besides, you're the one who encouraged me to dance with the others."

Alisa couldn't believe they were fighting like a couple of teenagers. Somehow she had an entirely different picture in her mind of how this night would unfold. "Well, you didn't have to make it look like you enjoyed it so much."

Sam smiled. "Aren't we just a wee bit jealous?"

She glared at him and stood to leave, but he reached to stop her. She looked at him coolly before she pulled her arm free and marched past the tables where her friends were seated.

In the ladies room, she freshened up. "Jealous," she muttered to herself. Her irritation rose at the thought of him purposely flirting to make her feel this way.

When she stepped out of the ladies room, Sam was waiting for her. She attempted to walk past him but he stepped in front of her and held her by the arms. "We need to talk, Beth."

She was powerless to move away from him. "It's Alisa," she murmured.

She felt small and vulnerable as he towered over her. She tried to back away, but was already against the wall. Her heart pounded fitfully as the intensity of his gaze bore through her.

He cupped her face in his hands, slowly moved against her and murmured, "Whoever you are, you're driving me crazy."

They studied each other and she tried to read what he was thinking. She could only see a simmering darkness behind the powerful force within his gaze. She placed her arms around his neck and gently pulled him close, attempting to break through the self-controlled barrier he had placed between them tonight. Brushing his lips against hers lightly at first, her resistance quickly melted away. She closed her eyes and allowed the kiss to deepen, not wanting this emotion to stop.

He pulled her into the shadows, wrapped his arms around her and pressed against her. Hardly able to breathe, she began to awaken, as if from a trance. Suddenly, just kissing him was no longer what she desired.

She opened her eyes and for the first time in ages, she sensed a passion that clearly matched his. She tipped her head back and he kissed the nape of her neck and followed the line of her shoulder as if he wanted to consume her. She was confused when he stepped away and whispered hoarsely,

"We'd better stop. I can't hold you like this any. . . "

Her pulse continued to race as she gently placed the tips of her fingers against his lips to hush him. "I don't want you to stop."

Sam's questioning gaze silently pleaded, as if he wanted desperately to understand the full meaning of her words. "Are you sure?" he asked.

She guided him until their lips met once more. She kissed him with the hunger of wanting to make up for the past two years. When she broke away for an instant, her head tilted back so his kisses trailed along her jaw line to the nape of her neck. "Let's go home now," she whispered, "before I change my mind."

* * *

Beth opened her eyes the next morning and was thrilled to find herself wrapped in Sam's arms. She smiled anxiously and felt the radiance from the love they shared. The drive home was torture for both of them, as Sam tried to keep his eyes on the road and his hands on the steering wheel, while Beth couldn't keep her hands off of him. She glanced at the trail of clothes scattered on the floor from the door to the bed and waves of excitement filled her when she thought about losing herself in his arms. Lightly she touched his whiskered face, his wonderful, gentle, loving face and knew she would never have reason to fear intimacy with Sam again.

Sam opened his eyes and held the palm of her hand to his lips. He returned her smile, then frowned when he studied her. "Why are there tears in your eyes?"

She smiled through the tears. "I'm just amazed that piece by piece you keep putting me back together."

He rolled onto his side, wrapped his arms around her and gently caressed the softness of her skin. "I won't stop until our lives are whole once more," he murmured.

She melted against him to safeguard the fragile bond between them, understanding fully she could never again live without the tenderness they shared. "Will this all disappear when I go back to work tomorrow?" she wondered out loud. "These past few weeks feel as if I've lived in another time." She sighed wistfully when Sam kissed her neck. "A safe, peaceful time." She held him close and needed the strength of his love to shelter her from the menacing thoughts still lurking in the dark reaches of her mind.

* * *

Sam parked the car in front of the school the next morning and turned to say goodbye. He searched her tired eyes. It had been a long night for her. She tried to hide the fact another dream had awoken her and she made little noise as she left the bedroom to keep from disturbing him. He immediately followed and found her weeping alone in the bathroom, the water ran in the shower to disguise her anguished cries. It frustrated him he wasn't able to destroy the foes whom waged this private war against her. He wanted something real to fight! He'd gladly face anything to help her find the peace she deserved.

When she kissed him, he sensed her uncertainty and held her close. "It's alright, babe."

* * *

He watched as she walked toward the main entrance of the school, his mind wandered to the conversation they shared over breakfast. She fretted about the possibility of their location being traced if he got a job. He attempted to reassure her he'd only accept a job that paid cash under the table. She agreed it wasn't reasonable for him to sit around all day while she worked. He convinced her he needed to pay off his student loan and more importantly, the need to move forward with their life together.

* * *

Beth arrived home late one evening after her college class and dashed up the steps to her apartment. She was convinced she'd never be able to shake the uneasiness someone would jump out at her. She closed the door to the apartment quietly when she found Sam asleep on the couch and set her textbook and supplies on the table. She turned when he stirred. His hair was rumpled and his eyes were groggy, but he looked wonderful. "Hi," she smiled, feeling such tenderness toward this man.

"How was your new class?" he asked and helped her out of her coat.

"It's going to be a tough one," she frowned. "You don't need to wait up for me, Sam."

He led her to the table and pulled the chair out for her. Wearily, she sat down. "I'm not really hungry. I hope you didn't go to any trouble." She rested her elbow on the table, sank her head onto her hand and closed her eyes.

He opened the oven. "No trouble at all," he replied as he set a plate before her.

She opened her eyes when the scent of roasted chicken woke up her taste buds and she smiled at him as she reached for a fork. "Maybe I am just a tiny bit hungry."

After dinner, Sam dried the dishes while Beth washed. She handed him another plate. "Any job prospects today?" she asked.

As if he sensed her uncertainty, he pulled her to him. "You're going to have to learn to trust my judgment. I would never do anything to put you or I at risk."

She looked down and felt the ever-present insecurities under the surface. "I trust you with my life."

He tucked his finger under her chin and gently tilted her face so he could look into her eyes. "I have a few leads to follow up on. One in particular sounds promising." When his lips met hers, she knew he depicted the doubt behind her smile.

* * *

The terror began as the smell of smoke woke her from a deep sleep. She jumped out of bed and threw the bedroom door open, startled to discover the entire apartment filled with smoke. She dropped to her knees and crawled to the front door as smoke engulfed her. She coughed uncontrollably and fought to make her way to safety. Each second seemed like hours as she inched her way across the carpet. Fearing her lungs would burst, she reached for the doorknob and struggled to open the door. She fell onto the cold cement landing and desperately gasped for fresh air. When her breathing returned to normal, she weakly pulled herself to her feet.

"Sam!" she screamed and pounded on the door. She turned the knob, but panicked when she discovered the door locked.

Sam gently shook her awake and she fell against him, her breathing labored. He tenderly soothed her with gentle words as sobs jolted through her body. "I. . . thought you were dead."

He covered her trembling body with the blanket, all too familiar with the course following the aftermath of her night terrors. Silently, he laced his fingers with hers and cradled her until her breathing was soft and regular. Unable to fall back to sleep, Sam's heart pounded from the helplessness he found so baffling. What were the secrets she was so determined to shield? He wasn't certain how much longer he could sustain his end of the bargain by not pressing her for answers. How could he sit idly by and watch her struggle in vain while this sinister web of silence twisted itself around her? He lightly kissed the top her head. She was much too vulnerable to fight this battle alone. When would she feel safe enough to confide in him before the secrets entangled her beyond the boundaries of his protection? These same questions continued to circle in his mind. When?

* * *

While waiting for Sam to pick her up from work, Beth rested her head on the door at the front entrance of school. Fatigue settled in quickly as she closed her weary eyes. The dull ache in her head had plagued her all day without a moment of relief. All she wanted was to soak in a hot bath and head straight for bed.

Her mind drifted to the panic she felt yesterday when she received a message at school from Gram to contact her right away. Beth raced to the phone, only to learn the house down state had sold. Lena signed the papers the day before which closed the deal for a price well above market value. Beth wanted Gram to have the money, after all, Gram supported her all these years. At first Beth stubbornly refused to accept anything from the sale, but Gram insisted she'd put the money into a trust for Samantha.

Samantha. The name brought an immediate wave of guilt that washed over her like a tidal wave.

She opened her eyes and checked the time. It wasn't like Sam to be this late. Her mind was in the process of conjuring up horrible images when she looked out the window in time to see Sam park the car in front of the school. She sighed with relief and rushed to meet him.

Sam smiled to greet her when she eased into the passenger seat and threw her arms around him. "Did you miss me?" he asked.

"I was worried about you." She stretched to kiss him, and felt the tension in her head begin to fade.

"I'm sorry you were worried. I was delayed at my new job." He smiled at her confidently. Beth remained silent and waited for him to continue. "Now don't get upset before you listen to the details." He noted a slight smile form on her lips.

"I'll be paid in cash working for a self-employed chemist. His name is Craig Johnson. He has more work than he can handle testing well water. The job is exactly what I was doing at home. I start work on Monday." Sam paused, as if expecting a reaction. She only held his hand tighter. "I didn't give him my social security number. He thinks my name is Sam Carson."

She smiled faintly. "It sounds great." She tried to make the words sound convincing. "Why don't we go out to celebrate?"

Over dinner, Beth watched Sam talk excitedly about the details of the new job. "I'll drive a company truck, so the car issue is resolved."

Between the effects of the beer, one too many pieces of pizza and watching how happy Sam was, Beth was able to relax a bit and share in his happiness. His face beamed warmly as he took her hand into his. "Looks like we can start planning our future, again."

Suddenly the glow of the moment halted abruptly. She looked away for a brief second, then back to him. "You'll have to remind me what it's like to look beyond today, Sam. I don't remember how." She could see how deeply touched he was by her words.

"My life was one huge void the entire time you were gone. We can re-learn together," he said gently.

Afraid to share the doubts spinning aimlessly in her mind, Beth didn't speak.

"We can finally get married and start a family. Like we had planned to do before all of this happened," he said gently.

Tears filled her eyes. "I can't promise you I can do the things we dreamed about before. The problems haven't disappeared because you're here. In fact, they seem more real to me now than before." She rubbed her temples, the headache returned with gusto.

She saw his patience fade. "If I had a chance to understand the problems, then maybe I wouldn't minimize them."

Beth motioned for the waiter to bring the check. She was too tired to deal with these issues right now.

Sam took her hand again. "I don't mean to pressure you, but I don't know what we're waiting for. When will it be okay for us to move forward?" His eyebrows raised in a questioning manner.

"I wish I had the answer." She squeezed his hand, afraid her constant struggle with the past would eventually build a wall so great it would force them apart. "There's nothing in the world I want more than to marry you, Sam. You know I love you, don't you?"

Nodding, he smiled tenderly. "I love you too, and you know damn well I'll wait if I have to." He reached to catch a tear and smiled suggestively. "Let's go home so you can show me exactly how much you love me."

She laughed softly as he pulled her to her feet. She leaned against him, sighed. "I'm in as long as it involves a hot, steaming bath and a couple of aspirins."

* * *

Beth hurried into the apartment and placed the groceries on the counter. She studied the recipe Ann had given to her earlier. Sam wasn't due home for an hour yet. Could she possibly master clam linguine before then? Ann assured her it was easy to master. Beth didn't have the nerve to inform Ann she was still mastering the art of preparing a grilled cheese sandwich.

As she filled a pot with water, she had her doubts. Just finding these ingredients at the grocery store was nearly impossible. If she hadn't enlisted the help of a young stock boy, she'd still be at the store searching for this stuff. She opened a bottle of clam juice and wrinkled her nose. She carefully crushed garlic, chopped onions and sautéed the concoction in butter until a tantalizing aroma filled the apartment. When all the ingredients simmered on the stove, Beth tossed a Caesar salad in an attempt to make it look more glamorous than a salad-in-a-bag.

Next, she set the table with the dishes, silverware and wine glasses she and Sam had recently selected together. She lit candles, arranged fresh flowers in a vase and surveyed her work with a critical eye. Everything had to be perfect. It wasn't often she took care of Sam. He'd worked long hours outside in the frigid weather for over two weeks and every night arrived home exhausted.

After she fixed her hair and makeup, she studied herself in the mirror and noticed for the first time, the dark circles under her eyes had vanished and the gaunt appearance was replaced by a healthy pink glow. She smiled and knew Sam made the difference. Even her nightmares had become less frequent.

Her heart fluttered when she heard the door open. "What smells so good?" Sam called out.

Beth joined him in the living room and smiled confidently when he looked at her with surprise. She helped him slip out of his coat and boots and took him by the hand.

He lifted the pan lids to peek inside and closed his eyes to savor the aroma. "You did all this?"

"It's a surprise for you."

He smiled and pulled her close, then stopped when he looked down at his mud-covered hands and clothes. "Let me take a quick shower first."

When he rejoined Beth in the kitchen, she was straining pasta. He stepped up behind her and slipped his arms around her waist. She turned in his arms. "Are you hungry?" she asked.

His lips pressed against hers and lingered tenderly. "Only for you." She directed him to be seated and filled the wine glasses.

The flickering light from the candles cast a soft glow about the room. His eyes danced warmly as he pulled her onto his lap. "What's the occasion?" he asked. "Your birthday isn't until May and mine was in October."

"Does there have to be an occasion?" She beamed. "Because I love you and need to take care of you."

"You're going to make me forget about dinner." His voice deepened with passion and he reached until his lips pressed against hers.

"Hey," she laughed. "That's for dessert."

After dinner, he leaned back in the chair and patted his full stomach. "That was great!" he groaned.

"Ann gave me the recipe today." She looked at him skeptically. "Now I suppose you'll expect something like this every night." She reached under the table to produce a gift wrapped in bright paper and ribbons.

"What's this?"

"A little something for you because you are the most wonderful man in the world."

He reached to kiss her and smiled as he opened his gift. It was a book about the Great Lakes. He thumbed through the pages and read the back cover. "Wow, it covers the lakes from millions of years ago when glaciers formed the basins up to modern times." He kissed her once more. "Thank you, babe."

His smile was replaced by a slight frown. "What?" she asked.

"I'm going to start traveling to the Upper Peninsula next week."

He held her hand tightly while her gaze searched his.

"Will you be gone long?" she asked, not wanting the disappointment to destroy the cozy mood they shared only moments ago.

"I'm not sure what to expect. Craig has tried to get a contract with this company for some time. He never had the manpower to handle the extra work before I came along." He squeezed her hand. "Don't start worrying about it yet, Beth."

She wondered why she wasn't elated he'd finally be out of harm's way. Why her heart questioned how he could leave her when she was only beginning to feel secure again. This is what she wanted, wasn't it?

"I won't go if you want me to stay." At the sink, he turned her to face him and whispered against her hair, "I don't want to leave you."

"I want you to go." The doubt in her mind shadowed her smile. "You'll be safer."

He tipped her head back so he could see her clearly. "My plan is to get a permanent job far away from here so we can both move. Then maybe you'll stop looking behind you all the time." He brushed her lips with his. "Maybe you can begin to live again."

* * *

Jack woke from a nap to the sound of the ringing phone. He sat upright, groggy from lack of sleep the night before.

"Hi, Jack. It's Tom."

Jack yawned. "Yeah, Tom. What's going on?"

Tom lowered his voice. "I discovered something today I need to talk to you about."

Something in Tom's voice caused Jack's mind to suddenly jerk awake. "What information?" he asked, guardedly.

"I can't tell you on the phone. Can you meet me in an hour at Willy's?"

Jack detected the secrecy in Tom's voice. "I'll be there."

As Tom set the phone down he nervously scanned the room to make sure no one had overheard his conversation. He was only marginally relieved to discover he was alone in the back room of the police station. Standing, he gathered the completed paperwork to take to the clerk. Tom returned to his desk and gulped down the last of his lukewarm coffee, shuddering from the bitter taste. He began to type one more report before his shift ended. Unwillingly, his mind wandered to the disturbing events he discovered earlier. He forced his thoughts back to the report and wouldn't dwell on the sensitive matter until he could talk freely with Jack.

When it was time to leave, he waved good-bye to the dispatcher on his way to the parking lot. As the door closed behind him, he held onto the doorknob to steady his wobbly gait. He wondered if he was coming down with a sudden case of the flu and attempted to shake the effects of lightheadedness aside. His thoughts were disoriented. What was happening? Why was everything moving in slow motion?

While Tom staggered to his car, Andy Thompson watched from across the street. He casually lit a cigarette and slowly pulled his car onto the street to follow Tom's at a distance. Andy watched Tom's car weave in an erratic manner. He felt a pang of regret he had to be the one to do the dirty work, especially when it involved his own partner. He was left with no other option when he discovered Tom spying on him earlier. He had no doubt Tom saw him exchange drugs for money with one of his contacts. Andy had to protect his interests, which meant Tom's silence. There was no alternative, but it still ticked him off.

Tom's car swerved over the centerline and wove back across two lanes as he tried to focus his blurred vision on the road. He attempted to bring his car to a stop, but his thoughts were so distorted he had no concept of time or space to determine which direction he traveled. Suddenly, he gasped for air and grabbed his chest as his heart raced out of control. In a panic, he blindly groped for the door handle and desperately attempted to alert someone for assistance.

Tom's car came to a stop and blocked traffic on the opposite lane. Car horns blared, but were muted and distant as he slipped into darkness.

Andy drove by, quickly looked inside to see Tom's head resting motionless on the steering wheel. Andy felt confident there was little chance Tom would survive the heavy dose of Fentanyl Andy had slipped into his coffee at the station. He quickly stepped on the gas pedal and vacated the area before someone identified him at the scene.

* * *

As Jack flipped through the juke box selections at Willy's Bar and Grill, he inserted a few coins and punched the buttons to make his selections. He returned to the booth and enjoyed the soft crooning of his favorite Blake Shelton tune. When the five selections were over, he glanced at his watch. Tom was over half an hour late. Maybe he got held up at work. Jack dialed the station on his cell phone.

"Hi, Marge. It's Jack Walsh. Is Tom Hutchins still there?"

There was a long pause before she spoke. "Tom's been in an accident, Jack. He's on his way to Lenawee General."

Jack disconnected the call as his heart pounded. This sounded too familiar for his liking. With a sudden feeling of alarm, he tossed a few bucks on the table to cover his tab and rushed to his car to drive straight to the hospital.

He entered the emergency room and found Tom's parents, Marv and Gail Hutchins, who clung to each other. Gail Hutchins cried softly as her husband tried to comfort her. Marv spotted Jack and turned to face him.

"How is he?" Jack asked while he clenched his fists together.

"It doesn't look good, Jack. They don't know how long he was down before CPR was started." Marv's voice was choked with emotion. Jack led them to the waiting area, where fellow officers waited, anxious for news of their comrade's condition.

* * *

When time permitted, Sam and Beth spent every possible moment together doing nothing at all but making up for time lost. One such weekend, Sam set his book down and laid his head on Beth's lap, across the papers she corrected. She smiled when she saw the mischievous twinkle in his eyes. He reached and pulled her down beside him as papers slid from her lap, across the bed and onto the floor. "I want to show you something." He opened a map of Michigan and unfolded it across the bed. Beth rolled onto her stomach and looked at him curiously. He pointed to the town of Marsquete, located on the northern coast of Michigan's Upper Peninsula. "I have to decide if I want to work here for the next two years."

"Two years?" she said. "I thought the job was temporary."

He brushed a lock of hair away from her face. "It is temporary, for two years."

She studied the map. "It's so far away."

"It's about a six hour drive," he confirmed."

She rolled onto her back and wrapped her arms around his neck to pull him close. "I know what this job means to you, Sam. I would never ask you to stop doing something you believe in so strongly."

He kissed the tip of her nose. "I know you wouldn't, that's one of the reasons why I love you so much."

She laughed coyly. "What are the other reasons?"

He stared at her thoughtfully. "The main reason is because you drive me wild." He playfully nibbled her ear lobe.

She giggled and pushed him away so she could look into his eyes. "But two years! It doesn't mean I have to be happy about it." She sulked.

Again, he pointed to the map. "I looked at a cottage for rent on Lake Superior, right here."

Beth squinted her eyes to read the small print. "You're going to move there?"

"I have to live somewhere. Besides, there's an option to buy." Again, she frowned. "It sounds so permanent."

""The Upper Peninsula is beautiful. You could spend your days off from school with me in paradise." He reached to kiss away the frown. "I know you'll fall in love with the area."

She continued to stare at the map. "It looks so remote."

"I think you would feel much safer there, than living here alone," he added.

She was touched by his thoughtfulness. "I do have a lot of vacation days to take."

He continued to sell her on the idea. "I'm told the summers are the best. Look how close it is to Pictured Rocks and Tahquamenon Falls. They say the water is the color of root beer from the minerals in the area."

Beth searched his face. "It sounds like you've already made up your mind. You don't need my approval, you know."

"I want you to be happy and part of this decision."

She kissed him tenderly. "I don't care where you live, as long as I can see you."

"Wait until you see the cottage. It needs a lot of work, but the price is unbelievable."

Beth reached for her calendar. "I'm off school for mid-winter break next month. Why don't I drive up to see you then?"

He pulled her close to kiss her and said is a soft, low voice "I was hoping you'd say that," he said as he pulled his tee shirt over his head.

* * *

After a long day at work, Beth wanted nothing more than to crawl into bed. Sam wouldn't be home until Friday, so she had a few days to catch up on her studies. Tonight, she felt particularly lonely. When she pulled her car around the back of the apartment, she was delighted to find Sam's truck already parked.

Her heart soared as she ran up the stairs and unlocked the door to greet him. When she opened the door, Sam sat up from his nap. "I'm sorry I woke you." She frowned when she saw the troubled look on his face. "Is something the matter? Why are you home during the middle of the week?"

He appeared solemn as he took a step toward her. "We need to talk." Something about his tone made her feel uneasy.

"What is it, Sam?" she asked as she slipped out of her coat.

"I called Jack this morning."

Beth sank into a chair and suddenly felt the tension in the room fill her with a greater sense of apprehension. "What's wrong?" she asked, and bit her lower lip. Her gaze followed as he paced the room. Her stomach muscles contorted.

He stopped pacing, placed his hands on his hips in a confrontational manner. His jaw was firmly set. "A few weeks ago, Tom Hutchins was killed." His voice was quiet, yet controlled.

"How?" she asked calmly, even though the fragile, thinly veiled guise of security she had shared with Sam these past few months was viscously stripped away.

"Evidently, Tom died on his way to meet Jack with some information he discovered." Beth closed her eyes to block out his words. "Someone drugged him with a lethal dose of Fentanyl."

She covered her face with her hands and refused to believe this had anything to do with her.

Sam knelt down in front of her. "It's time for you to tell me everything. Before someone else is hurt," he pleaded.

She bolted from the chair, but her knees buckled. Sam reached to steady her. "This isn't something you can keep to yourself any longer. People are still getting hurt, even though you've remained silent."

"You don't know if this has anything to do with me."

"You know damn well these events are related, Beth." He forced her to face him. "Tell me, damn it!" The determination in his eyes made her back away.

"You knew I wouldn't tell you when you made the decision to stay with me." She crossed her arms to hide the trembling .

"Tell me before something happens to you," he shouted.

She flinched and broke free from his grasp. He reached for her but she pushed him away. "Leave me alone," she cried as she locked herself in the bathroom.

When he pounded on the door, it sent waves of nausea through her. What had Tom Hutchins discovered that cost him his life? She thought about Jack's near brush with death. Who would be next? Sam? Perhaps Gram? She thought of her baby and wondered how long she'd be safe. What would happen if she confronted those who wanted her permanently silenced.

"Beth, open the door," Sam called out. "Please."

Something in his tone made her want to reach out to him. Slowly she opened the door and fell against him. "I can't tell you," she choked.

Sam held her away. "I can't sit by any longer and watch this thing destroy another person. If you don't tell me, then. . ." He stopped.

"You'll what?" she demanded.

His hands remained clenched at his side as he faced her. "You have this part of you I can't break through. You were like this when I asked you to marry me in college. Something always stopped you from making the commitment."

"Sam, I. . ."

"Even though you say you trust me, you continue to hold back." His eyes were angry, she detected the hurt in his voice and it killed her. "Until you can trust me unconditionally, then what we have isn't worth a damn!" They stared at each other for several moments. "If you can't tell me, then I'm leaving. These secrets of yours will eventually destroy us. We can either face this together, or you'll have to hide from it alone." He reached for his duffle bag and stepped to the door.

A small sob escaped her. "Damn you, Sam." She saw his shoulders slump as he stepped out of the apartment. "You promised you'd never leave." Her words were lost as the door closed.

Beth stared at the closed door and felt more alone than ever. Her precariously fragile world began to shift once again. She stumbled to the bathroom and held her stomach, the nausea churned inside of her like a caldron over a burning fire. How much longer could she endure this pain?

"If you're coming to get me, then get it over with!" She screamed at imaginary demons. She cried once more and felt the jab of Sam's words pierce through her heart. Perhaps he was right. Maybe it was her fault Tom Hutchins died. What good had her silence done so far?

How she longed to be free of this constant struggle for peace. By facing her foes, would this suffering stop?

In a dream-like trance, she searched for her car keys and stepped outside without a coat to shield her from the bitter, northern winds.

* * *

By the time Sam reached Mackinaw City, his anger had died down to a sick feeling of guilt in the pit of his stomach. He turned the car around before he crossed the Mackinaw Bridge to the Upper Peninsula, and headed back to Beth. He was mad and worried beyond reason, but how could he act like such an idiot?

After he parked his car in front of the apartment building, he raced up the stairs, but was surprised to discover the door wide open. He cautiously searched the apartment, but she wasn't inside. Where would she go in the middle of the night? The answer was simple: there was only one place Beth would seek shelter. He jumped back into his car and drove like mad to Rose Brockton's house.

The house was dark when he knocked lightly on the door. There was no answer so he pounded harder. Finally, Rose called out, "What do you want, Sam?"

"Please let me in Mrs. Brockton, I need to see Beth." For several long seconds he refrained from breaking the door down. When he heard the lock set free, he pushed open the door and stepped into the house. "Where is she?" he insisted, his patience shot.

"Hold on just a minute." Rose scolded him. "She just went to sleep. I won't let you disturb her now. Come into the kitchen."

Rose opened the refrigerator and passed him a bottle of beer. Gratefully, Sam accepted and sat at the table when she motioned for him to have a seat.

"How is she?" he asked.

Rose poured her beer into a glass. "You tell me. I couldn't make sense out of what she was saying."

Sam rubbed his strained eyes. "We had a fight. I said some stupid things." He took a healthy swig of beer and wiped his mouth with the back if his hand.

Rose patted his arm. "It would take more than hurtful words to destroy her love for you, Sam."

He took another swig of beer. "I hope you're right."

Rose's smile hinted of sadness. "My husband and I would get into some real doozies over nothing at all." He watched a slight blush tint her face. "It was the passion responsible for such words. You and Beth will be just fine."

Sam wasn't so certain. "What do you know about the reason she left Aidan?"

Rose frowned. "Why do you ask?"

He searched her face for any clues. "I know part of the story. It's time for her to tell me the rest. Her life is in danger, others are in danger, too. She thinks she's protecting all of us by not confronting what happened."

Rose looked at him with alarm. "Do you really think she's in danger?" Sam opened the refrigerator for another beer and turned to Rose.

"I know she isn't safe. Neither are you or anyone else who continues to shelter her from facing the truth about the night she was raped, beaten and terrorized." He pounded the table to emphasize each word.

"Sam, don't. . . please. . ."

When he discovered Beth leaned against the doorway, appearing pale and fragile, he rushed to her and lifted her into his arms. Rose led the way to the bedroom where he gently laid her on the bed and covered her with the blanket.

"God, Beth. . ." his voice choked with emotion as he leaned over her. "I'm sorry. . ." He rested his head against her forehead, unable to speak.

"I know you were speaking the truth." She curled against him as he drew her close.

"I was scared and angry. My words were meant to provoke you into telling me what happened." He kissed her. "Forgive me," he whispered.

They clung to one another as Rose closed the door behind her with a heavy sigh. She returned to the kitchen to finish her beer. By God, if she knew what really happened that night, she would tell Sam every last, ugly, sorted detail.

CHAPTER TEN

While Beth drove the distant miles to Sam's cabin on Lake Superior, she observed the breath-taking landscape of Michigan's Upper Peninsula. The trees became more abundant and the hills became steeper as each mile brought her closer to Sam. She longed to have him near to help calm the growing discontentment she had felt since the news of Tom Hutchins' death.

Although they had not spoken of the incident since the night of their argument, she sensed a subtle distance between them. Sam's words continued to gnaw at her, which only added to the confusion and doubt in her mind. But in her heart, she knew he was right. She didn't really know the meaning of the word trust. She'd learned at an early age to be wary, to fend for herself and fight each day to maintain her sanity through the neglect and harm she faced at every corner. She learned to shelter herself through the bullying at school, through her Mom's drunken anger, through the times she was ill or lonely and had no one to turn to. The trauma did not harden her, it created a vulnerable strength and compassion within her. She trusted Sam and Gram and Jack as best she could. Sam wanted total commitment. How could she give him what he wanted and not put him at risk? A marriage license would be easy to trace. She'd have to devise a plan, or risk losing Sam forever.

She looked out of the window at the beautiful, clear blue water of Lake Superior as she drove through the town of Munsletier. The water stretched to meet the sky at the horizon and gave the appearance to continue on forever, like a great, vast ocean. When she gazed at the magnificence of the great lake, she could appreciate why Sam's passion to protect them from man's ignorance remained a mission he was determined to pursue.

She followed the direction's Sam had mapped out and drove slowly along the snow-covered side roads off the main highway. Sam was concerned about her small car handling the heavy snow known to easily accumulate higher than ten feet in this part of the state. He made her promise to be careful. She finally stopped the car in the driveway of the address on the map and with suitcase in hand she trudged through the drifting snow. She marveled at the height of the cleared snow in the form of a white labyrinth to the door of the cabin.

The front door was unlocked, just as Sam promised and even though she knew he wouldn't be home from work until later in the evening, she was still disappointed he was not there to greet her.

She stood in the entrance to observe the quaint cabin. The rich, warm honey color of the embers in the fireplace lent a feeling of immediate welcome. When she switched on the track lighting, located on the beams high above the upstairs loft, the glow of the room grew more inviting.

She curiously explored the rooms on the main floor and was relieved to discover a bathroom with a shower. At least the plumbing was indoors. To be honest, she wasn't sure what to expect.

In the bedroom, she found a queen-size mattress on the floor. Sam's clothing was placed in neat piles on top of the mattress. There were no other furnishings in the room. The kitchen was small, but efficient. Beth smiled as she peeked into the cupboards and discovered them empty. Sam had the nerve to tease her about the state of her kitchen at the apartment; she couldn't wait to chide him when he got home. At least she had her beloved pan to cook with.

The kitchen, dining and living area were one open room designed to utilize the heat of the large fireplace situated in the great room. She opened the double glass doors of the fireplace and stoked red embers glowing inside. She added some kindling to start a fire. This place was freezing. Once she was certain the flames were strong, she set more logs on the fire and stood on the hearth to rub her gloved hands together. Before long, the warmth heated the room enough so she was able to unzip her coat. She sat at the picnic table near the fireplace and dreamed about what it would be like to live in this cabin with Sam and Samantha on a permanent basis. Maybe when the school year was over she'd take the risk. The thought jolted her. Never had she allowed herself to believe she could live her dream.

She rummaged through the kitchen and found a package of tea bags. The gas stove was a relic; after two attempts to light the burner, she gave up trying. With her luck she'd blow up the place. She spotted a down-filled sleeping bag rolled up on the couch. As the room grew warm, she became acutely aware of how tired she felt. A little nap was just the thing she needed after the long drive. She slipped inside the sleeping bag, closed her heavy eyelids and had no trouble falling fast asleep.

Sometime later, a knock at the door awakened her. She stepped to open the door, still half-asleep, but hesitated.

"It's Mildred Simon. I live next door." The woman raised her voice to be heard over the howling wind.

"Come in." Beth said as she held the door open.

Mildred untangled the scarf bundled around her neck and removed her hat. She smiled at Beth as she set a basket on the floor. "So you're the pretty little lady Mr. Sam is all worked up about." Mildred studied Beth for several moments. "You're even prettier than he described you." Beth felt a hot flush, but relaxed instantly. It was impossible to be nervous with this outgoing woman.

"Hi. I'm Beth."

Mildred continued to smile. "I know exactly who you are. I promised your young man I would come over to make sure you feel right at home." Beth returned her smile.

"Thanks. It's very kind of you, Mrs. Simon."

Mildred began to remove her coat. "Call me Millie."

"Come in, Millie. I'd make some tea, but I haven't figured out how to light the stove yet." Beth followed Millie's scowl to the fireplace.

"First we need to get some heat in this place," said Millie. "Get your coat on, and I'll show you to the wood pile." Beth threw on her coat and Millie pointed to Beth's ankle high boots. "If you plan on spending anytime up here in the winter, you'd be smart to invest in some real boots." Beth followed Millie outside to a huge woodpile behind the cabin.

They loaded up with logs and returned to the cabin.

Millie set several logs in the fireplace and chuckled while Beth rubbed her wet ankles and changed into a dry pair of socks.

"Now, let me show you how this cook stove works. Heaven knows it's a crotchety old thing." Before long, the cabin was warm and cozy while the two women drank tea at the table and talked as if they'd known each other for years.

"I've lived next door for over twenty years. Me and my husband moved here when the kids grew up and left us," said Millie as she unpacked the basket of food items. "I figured you didn't get to the store yet, so I made a pan of lasagna for your dinner." Millie winked. "I know you young people have more important things on your mind than food."

Beth laughed. "Thanks, Millie. You really went to a lot of trouble and I'm very grateful."

Millie waved her hand. "No trouble at all. That young man of yours has helped me and Pete out shoveling our snow. I'm glad to return the favor."

Beth's mouth watered as she stared at a plate of oatmeal raisin cookies. Millie smiled and passed the plate across the table. "Help yourself. I made plenty."

Beth looked around the cabin and enjoyed the feeling of being at home in such a short time. "What kind of work do you do?" Beth asked between bites.

"Pete and I own the bait shop down the road. In the winter we build log furniture to sell at shops down state. It keeps us busy enough to sustain the long winters. You need something to keep you busy this time of year."

"I'd love to see your work."

"Come over anytime. We have a workshop in the basement. In fact, Pete is helping Sam make a piece."

"Really?" Beth asked, surprised.

"Yes indeed. They're working on a log bed. Have Sam bring you by this weekend so he can show it off. But you'd better act surprised when you see it."

Beth smiled, tickled with delight. "I will."

Millie began the task of bundling up and pointed out the window. "See that brown house over there?" Beth nodded. "You come over if you need anything, you hear?"

"I will and thanks for everything, Millie. You have made me feel very welcome."

"I promised your man that I'd look after you. So don't disappoint me or him by not asking for anything you may need."

After Millie was gone, Beth unpacked the schoolwork she brought along and lost track of time. When she heard the sound of a car door closing, she looked up surprised to see how dark it was outside. She ran to open the door, elated to see Sam who trekked through the snow toward the cabin. She smiled happily when she saw the grin on his face and jumped into his arms. "It's so good to see you." She brushed snow from the dark stubble on his face as he lifted her into his embrace, carried her into the cabin and kicked the door closed. All the while their lips hungrily sought resolution to their building passion.

"It's been a long week without you," he whispered as he cupped her face between his gloved hands. He bent to kiss her again, this time gently.

"I've missed you so much, Sam. You feel so good." She snuggled against him for warmth.

"How do you like the place?" he asked.

"I love it. I feel as if I'm home."

His grin deepened as he pulled her closer and kissed the tip of her nose. "I was hoping you'd feel safe and protected here." He pointed to the loft. "I plan to make two rooms up on the loft. There's a lot of potential, don't you think?"

"Yes, I do. Millie Simon brought dinner over. She's wonderful."

Sam smiled. "Wait until you meet her husband, Pete. They're both great." He pulled her to him. "I'm glad you're here."

Beth wrapped her arms around him and felt safe. "Not as much as I am."

He looked at her questioning. "Are you sure?" he asked. "I still see shadows behind your sexy smile."

"When I move here, I promise to share those secrets with you." A slight smile tugged at the corner of her lips as she unbuttoned his heavy oilcloth coat. "But right now I'd rather we share something else." She frowned when she unzipped his sweatshirt, only to find canvas overalls underneath. "How do you manage to move with all these clothes on?"

He grinned at her hungrily. "I have no problem." He removed her jacket and slipped his hands beneath her sweater so fast it made her head spin. "See?" he whispered in her ear as he planted warm kisses along her neckline.

She rubbed his heavily whiskered face and laughed seductively. "You look like a wild mountain man."

He scooped her off the floor, into his arms. "Women, come! Take shower," he grunted as he carried her into the bathroom.

Beth laughed with delight as he set her on the floor. "We'll freeze to death in here!" she cried as he began to unfasten her jeans.

He turned on the water in the shower. "I'll keep you warm," he whispered and gently reached to kiss her as steam surrounded them.

* * *

During the next four days, Beth felt as carefree as she did when she spent summer months in Maine with Gram and Aunt Lily. She relaxed for the first time in years and made plans with Sam for their future together. It was as if their life up north existed in another world.

She fell in love with the cabin and the surrounding area. The peaceful solitude enabled her to experience a sense of security she hadn't felt before. Just the thought of future plans had always sent her into a near panic attack, but at the cabin with Sam, she felt safe enough to venture a risk.

Sam cleared a path from the cabin to the lake so he could show Beth the spectacular view they would enjoy when the snow melted. Together they stood at the icy edge of Lake Superior.. The wind had blown the crashing water into a frozen ice cave. They explored the water's edge for hours. They ventured into the nearby town of Ashkelon and enjoyed dinner at a quaint lodge.

They visited Millie and Pete Simon's workshop where Beth watched firsthand the homemade furniture business. Her smiling gaze met Sam's when Pete showed off the bed he and Sam were creating. The bed was made of logs, which Beth smoothed her hand over. She marveled at the headboard made of gnarly bumps of the tree. Tears streamed down her cheeks as Sam watched with pride.

But the nights in Sam's arms were the most glorious times of all. When he touched her and kissed her she forgot the horrors and the darkness always close enough to send her into a terrified panic.

One stormy evening, Beth curled up next to Sam in front of the glowing fire. She dreamily watched the flickering of lights as they glowed around the room while Sam played with a lock of her hair and gently twisted it around his finger. He traced his finger up her chin to her lips.

She stretched lazily and thought if she were more content than this, she would be in heaven.

"Why don't you move here now and live with me?" he whispered and nibbled on her lower lip.

"I'd love to move here," she yawned. "But not until the school year is over. I can't just leave without notice or a replacement." Her heavy eyelids fluttered shut.

Sam watched over her long after the tension in her body slumped and gave way to peaceful slumber. He was determined to convince her this was where she needed to heal and give her entire self to him… secrets and all.

When the time came for her departure, his heavy heart dreaded saying goodbye. How long would it be before they saw each other again? He was sure he wouldn't be able to get away for at least three weeks, maybe more.

Beth turned to him at the door and reached to kiss him. "Maybe I'll surprise you and drive up for a long weekend," she said as she held him close.

He felt her apprehension and crushed her to him in a fervent embrace. "I'd feel much better if you'd move up here."

"I do love it here with you, Sam. But I need to finish this school year."

Sam refrained from speaking, the thoughts strained to be said and looked into her eyes before she diverted her attention. He wondered if the time would ever be right for them to be together without unknown conflicts driving a wedge between them. He picked up her suitcase and walked her to the car. "You'll be careful driving home?" he questioned.

Beth smiled, even though tears sprang to her eyes. "I'll be careful."

"Don't forget to exercise and eat right," he added, noting the tears. "You have the phone where you can reach me anytime right?" She nodded, reached into her pocket and produced the phone. He pulled her to him once more. "I love you, Beth."

"Oh, Sam," was all she could manage as she buried her face in the thick fabric of his coat and choked back tears.

Sam clenched his fists tightly to fend off the frustration as he watched her back out of the driveway. He'd been patient, more patient than he could ever imagine. He fought the urge to stop her from leaving and attempted to ignore the ominous feeling that loomed over him. He'd give her until the school year ended to come to terms with her decisions.

* * *

Beth arrived home late afternoon and wanted nothing more than to soak in a hot, steamy tub to ease her weary, tense muscles. She forced her thoughts to dwell on the fun she and Sam shared over the long weekend. It seemed like a winter wonderland far from reality, much to wonderful to be real. The cabin. The love. The soft glow of Sam's face when he bent close to kiss her.

She knew he was eager to move on with their life together, but she wanted things to remain the way they were. She was afraid to make further commitments, afraid she'd lose everything if she became greedy for a normal life filled with all the wonderful hopes Sam had to offer. Her tranquil thoughts were interrupted by the sound of the phone ringing. Beth jumped out of the tub and hurriedly dressed. Her heart raced, she wondered what was so important for Gram to contact her. Beth tucked her damp hair into a wool hat and dialed Gram's number.

Rose answered immediately. "Beth! I've tried to reach you all day!" said Rose.

"I was visiting Sam at his new cabin. What's wrong?"

When Gram sighed, Beth felt her heart sink. "Aunt Lily has suffered a stroke."

Beth felt the impact of Gram's words hit her full force as if they were delivered by a freight train. "Oh, no! When?" Her voice sounded distant as she thought about the ramifications of this new development. Where was Samantha?

"Lily's neighbor, Mrs. Felsworth, phoned me this morning. She has Samantha in her care. I'm leaving tonight on an eight-forty flight from Tri-County Airport."

Beth swallowed and tried to rid herself of the lump in her throat. "I'll be over to take you to the airport as soon as I get ready." On the drive to

Gram's, Beth's thoughts were troubled by the past rapidly closing in on her. Events beyond her control were happening so quickly, it wouldn't be long before she was forced to face the secrets she had worked so hard to keep at bay.

Rose opened the door and they clung to one another for several moments. "How's Aunt Lily?" Beth searched her grandmother's distressed face.

"She's not responsive. Mrs. Felsworth made it sound as if the stroke is fairly serious. I'll call you after I arrive and see Lily for myself."

Beth shook her head no. "Let me call you."

Rose agreed and cupped Beth's cheek lovingly. "I'll stay as long as I have to, honey. Don't you worry about. . ."

Beth's eyes filled with tears as she took the cloth doll out of her bag and handed it to Gram. It was the same doll Sam had given to her the night they fell in love so long ago. The one Gram had brought back after the funeral. "Give this to Samantha. Tell her it's from her Daddy." Beth could barely manage to utter the words that had never been spoken above a whisper. "I haven't said her name out loud in so long," she cried.

"It's going to be all right. No matter what happens, I'll stay in Maine with your baby until we can figure something out." Beth looked into

Gram's eyes, also wet with tears. "Mrs. Felsworth is watching Samantha until I arrive." Gram wrote down a number. "Call this number in the evening when you want to talk."

Rose slipped on her coat. "We'd better leave. I don't like to rush at the airport."

As the plane disappeared from sight, Beth felt as if a part of her would finally hold her little girl. When Gram talked to Samantha, it would be as if Beth was there to share in the joy of seeing her daughter for the first time since she was born. As she inhaled deeply, she felt the loss she had been forced to endure in order to protect the innocent ones she loved and it hurt like hell to breathe.

* * *

Andy Thompson entered the dark, smoky tavern of Max's Lounge and sat at the bar. He nodded his head at the bartender, Charlie, who placed a full pitcher of beer on a tray for a waitress. Charlie walked over and set Andy up with a scotch on the rocks. "What's happening, Charlie?" Andy took a healthy swig of the scotch and directed his glassy stare at Charlie.

"Not much. Bill in?" Andy slurred and attempted to focus on Charlie's broad face.

Charlie motioned toward the back room. "You want me to send one of the girls to get him?"

Andy slid off of the barstool and picked up his drink. "Naw! I'll just mosey on back." He pushed open the double doors, passed the restrooms and pay phone. He entered the cold storage area and followed the maze created by cases of booze stacked higher than he was tall. He knew the way to the office located by the receiving doors on the outer wall of the storeroom. When he approached the glass windowed office, he saw Bill Tanner was talking on the phone. Bill noticed Tanner's eyes open wide with surprise as he slammed down the phone.

"What the hell are you doing here during business hours?" Tanner demanded.

Andy paced restlessly, reached into the pocket of his leather jacket and held up his pager. "You contacted me." He pressed the button to demonstrate the number on the pager's display window.

Andy didn't like the way Tanner's face flushed as he closed the door to the office. "I didn't expect you to answer in person, for Christ's sake!" Andy looked at his business partner with surprise.

"I was passing by on my way to Sal's place. What's the big deal?"

Tanner glared at him. "Look at you! You're stoned out of your mind. Your carelessness will be the downfall of us yet."

Andy clenched his fists tightly to his sides, in a half-hearted attempt to control the rage building inside. "If you mean the business with Tom Hutchins, I didn't have a choice."

Bill jumped to his feet and leaned across the desk to glare into Thompson's eyes. At six foot two, he easily towered over Thompson by five inches. Yet, what stature Andy lacked in height, he easily made up for in his compact, sturdy build. He outweighed Tanner by fifty pounds.

"Keep your voice down!" Tanner spat under his breath. "You don't know who might be listening." His narrowed eyes darted around the storeroom before resting back on Thompson. "You're getting sloppy, Thompson. My patience is wearing thin."

Tanner's dark, menacing eyes permeated the temporary sense of confidence produced by the hit of coke Andy snorted in the parking lot. "So, what did you page me for?" he asked, false pride overshadowed his nervousness.

Tanner sat down and rested his feet on the desk. "Do you have any information about Beth Brockton?"

Andy continued to pace the small office and felt the walls closing in. He leaned on the desk and stared at Tanner accusingly. "You're the one who is stirring things up by wanting to locate her!" Andy felt a bead of sweat run down the side of his face. The way Tanner looked at him made him uneasy. "Why in hell can't you let her be?"

Tanner calmly stood and reached across the desk to grab the front of Andy's jacket. "It's not your place to question why. Just find her and bring her to me, unharmed."

Andy searched Tanner's eyes before he pulled away to smooth his jacket. He knew Tanner's weak spot was Beth Brockton and it made him furious, he wanted no part of this, but Tanner had him by the short hairs. "I'll see if Sally found anything out from Lena McCray."

Bill watched as Andy moved toward the door. "Be careful, Thompson. With the heat from Tom Hutchins' death, things are getting way too close for comfort. I don't want anyone else getting hurt."

After Andy left the storeroom, Tanner opened the desk drawer to find the college graduation picture of Beth, Linda Brockton had given to him. He studied her lovely face, full of youth and promise. He'd never accept the reasons why she chose not to share her life with him. Angrily, he tossed the picture back into the drawer and felt the humiliation of her rejection as if it happened yesterday. Did the snooty little bitch think she was too good for him? By God, when he got his hands on her again, she'd pay dearly for the way she discarded him. He smiled to himself and wondered how she could refuse what he had to offer her now. He was the richest and most powerful citizen for miles around. Everyone in the community respected him. Didn't the fact he donated massive amounts of money to various charities warrant Beth's respect? Didn't he rub elbows with all the right people? He straightened his cashmere jacket and held his head high when he considered how far he'd come from being the son of a drunken bar owner.

Proudly, he admired the campaign poster on the wall behind his desk. He was running for a senate seat in the next election, with strong backing from some of the most prominent and powerful people in the state. According to results from the latest polls, he was as good as elected. The rest was merely a formality. He wanted Beth by his side as he accomplished his goals.

He frowned and the blood pounded through his veins when he thought of her in the arms of Sam Andrews. He shook the image out of his mind. She wouldn't be so stupid to let Sam back into her life after the warning he'd given her before she disappeared from town almost two years ago.

Tanner felt a momentary twinge of guilt as he recalled the night he forced her to leave town. Somehow he'd make it up to her and prove how sorry he was for hurting her. She'd have no choice but to forgive him when she was finally by his side.

His thoughts turned to a more pressing issue. What was he going to do about Andy Thompson? He couldn't afford to keep that particular liability around much longer. After Thompson found Beth, he'd just have to meet with some untimely accident by way of Tom Hutchins.

* * *

Sally jumped to her feet from the abrupt pounding and unlocked the door for Andy. "Hi, Hon." She set down the book she was reading on the new sofa table, situated in front of the new sofa.

Andy scowled as he brushed past her and slumped down into the soft, pastel cushions of the couch. He looked around the room and sneered at the color scheme. Christ! It looked like rainbow sherbet. The way Sally frowned at him irritated him further.

"What's wrong now, Andy?"

"My life is a mess!" he whined and reached for her.

She smoothed his hair. "Do you want me to fix you a drink?"

He held her against him. "Has Lena McCray told you where I can find Beth Brockton?" he asked.

"No, she hasn't. I already told you what she said."

Andy walked into the kitchen and opened the refrigerator. He helped himself to a piece of cold fried chicken, shook some salt onto a drumstick and turned to her. "I paid for all of your new crap here. Now I want some answers," he blared at her, his mouth full of food.

"How can I get her to tell me? I've already tried everything I can think of," she said defensively as she folded her arms across her chest. Andy tried to think rationally, but he couldn't shake the sneaky feeling Tanner planned to set him up to be the fall guy. If that became a reality, Tanner was in for a big surprise if he thought he could walk away from this mess unscathed. Andy had photos and secret recordings of their "business" dealings and conversations.

"Look, Sal. I have reason to believe Beth Brockton is involved in the death of Tom Hutchins."

Sally's head jerked up to look at him. "What?" she asked, surprised. "You've got to be kidding."

"I'm serious. She always had a thing for older men." He could tell he'd piqued Sally's interest. He watched her eyes narrow. He knew Sally had been in love with Bill Tanner for years and was insanely jealous of the way Tanner lusted after Beth.

Sally snickered faintly. "And the way she flaunted herself at Tanner. It served Tanner right when she wanted absolutely nothing to do with him. I'm sure the only reason Tanner was attracted to her was because she wasn't interested, and Lord knows Tanner is used to getting everything he wants." She frowned at him. "But what does it have to do with Hutchins' death?"

Andy was desperate and he needed Sally to press Lena McCray for details on how to locate Beth. He was quick to come up with a convincing story. "Hutchins was blackmailing Beth because he found out she was involved with drugs and prostitution."

Sally laughed, sarcastically. "Oh please!"

Andy shrugged. "Think about it. She left town without a trace because Hutchins threatened to turn her in." He reached over to pull her into his arms. He knew Sally hated Beth Brockton and this was the type of crap she'd want to believe. "Come up with a story to tell Lena how concerned you are about Beth."

Sally smiled as Andy started to unbutton her sweater. "I'll think of something," she whispered as he kissed her.

* * *

Andy drove well over the speed limit to meet his contacts in Detroit. Damn! He was late and these weren't the types to keep waiting. He hadn't planned on spending so much time with Sally, but he smiled wickedly and didn't feel the least bit guilty.

Cautiously, he looked into the rearview mirror and noted the cars behind him on Interstate 94. He altered his speed to allow the surrounding cars to pass. Ever since the incident with Tom Hutchins, he was much more alert to anything suspicious. He quickly exited the freeway and was relieved to find no one followed as he stopped the car at a gas station. After he topped off the gas tank, he merged back onto I-94 and traveled east toward Detroit.

He reflected on his earlier conversation with Tanner. Why he was so hung up on Beth Brockton, Andy couldn't figure. She was just a kid, and a scared one at that. If Tanner was so hell-bent on finding her, why didn't he do it himself? Andy was used to doing all the grunt work for Tanner, but he was getting real tired of it. Something about this business with Brockton made him feel uneasy. Normally, Tanner was the mastermind behind their operation, but it was obvious he wasn't thinking with his brain when it came to Beth.

Andy exited at Michigan Avenue and headed toward the old Detroit Train Station. He reached over to a make sure the briefcase with the cash was still sitting on the passenger's seat. It made him real nervous to carry this much money. He popped three antacids and lightly skimmed his fingers over his piece hidden under his jacket. He was getting too old for this risky, double life. Maybe he should start thinking about retirement, but chuckled sarcastically knowing it was futile to consider. His involvement ran too deep for him to up and quit, besides, Tanner wouldn't allow it. Again, he checked out the car when it exited behind him and turned left on Michigan Avenue and stopped at the first street he came to. He waited until the car passed him before he turned around and drove east to his destination.

* * *

After she talked to Sam, Beth disconnected the phone. He wouldn't be able to visit for the weekend as planned. She looked into the mirror at her reflection and thought it was just as well. He'd be worried about her if he saw her. Ever since Gram left for Maine, Beth had lost weight again. She applied a cool washcloth to her bloodshot, burning eyes. Her nightmares had returned in full force and kept her from sleep most nights. Fears she thought gone were back with a vengeance, greater than before. It was as if her sense of anonymity had slowly eroded and left her exposed and vulnerable.

She glanced around the apartment and felt the emptiness more acutely without Sam close by. Should she leave this place to start over somewhere else? The thought seemed ludicrous, totally out of the question. She could never survive living without Sam. But she was afraid she would soon be faced with the decision to choose between his safety and a life without him.

She wrapped her arms around her more for comfort than warmth and struggled to force herself to place her nightly call to Maine. Each night became more of a burden to talk to Gram. It was impossible to tune out the happy sound of Samantha's voice which chattered in the background. Gram had tried to put her on the phone, but Beth wouldn't allow it. She couldn't bear to long for her little girl more than she did.

* * *

After knocking lightly on Sally Cantrell's door, Lena inspected her reflection in the window and fussed with her windblown hair. Sally opened the door and greeted Lena with a smile. "Come in, Lena."

Sally watched Lena study the room with a critical eye. "This looks great, Sally. Do you like it?"

Sally smiled appreciatively. "I'm still surprised when I come home. I have to think twice whether I'm in the right apartment or not. I love it." She motioned toward the couch. "Have a seat, Lena." When Sally re-entered the living room, she placed a tray of coffee on the shiny new surface of the coffee table. She couldn't help but beam with pleasure. "I just love the way my grandmother's China fits the decor. Isn't it odd I never liked these dishes before?" Again, she smiled lightly at Lena. "Before I forget, here's your check."

"Thanks for having enough confidence in me. I'll have to warn our regular decorator to be wary of the competition."

Sally's mood turned serious. "I must confide in you, Lena." Lena turned her full attention to Sally.

"What is it?" she questioned.

"I have a friend on the police force. He told me some disturbing information about your niece, Beth Brockton."

Lena frowned. "What news could possibly concern Beth?" Sally swallowed her coffee and hoped Lena would take the bait.

"He told me about an investigation he's involved with and the possibly links Beth to Tom Hutchins' death."

Lena gasped, setting the coffee cup on the table. "That's ridiculous! Beth couldn't be involved!"

"I'm only telling you this because of my concern for you. Don't you think Beth has a right to know?"

Lena stared at Sally, but appeared to be lost in her own thoughts. "I don't believe it."

Even when she made this statement, Sally saw the doubt in Lena's eyes. She cleared her throat. "Well, I'm only telling you what I heard."

"I guess you're right. If the police are questioning her involvement she should be informed. I'll call Beth's grandmother right away. She knows how to get in touch with her." Lena stood, obviously troubled by this news.

"Where does her grandmother live again? Linda told me once, but I've forgotten."

Lena reached for the doorknob. "In Pineville, north of Cabot's Bay."

Sally leaned against the closed door, relieved with her successful bit of sleuthing. Now maybe Andy would get off her back about spending so much money to redecorate the apartment.

* * *

Sam leaned over the plant blueprints spread out on his desk. He wasn't able to concentrate on work. He tossed and turned most of the night after he'd talked to Beth and although she made every effort to sound cheerful, he could hear the underlying sadness in her voice. He stared at the geometric patterns of the doodles he scribbled on the blueprints and quickly erased the marks. He questioned whether or not he was doing the right thing by working so far from her. He'd make up for his absence the coming weekend. Still, the feelings of guilt churned in his gut.

He glanced outside and studied the streaks of condensation frozen on the windowpanes that resembled tiny crystallized snowflakes. He forced his attention back to the blueprints and tried to push thoughts of Beth to the back of his mind.

* * *

Andy Thompson rubbed the fog from the windshield with the sleeve of his jacket, opened the window a crack and lit another cigarette. He'd been parked across the street from Rose Brockton's house for two days and hadn't observed any activity inside. Maybe the old lady went to Florida for the winter. If he didn't see Rose Brockton by the evening, he'd break into the house to see what he could find. He blew smoke rings out the window and waited.

When darkness fell, he slipped around to the back of the house and easily picked the lock to gain entrance into the kitchen. He opened the refrigerator and guessed no one planned to live here for a while. All of the perishable food items were gone. He searched the counter tops for clues about Beth Brockton. Grandma was extremely tidy, as everything was neatly arranged in the cupboards and drawers in proper order.

He entered the living room and stopped to study a framed picture of a man who had to be Beth's old man. He opened a roll-top desk and sorted through various piles of letters. As he scanned each note, no reference was made about Beth. Expertly, he placed each item exactly as he found it and rummaged through a stack of bills. He tucked a phone statement into his pocket to review later. Could be one number on the list would lead him to Beth. In an address book, he found Beth's name listed at her mom's address in Aidan. Grandma had done a good job to protect the identity of her grandchild.

Andy completed his search disappointed he didn't have more than a phone bill to help with his investigation. Hastily, he covered all traces of his presence and locked the door securely behind him.

* * *

Just one more day! Beth sighed as she closed her eyes. She could almost feel the security of Sam's arms wrapped around her, almost delight in the taste of his lips pressed against hers. Her pulse rate quickened at the thought of him touching her. The week had dragged on endlessly, but by this time tomorrow, the pleasure of lying in his arms would be worth the long wait.

"Miss Rose?" Her eyes popped open and the fantasy vanished instantly. All of the children were watching her curiously. She felt herself blush as she quickly directed her attention to the list of spelling words in her hand. She calmly called out the next word "Dictionary, I searched for the word in my dictionary."

Slowly, her pulse rate returned to normal. Secretly she smiled to herself and watched the students diligently write on sheets of paper. How embarrassing to be caught fantasizing about Sam in front of her students. Sam was turning her into a sex fanatic! She fought to control the urge to giggle when she realized the thought thrilled her. Finally, the bell rang to dismiss the children from school for the weekend.

After she stopped at the grocery store, she parked her car in front of the apartment building and ran the bags of groceries up the stairs. She unlocked the door, set the bags inside and made another trip to park her car in the rear of the building. She raced up the stairs once more and securely locked the door behind her. She hummed softly to herself while she put the food away and paused to read the recipe on a package of pasta, making sure she purchased all the necessary ingredients. While she placed eggs on the tray in the fridge, her thoughts were interrupted by a sound in the next room. She turned and looked toward the living room; her heart lurched in her chest when she saw snow melted footprints on the carpet. Her gaze followed the steps. They disappeared at the hall toward her bedroom. She was frozen with fear, someone must have entered her apartment when she moved her car. The scent of cigarette smoke caused her heart to lurch to her throat.

She began to inch her way toward the door as quietly as possible but her legs wobbled with terror. When someone stepped into the living room, she screamed out and jumped toward the door.

"Hello, Beth." Andy Thompson smiled, casually leaned against the wall and took a drag of his smoke.

Beth dropped the carton of eggs and watched in horror as a puddle of broken, runny egg slime oozed onto the carpet. She turned and ran to the door, but Andy was quick to grab her. She spun around and hit him with her fist. Andy looked at her with rage in his eyes and hit her on her cheek. She continued to struggle and cried out as she kicked his shin.

"Stop it!" he yelled as he shook her violently.

Tears blurred her vision as her head reeled from the impact of his fist. "What do you want?" she whispered, her voice shaking.

He leered at her. "I'm taking you back to Aidan." At first, the dreaded words did not penetrate her frenzied thoughts. Confusion clouded her reasoning. "Bill Tanner sent me to fetch you. He wants you to come back to him." His mocking smile contradicted the evil gleam that emanated from his eyes.

"Please don't take me back," she pleaded.

He roughly dragged her along and grabbed her coat. "Put this on," he harshly demanded.

Her gaze darted toward the kitchen counter and she reached for her purse. Andy latched onto her wrist and squeezed tightly until she dropped it. He searched the contents of the purse and handed it back to her.

She stumbled as he led her to the door. She toyed with the pepper spray on the key ring in her pocket. She aimed it at his face, but before she could press the nozzle, he slapped it away. Helplessly, she watched the key chain land on the floor. When he hit her once more across the face, she stumbled against him. Tears blurred her vision as he glared at her.

"Don't try anything stupid." He searched her coat pockets and held the burner phone. When he threw it to the carpet and crushed it with his boot, Beth cried out and he smacked her again.

Her eyes followed his hand as he produced a gun from the waistband of his pants. He placed the gun against the side of her head. "I won't have any problem using this." He shook her. "You got that?"

She nodded her head as tears ran down her cheeks and mixed with the blood from the cut on her lip. Disgusted, he reached into his pocket and shoved a wad of tissue at her.

As he dragged her to his car parked at the end of the street, she looked around to see if anyone could assist her. Her hopes were dashed when she discovered no one in sight. Andy pushed her onto the passenger's seat and closed the door with a loud thud. Beth closed her eyes, her head throbbed and her heart beat so violently against her ribs she thought it would explode. Andy sat in the driver's seat and watched her for a moment before he started the engine.

The drive was quiet; Beth was lost in desperate thoughts of escape. She wouldn't go back to Tanner, no matter what happened. Images too frightful to fathom flashed through her mind.

She opened her eyes and stared out the window as each passing mile brought her closer to Aidan. Briefly, her thoughts wandered to Sam. Beth shuddered, afraid to even think of what might have happened had Sam been there when Andy broke in. What would Sam do when he discovered her gone? She couldn't think about it. She had to force herself to remain calm to devise a plan of escape.

She grabbed the door handle when they passed through the town of Jane Arbor. She quickly looked at Andy behind the wheel of the car and he turned to face her. "What?" he demanded.

"I need to use the restroom." Again, her heart lurched in her throat. He diverted his attention back to the road, clearly not concerned about her comfort. "Please stop the car, I'm going to be sick," she pleaded.

He motioned toward a gas station ahead. "I'll pull in there." He parked around the side where the restrooms were located and turned to her. "I'll go first."

He grabbed her arm and locked a set of handcuffs around her wrist and the steering wheel. Beth's heart sank as she futilely struggled against the shackles.

She watched as Andy disappeared into the station. He reappeared several minutes later with a bag. He opened the door and placed a cup of coffee on the dashboard while he slid into the driver's seat. He searched for the key and unlocked the cuffs. "Go ahead," he nodded toward the bathroom. "Just remember I'm out here watching." He opened his coat just enough to expose the gun tucked into the waistband of his trousers.

Inside the temporary shelter of the bathroom, Beth surveyed the damage to her face. Quickly, she splashed water onto a paper towel to dab away the blood that still trickled from the split in her lip. With trembling hands, she pressed the cool towel against the throbbing, ugly bruise on her cheek.

She jumped to the blast of a car horn and reached for the doorknob. She debated for a moment whether or not to make a run for it, but decided he would only chase her down and possibly kill her.

When she was seated next to him, he grinned at her and sipped his coffee. "Nowhere to go, is there?"

Feeling nauseated, she turned away, sickened by his cruelty. When he didn't start the engine right away, she looked at him questioning. He rolled a dollar bill and produced a small plastic bag of white powder. He poured a thin line of the powder on a magazine and turned to her before snorting the drug. "You want some?"

She shook her head and as he placed the rolled bill into his nostril she lunged at him, the hot coffee spilled in his lap.

"Shit!" he hollered as the cocaine spilled everywhere. He snatched her arm, but she struggled out of his grip as he desperately tried to fan the area where the hot coffee burned his skin. Beth grabbed her purse and seized the opportunity to dash out of the car.

Outside in the dark, she ran, her heart pumped wildly as she stumbled toward the wooded area behind the gas station. She didn't have a clue where she was, or what direction to travel, but her only concern was to get far away from Andy.

She ran until her lungs felt as if she couldn't take another breath, yet she mustered the strength to keep going. It wasn't long before she heard his footsteps in the distance behind her. She covered her mouth to stifle a cry as she turned back to make out his blurred silhouette several yards away. A tree branch slapped against her face, but she was numb to the pain. She continued to outrun him, yet he gained ground and narrowed the distance between them.

She screamed as he tackled her to the ground and fell on top of her in the snow. He stared down at her. The moonlight was casting enough light so she could read the fury in his eyes.

He pulled his fisted hand to deliver a full blow to her face. Beth futilely struggled to free herself, but could only turn her head to divert some of the impact.

"You stupid bitch!" he yelled as his clenched hand met her chin.

Beth momentarily felt the ground spin beneath her. Her senses were dulled, but she saw him pull out the gun.

Without hesitation, she grabbed the gun and forced his aim upwards. He yelped in pain when she bit his arm and he dropped the gun. Again, he moved to strike her, but she quickly wrapped her hand around the gun and pointed it at his face. "Get off me!" she screamed.

Andy lunged for the gun as they struggled to gain control of the weapon. He rolled and pulled her over on top of him. "Let go!" he yelled, but her grip tightened around the gun. As he attempted to pry her fingers loose, the sickening sound of gunshot pierced the otherwise still night air.

He stopped fighting. His startled eyes focused on her for a second before his facial muscles contorted in a grimace of pain. He clutched his chest and looked down to see a dark stain already soaked through the front of his jacket.

Beth covered her mouth to keep from screaming. He growled and helplessly watched as she struggled to her feet.

His hand latched onto her scarf and pulled it from her as she scrambled out of his reach. Her leg muscles betrayed her; she attempted to stand but stumbled forward. Andy made one last attempt to grab her foot, but she jumped out of reach. She glanced at his face. His eyes stared at nothing in particular as his body jerked then relaxed.

Fear rendered her incapable of moving her body voluntarily. The gurgling sound of Andy's breathing became faint then ceased altogether. Frantically, she turned away from his lifeless body.

Her stomach muscles contorted as she retrieved her purse from the snow. "Oh, God," she whimpered and ran further into the woods.

Her adrenaline pumped so hard she felt as if she could run all night without stopping. She had to get out of this area before it swarmed with police. She ran as if the devil himself were in hot pursuit until she could run no more. She gasped for breath, sank to the ground and covered her face with her hands.

* * *

Sam smiled to himself when he parked his car next to Beth's at the back of the apartment. She wasn't expecting his arrival until tomorrow. He glanced at the time; it was just after midnight. He could hardly wait to crawl into bed beside her and hold her while she slept soundly in his arms. He quietly closed the apartment door and removed his heavy outer clothing. He walked toward the kitchen in the dark, but jumped with surprise when something cold and slimy soaked through his sock. He hopped into the kitchen and turned on the light above the sink. He found the carton of broken eggs on the floor and looked at the other groceries on the counter.

He frowned when he touched the container of milk and discovered it was room temperature.

He rushed to see if Beth was in bed; perhaps she was ill. After he found the bed empty, he raced to the bathroom. She was not in the apartment. His heart pounded when he picked up her car keys from the floor and stared at the pepper spray attached to the key ring. Alarmed, he spotted the smashed phone and drops of blood then sank onto the couch. He grabbed his cell phone and quickly punched in Jack's pager number.

He clenched his fists tightly as he paced back and forth. He felt the tension tighten inside of him like a mainspring ready to unravel. His heart filled with longing as he stood in the doorway of Beth's bedroom.

While he waited for Jack to respond to the page, he put away the remainder of the groceries and then cleaned up the mess from the carpet. After several long moments, he jumped to answer the phone.

"Jack!" Again, his heart pounded.

"Sam! Where are you?" Static from the cell phone distorted the clarity of Jack's words.

"I'm at Beth's apartment. It looks as if she left in a hurry."

Jack paused. "You need to come home, Sam."

Sam was surprised by the guarded tone in Jack's voice. "Is she all right?" His words were forced in an attempt to hide the panic rising inside of him.

"I hope so. Right now I'm trying to locate her."

Sam frowned. "What aren't you telling me? What's going on, damn it."

There was momentary silence. "Come home, Sam. I'll meet you there as soon as I can." Jack pressed the button on his cellular phone to disconnect the call and stared ahead at the road before him. He felt a lump in his throat as he tried to shake the sound of anguish in Sam's voice from his mind.

Again, Jack pieced together the events of the night. A call came into the station around ten o'clock reporting Andy Thompson had been shot. Jack joined the local police at the crime scene, where they led Jack to Thompson's body in the wooded area behind a small gas station just south of Jane Arbor. He examined two set of footprints in the snow, one large set, the other small. Only the smaller footprints led to the highway where they disappeared. He clearly pictured in his mind the scarf he found in Thompson's hand. Without a doubt, it was the scarf Suzy had purchased years ago for Bradley to give to Beth as a Christmas gift. Beth wore it all the time.

Jack gripped the steering wheel tightly. He knew Beth was at the crime scene. But what logical reason could there be? It didn't make sense why tens of thousands of dollars' worth of cash, drugs, and weapons were found untouched in the trunk of Andy's car. This was not a clear-cut robbery.

His thoughts raced, he wondered what connected Beth to Andy Thompson, and the recent death of Tom Hutchins. Why was Beth running from the scene? What did she know?

He stared ahead and followed the route of a bus headed for Chicago out of Jane Arbor. The ticket clerk at the bus station gave him a description of a frightened, battered young woman who purchased a ticket to Chicago around ten o'clock. The description was a ringer for Beth.

Jack checked the time; it was after midnight. According to his calculations from tracing the bus route on the map at the station, he should catch the bus at a scheduled stop in White Rapids Creek. He stepped on the accelerator, turned on his flashers and pushed his speed past eighty.

* * *

In the ladies room at a bus stop east of White Rapids Creek, Beth splashed cold water onto her bruised face. Any attempts to steady her trembling hands only made them shake more violently. She looked into the mirror at the reflected image. The blood and bruises made her skin appear deathly white. She leaned over the toilet as wrenching dry heaves assaulted her.

What would she do when she arrived in Chicago? She tried to rid herself of the raging panic. She forced herself not to cry. She had to remain calm until she was safely out of the state.

She glanced at her watch, her scheduled bus wasn't due for an hour. She decided to hide out in the ladies room rather than wait in the open station. When she closed her eyes, all she could see was the shock of Thompson's lifeless face.

When the hour finally ended, she gathered the courage to step into the main lobby of the bus station. Beth made her way to the door so she could board the bus as soon as it arrived and pulled the hood up over her head to help disguise her battered face.

When someone tapped her on the shoulder, she turned with a start and struck out defensively. Her heart sank as a mixed feeling of relief and dread overcame her when she stared into Jack's troubled eyes. When he reached to touch her bruised cheek, she collapsed against him. He gathered her close and gently rocked her, as she trembled in his arms.

"Tell me what happened," he asked softly when she finally looked at him. He patiently waited while she wiped the tears from her face. She felt his anger as he examined the cuts and bruises on her face more closely. "Did Andy Thompson do this to you?" he asked and held a tissue against the cut on her lip.

She winced and nodded her head. "He broke into my apartment." Her voice was hoarse from fatigue.

"Why?" Jack asked and gently placed his fingers under her chin to tip her head up so their eyes met. She didn't answer. "Did you shoot him in self-defense?" Her gaze met his for a brief instant before she looked away.

The high-pitched screech of brakes drew their attention to the bus arrival. Her protective instincts prompted her to flee. She turned to Jack. "Please let me go," she pleaded.

She heard him sigh, as if the burden of her words weighed heavily upon him. "Go where?" he asked, softly.

"Out of the state, I don't know. Just let me go so no one else gets hurt."

He shook his head. "For your own safety, I have to take you back to clear your name. Right now you are a fugitive wanted for a cop murder."

She closed her eyes and felt the room spin. "Oh God, Jack." Once again, Jack clutched her close. It broke her heart when she saw tears in his eyes.

He whispered into her ear as the sound of her sobbing drowned out the heart wrenching words he was forced to recite. "You have the right to remain silent. . ."

CHAPTER ELEVEN

June, 2023

Sandra Parker stepped out of the shower and wrapped a towel around her damp hair. It promised to be another hectic day in court. Her client was a low life piece of trash whose only defense was he's a stupid, son-of-a bitch who never took the initiative to make something out of his life.

She blow-dried her short, blonde hair and replayed the evidence against her client over and over in her mind.

She pulled on her navy heels, studied herself in the mirror and plucked a tuft of white cat fur from her navy wool skirt. She stooped to scratch Lucy's head. "I can't pick you up, sweetie. You'll make a mess out of my clothes." Lucy twisted between Sandra's legs, rubbed and made every effort to charm her into changing her mind. Sandra smiled when she heard the sound of Lucy's purr increase several decibels. "Oh come here!" she said, scooped the cat into her arms and nuzzled against the soft fur a few moments before she left for court.

* * *

Sam charged through the police station in search of Jack. He didn't stop at the front desk to check in, but made his way toward the back room where the officers were located.

"Excuse me, Sir." Sam turned toward the receptionist. "Civilians aren't allowed in back. Can I help you with something?"

Sam ignored the warning and opened the door. "I know my way." The receptionist followed and increased the tone of her voice. "I said you aren't allowed in here."

Jack stood when he saw Sam enter the room. Sam briskly shook the receptionist's hand from his arm.

"It's all right Tina. He's my brother-in-law," said Jack.

Tina narrowed her eyes to watch Sam before she returned to her desk. "Are you sure?" She glanced at Jack.

"Yeah. Thanks." His gaze never left Sam. "That's Tina, our new third shift clerk. She takes her job seriously. Do you want a cup of coffee?"

Sam paced and appeared restless. "This isn't a social visit."

Jack eased himself into the chair. "Sit down and tell me what's on your mind."

"This is on my mind." Sam tossed a newspaper onto the desk. "I already read it," Jack said without looking at the paper.

Sam slapped both hands on the desk and faced Jack. "Why did you bring her back here?" His expression revealed a combination of hurt and bitterness.

Jack bolted from his chair and stood nose to nose with Sam. "What the hell was I supposed to do? Let her fend for herself?" He ran his hand through his hair. "Do you think she'd be better off if I had let her go?" Jack continued, "She'd be a fugitive on the run and fair game for every sleaze ball bounty hunter out there. I did what was best for her safety."

Jack followed Sam's gaze to the newspaper. His guilt rose to a new level when he read the headline in large, bold print: **COP KILLER.**

"I just left the jailhouse. She won't see anyone," Sam murmured.

Jack noted the anger on Sam's face had subsided.

"I know. I tried to talk to her this morning," said Jack.

"The paper is trying to link Beth to someone who disappeared the same time she left Aidan." Sam pointed to the newspaper.

"I don't believe it, do you?" Jack asked.

"No!"

Jack leaned forward and spoke softly. "Don't read the papers, Sam. You're going to hear a lot of speculation before this mess is straightened out. Beth has confessed to shooting Thompson as they both struggled to control the gun." He watched as some of the color brightened Sam's face. "She needs a strong lawyer to defend her."

Sam settled into the chair, exhausted. "My mom has a friend from college who's a defense lawyer. I understand she has quite a reputation in Jane Arbor all the way up to federal court."

"Look Sam, I know how hopeless this seems. I'm afraid it is only going to get worse. I'm doing all I can to investigate some loose ends." He patted Sam's arm. "Hang in there."

"Give me something to do, Jack. This waiting is driving me crazy." Jack walked to the door with Sam.

"Get the lawyer over to see Beth as soon as possible. She's going to need expert legal counsel. This friend of your mom's better be dynamite."

Sam stopped at the door. "You have the connections, Jack, isn't there some way you can find out how Beth is doing?"

"I'll try to pull some strings to get in to see her. Hopefully, I'll know something by tomorrow."

* * *

Beth looked up from the pages of the book she read, interrupted by the sound of footsteps echoed down the long corridor of the cellblock. Her pulse quickened as the steps drew near and stopped in front of her cell. She purposely buried her face in the pages of the book.

"Brockton, there's someone to see you."

The husky voice belonged to Angela Medico, one of the day shift wardens at the county jailhouse where Beth was to spend her time until the preliminary hearing and perhaps until the trial if she wasn't awarded bond. Beth stared at the tall, large women whose features were hardened by working several years in this harsh environment.

"I told you I don't want any visitors."

The guard walked away. "Tell him yourself."

She averted her face and did her best to remain indifferent.

"Hi, Beth."

Her eyes shut instantly. It would be impossible not to recognize Jack's voice. "Go away, Jack."

"Come on, Beth. You don't know what I had to do to get in here." He pleaded with her.

"I don't care," she said quietly.

"If you're mad at me for bringing you in, I understand, but try to see my side for a moment."

Beth flashed him a look of contempt. "I said I don't want visitors, Jack. Go away!" Her voice quivered and betrayed the uncaring facade she attempted to portray.

Jack wrapped his fingers around the bars that separated them and Beth watched his knuckles turn white as he squeezed tighter with each word. "Sam asked me to see how you're doing."

Beth refused to let him see the tears in her eyes. "If you don't leave right now, I'm going to scream until the guards come running."

Jack stood his ground for a moment and then backed away. "All right, I'm leaving. But I'll be back to see you whether you like it or not."

Beth listened to the sound of Jack's retreating footsteps, and when the clanging sound of the door opened to let him out of the compound, it took every ounce of effort not to call out to stop him. She turned restlessly on the hard, narrow bed and stared blankly at the ceiling. She felt so alone. There wasn't anyone she could turn to for help. She was on her own.

Somewhere in the distant realm of the cellblock the sound of soft weeping broke the gloomy silence. Her heart reached out to the faceless inmate and she felt an unspoken bond to the one sharing her similar despair. Yet, Beth's eyes remained dry. What good would tears do her now? Then she thought about Sam. He must be confused by her decision not to accept visitors. It was the only way she could steal her feelings to endure this present madness. Sam could break her down with one word. With one touch.

Beth shivered and rested her feet on the cold tile floor. The last few days seemed like a dream from hell. The humiliation of being brought to the station where she was booked, finger printed and posed for mug shots. Several photos of her cuts and gashes were collected as well. The endless hours of questioning she was not able to answer clearly. Her mind was in a fog and she was nearly in a state of shock.

She used her one phone call to contact her grandmother. Rose was nearly hysterical when Beth told her the news. Beth was insistent Gram remain in Maine for an indefinite period of time, at least until this was resolved. Beth warned Gram if she were to come here now, it would put Gram and Samantha at great risk. Would the media frenzy surrounding her arrest travel to the northern shore of Maine?

She stepped to the bars and rested against the steel to let the coolness ease her throbbing, swollen cheekbone.

* * *

Sandra Parker stared at the message on her desk from Helen Andrews, her college roommate and friend, who wanted to be contacted right away. A slight smile formed on her lips when she thought of her dear friend. The smile slowly faded. Helen needed her legal expertise in a case that involved the fiancé of Helen's son. Sandra's gaze rested on the newspaper, well aware of the attention already surrounding the so-called "Cop Killer" case. She sighed deeply and hoped for Helen's sake, the case would be in favor of the defendant. Maybe it would be best if she referred this case to one of her peers, but somehow the media attention had piqued her interest. How she despised the way the media could make or break the judicial system with the half-baked pieces of information carelessly printed. She picked up the paper and sneered at a picture of Councilman Bill Tanner and read the article. She scoffed at his comments. It was so obvious he used the media for free advertisement.

He vowed to rid the streets of psychopathic stalkers, such as Elizabeth Brockton and made ridiculous promises to fight for stricter gun control laws with a hard-nosed crime prevention strategy.

Sandra tossed the paper aside, her irritation elevated at his pompous, self-serving method of politics. Why the public fell for slick, handsome politicians, who had their personal agendas at heart, was beyond her.

She filled her coffee cup and paced. Just the mere fact Tanner made such strong statements prematurely was enough motivation to represent the defendant.

Sandra studied the pale, confused face of the accused as she was led from the police station. Upon closer inspection, Sandra could see the dark bruises and cuts on her face and wondered what drama would unfold as each layer of this investigation was revealed.

She pressed the button on the intercom system to buzz her secretary. "Yes, Sandra?" the pleasant voice responded.

"I'm on my way to meet with a client at the County Jail. I might be a bit late for my one-thirty appointment."

"I'll offer Mr. & Mrs. Kline some coffee." "Thanks, Karen."

Sandra rushed out of the office. She'd have to skip lunch to drive across town to meet with this potential client and then rush back in time for her scheduled appointment. She sighed loudly as she merged with the traffic on the busy street. Skipping lunch was a regular habit in her profession.

* * *

As Sandra was led through the familiar security points at the jailhouse, the butterflies in her stomach increased. It didn't matter how many times she had done this, whenever she met with a client for the first time, she always questioned her own ability to represent the defendant fairly and accurately. It wasn't until she was seated in one of the security meeting rooms, waiting for the defendant to arrive, that she regained her self-composure.

When the door opened, Sandra closely examined the serious, battered face of Elizabeth Brockton. She was scared and appeared wary, but this petite, gentle looking young woman didn't fit the profile of a murderer. Then again, Sandra couldn't count the number of times she'd been fooled by appearances.

Sandra held out her hand. "Hello, Elizabeth. I'm Sandra Parker, defense attorney." She placed her card in front of Beth and waited.

Beth slid the card closer and read each line.

Law Offices of McBride, Parker, Leone

Sandra J. Parker, Attorney at Law

Criminal Defense

734-822-8120

She returned Sandra's firm handshake, but didn't speak as she sat opposite her.

"Helen Andrews is a close friend of mine. She asked me to consider representing you. I hope we can reach some sort of an agreement regarding your case."

"I have some money from the sale of my mother's house. What is your fee?"

Sandra hid a threatened smile from tugging at the corners of her lips. Here was a young woman about to be accused of murder and she was concerned about being able to pay her bills. "As I said before, I am close to the Andrews family. Don't worry about the fee. We'll work something out."

Sandra noted the way Beth jutted her chin stubbornly. "I do expect to pay you."

Sandra reached into her briefcase for a tape recorder and a pad of paper. "I said we'll work something out."

Beth stared at the recorder, feeling a sudden flutter of panic in her stomach as Sandra pressed a button to engage the tape. "I need to ask you some basic questions. If you allow me to take your case, I expect you to be completely honest with me." Sandra looked into Beth's eyes, but couldn't read her thoughts.

Beth cautiously watched Sandra. "I suppose it depends on what questions you ask."

Sandra flipped open the note pad. "The success of the trial will depend a great deal on how much you are willing to fight for your freedom. If you leave out even the most minor detail, it could drastically alter the outcome of the conviction. If you decide to hire me as your lawyer, I must tell you up front my expectations of total commitment of sincerity on your part."

Beth looked away. "I'll do my best."

Sandra continued to stare at Beth. "Your best isn't good enough. Your preliminary hearing is scheduled for next Thursday morning. Which means we have less than a week to prepare." She closed the notepad and shut off the recorder. "Think about what I've said. I'll be back tomorrow for your decision."

* * *

Beth stood in the shower and let the warm water beat against the tense muscles on her back. She felt trapped as she contemplated Sandra Parker's words. There was no choice to make. Beth couldn't tell the truth, yet Sandra would easily see through the deceit. When she stepped out of the shower, a sudden chill braced her damp skin. She nervously searched the room. Usually the shower room bustled with activity after breakfast. A sudden wariness settled upon her as she hastily dressed and wiped the steam from the mirror.

When she brushed her teeth, she was surprised by the sound of water splashing loudly from a shower stall. She was certain she was alone. Before she could turn to investigate, someone grabbed her from behind. She screamed out as someone twisted her arm against her back and pinned her against the wall.

"Shut up," a deep female voice threatened.

Beth closed her eyes and silenced an urge to cry out. When she struggled to free herself, her arm was twisted harder. "I have a message for you."

Beth tensed further as her senses came to full alert.

"Tell your lawyer you shot Thompson. He was forcing you back to Aidan where he had raped you before. If you don't follow these orders, you know what will happen to your loved ones. Do you understand?"

"Yes," Beth whispered.

The women pushed Beth harder against the wall and twisted her arm until the sound of a sickening snap echoed in the room. Sinking to the floor, Beth refused to open her eyes, afraid to see the twisted angle of her wrist and equally terrified to identify her assailant. Her soft weeping could barely be heard over the sound of water which poured from the shower.

* * *

The buzzing sound of the automatic door release startled Beth awake, but she didn't stir.

"What happened, Elizabeth?"

Beth could barely clear her head from the effects of the pain shot. She narrowed her eyes to focus on Sandra's blurred face. "I fell in the shower," she managed.

Sandra frowned and leaned closer to hear the words Beth whispered. She studied Beth's pale, taunt face. "Did someone threaten you?" Her voice held an edge of accusation.

Beth opened her eyes and Sandra saw a look of surprise before she shut them once more. Carefully, Sandra sat on the edge of the small bed and watched Beth cringe at the slightest motion. "Have you decided whether or not you want me to represent your case?" She watched the younger women nodded her head in agreement. "Good. I'll be back tomorrow when you are feeling up to talking. In the meantime, I'm going to see about getting you moved to a higher security area."

* * *

Sandra wrote another point of interest on a sticky note and handed it to her legal assistant, Chris Hammond. She glanced at the words as Chris rearranged several notes already stuck to the wall in Sandra's living room. He inserted the latest addition along the progression of notes stretched across the entire length of the Sandra's living room.

Sandra frowned as she caressed her cat, Lucy, and contemplated the many question marks strategically scattered along the process line chart. "Jack Walsh thinks he is on the trail of some shady dealings involving Andy Thompson. We need to press him for more details."

Chris stood back to study the details of information they had thus far. "I'll talk to Sally Cantrell and Lena McCray. They were not especially eager to share any information with me, but I get the impression they have a lot to say."

Sandra's eyes focused at the beginning and slowly reviewed the turbulent life of Elizabeth Brockton, starting with her childhood to the night she was raped. Beth had disappeared from town and changed her identity, which would be fodder for the prosecution and a weak link in the already unstable chain of events.

"What is she hiding?" The nagging question repeated itself. "Sam Andrews told me about the threats she received, but there's more to the story she's not telling."

Chris turned to her. "Do you think she's guilty?"

Sandra shrugged. "We need to discover the motive for shooting Officer Thompson, even if it was an accident or self-defense. Why was he taking her back to Aidan?"

Beth needs to open up about the facts. The prosecution is working overtime to come up with a strong connection there." Chris added.

Sandra shook her head. "This trial is not about Tom Hutchins, but someone is feeding information connecting his death to Beth."

Chris pointed to the wall and pointed to one particular detail. "What about Jack Walsh was almost killed when he started asking questions about why she originally disappeared from Aidan?" He pointed to another note. "What's the story about Officer Tom Hutchins death?"

Sandra stared blankly. "Jack is adamant Beth wouldn't hurt a fly. Their friendship goes back to grade school and it's clear they care about each other."

Chris studied Sandra for a moment. "What if she only meant to warn him and never intended for Thompson to get hurt?"

Wearily, Sandra massaged her temples with her fingertips. "There are too many holes in this story. We sure have our homework cut out for us."

* * *

Anxious for Beth's arraignment to begin, Sam fidgeted and finally stood up to pace as he waited in the hall outside of the crowded courtroom. He straightened his tie repeatedly, raked his fingers through his hair and picked at imaginary lint from his suit. He was deep in thought as he took a seat near the front of the courtroom. Various people shuffled in and out of the court.

There were cases before Beth's, yet he didn't understand why minor cases were more important than a murder case. He folded his arms across his chest and leaned back. He decided there and then how much time would be spent waiting. He just wasn't known for being laid back or patient when it involved his loved ones. Then his thoughts wandered to Beth. How was she faring?

It was hell for him to have to endure the unanswered questions. It had to be worse for Beth, locked away to wait out the lengthy judicial process.

Both Jack and Sandra Parker warned him of the emotional ups and downs he'd encounter in this media-crazed trial, of the frustration as one delay after another prevented the proceedings from occurring as scheduled.

Hopefully, Beth was sheltered from the television and newspaper's warped accounts and half-baked accusations regarding her guilt in the death of Andy Thompson. This period has been hard on his entire family, but Sam, with his family's support, stood firm in unwavering support of Beth's innocence.

Once in a while in the darkness of his room, a sight nagging voice probed his mind and made him momentarily question whether or not Beth was responsible for murder. It only lasted a moment, when he was tired or depressed by what he had heard from others, or when a particularly damaging article appeared in the newspaper. This slight weakness tortured him to the bone. How could she be guilty of such a crime? He knew her better than anyone and a killer she was not. He steeled his mind from creeping to such thoughts.

He decided from the start to ignore the gossip and accusations. It was all speculation. He had no control over what others thought. He listened to his heart, and it assured him Beth was innocent. Her actions were accidental.

Someone slid along the bench beside him and he was relieved to discover Jack's reassuring presence.

"How are you holding up?" Jack asked.

"I'll feel a hell of a lot better when I see Beth is all right." He swallowed hard. "I wish this was over, not just beginning."

Jack nodded. "It's not going to be easy for anyone, especially Beth."

"How's Suzy feeling?" asked Sam.

Jack frowned. "She's ready for the baby to come. Having to spend the last few weeks in bed has been tough on her."

A slight smile tugged at the corner of Sam's mouth. "It's probably harder on her because she can't be here to see what's going on."

Jack smiled. "When I get home, she'll make me go over every last word. I can tell her everything went fine, but she whittles me down until I'm going over full paragraphs of information. Women love all the details." The smile quickly faded. "I wish I could be with you during the trial, Sam."

Sam noticed the dark, telltale circles under Jack's eyes, indicating how difficult this was for Jack to be one of the witnesses for the prosecution. He reached out to place a reassuring arm on Jack's shoulder. "I'd like that, Jack."

They both looked up when the courtroom doors swung open and several people filed in. Sandra Parker and her assistant sat down at their respective table.

She turned to give Sam a reassuring smile. "How are you, Sam?"

Her sympathetic expression did little to comfort Sam's strained nerves. "I'll feel better when I can talk to Beth."

Sandra looked at him with a frown. "She says it will destroy her to see you now."

"Damn it! She can be the most obstinate person I know."

Sam followed Sandra's gaze to a tall, middle-aged man. As he walked by, they nodded stiffly to one another before he sat at the opposite table.

She again turned back to Sam. "That's Richard King, the prosecuting attorney."

Sam looked into Sandra's eyes and whispered, "That's Rich the King Cobra?"

Sandra covered a laugh with a slight clearing of her throat at his reference to the nickname the press has dubbed Rich King for the way his questioning had a tendency to mesmerize the witness before he struck. "I thought you weren't going to read the newspapers."

Sam's eyes fixed on the door Beth would enter. He hoped to get a good look at her to see how she was faring to life behind bars. To make sure she stayed strong and was willing to fight all these insane accusations. He was nearly at his wits end and he hadn't endured a life filled with abuse and neglect like Beth had.

Sandra flipped through a pile of papers on the defense table, occasionally consulting with her assistant, Chris.

The prosecuting attorney, Richard King, leaned back confidently in his chair and conferred with another associate on his team.

Sam observed as people steadily filed into the room and filled the seats well beyond capacity. He felt as if he was the center of attention as many eyes were focused on him. He nodded to several of his friends and neighbors. The room was packed with reporters already writing notes. He was relieved to discover cameras were not allowed.

Suddenly, his gaze was cast to the side door as it opened. He held his breath as Beth entered the room, escorted by two deputies, Sam's heart jumped to his throat. He had no clue how he remained seated, why he didn't bolt forward to whisk Beth away from this terrible nightmare. To hold her. To reassure her.

The deputies led her to the empty chair next to Sandra. As if she were a fragile, old women, she sank into the seat. She didn't lift her head to look up. Sam observed her diligently, the print dress she wore literally hung on her small frame, making her appear more vulnerable. Her face still bore the wounds of her struggle with Andy Thompson.

Desperately, his mind beckoned for her to look at him. He wanted to see her eyes, his heart ached to see her smile. Although Sandra told him about the "so called accident" in the shower, his gaze rested upon the cast that covered her left arm. It was big and clunky on her small arm. She looked defeated. "Don't give up," his thoughts raced.

As if she could hear him, she turned as if not able to stop and her gaze met his for a mere second. The color drained from her face, making the bruises and cuts and stitches more obvious. He concentrated on fighting the sick feeling in his stomach and the shakiness he had no control over.

The courtroom deputy led the Honorable Bentley T. Walker to the bench and proceeded to call out for all to rise as the judge took his seat. "Court is now in session for the arraignment of Elizabeth Brockton in the murder allegation of Deputy Andrew Thompson."

Hearing the murder word had Sam's knees weaken and he was grateful when the deputy motioned for all in the courtroom to be seated.

Judge Walker picked up the documents before him and took his time to study the affidavits. After briefly explaining to the court the reason for an arraignment, he addressed Beth and asked her to stand. "Miss Brockton, do you understand the charges that are brought up against you?"

"Yes, sir," she answered in a hushed voice.

"How to you plead to these charges?"

"Not guilty, Your Honor," she said softly.

Many whispered voices were heard and some gasps of disbelief. "Hold your commentary until court is adjourned." The judge's voice was stern and rose above the sounds in the court room.

"After reviewing the evidence, the court finds enough reason to set a preliminary trial. Say in one month?" Both the defending and prosecuting attorney conferred and a date was set. "In light of the defendant's flight risks, bail will not be set and Miss Brockton will remain in custody, for her safety and the safety of the general public."

Beth buried her face in her hands and Sam stood to protest, but Jack pulled him down to be seated. "Don't interfere with the Judge's decision. It could be much worse."

Sam reluctantly sat, but the desire to reach Beth was unbearable. "Besides, one thing is for certain, she is more protected in jail."

Sam abruptly turned to Jack. "Are you kidding? Look at her. She's starving herself, has a broken arm and is traumatized to the point she does not want to see anyone." He pushed Jack's hand away. "You call that safe?"

CHAPTER TWELVE

September, 2023

The weeks before the trial were long and difficult. Sam filled the hours with constant actively and drove himself relentlessly in an attempt to rid his mind of the nightmarish thoughts of Beth sitting alone and frightened in jail. He spent hours with his nephew, Bradley, while Suzy recovered from the birth of his new niece, Mary Kathryn. By avoiding the town folks, he steered clear of most of the gossip that ran faster than wildfire through the county. He continued to make weekly trips to the jail and never gave up hope Beth might change her mind about seeing him. He'd leave her letters of love and encouragement. Cross word puzzles, solitary games and books to help her mind carry her to another time and place. Each week he walked back to his car feeling more disappointed than the previous visit.

* * *

In order to prepare for the trial, Sandra badgered Beth constantly to level with her about what she was hiding. Sandra paced back and forth in front of Beth. As usual, Beth remained silent. Seated across from Beth, she stared at her client angrily. "How am I going to convince a jury of your innocence if you can't even convince me?" Beth looked away. "Damn it, Beth. I need to know what the hell I'm fighting for. I'm clueless here. I want to help you."

Sandra saw the look of contempt Beth flashed her way. "No one can help me," she whispered.

Sandra had seen this look before. "Tell me who you are protecting." Beth shook her head no. "The prosecution is going to tear us apart unless I have something more substantial to offer. At the rate we're going, we'll be damn lucky to get second degree murder. Forget about a ruling of accidental or self-defense."

For several moments, Sandra allowed the tension to mount while the room grew uncomfortably quiet. Finally she continued, "I want to go over questions to expect from Rich King."

Beth sprang to her feet and paced in the small room. "I'd rather not listen."

Calmly, Sandra watched Beth. "You need to hear this." Beth folded her arms across her chest. "The case continues to mount against you. There is so much evidence stacked up that proves you shot Andy Thompson. I need more information to defend you properly."

Beth held her chin up, the only outward sign of her defiance. "The gun went off as Thompson and I struggled with it."

Sandra smirked. "Rich King will come up with a logical story." Sandra noted the worried flash of doubt in Beth's eyes. "What might that reason be, Beth? Tell me!"

Beth covered her ears with her hands. "It was a struggle. I didn't intentionally shoot him. Both of our hands were on the gun."

"If I didn't believe you, I wouldn't be wasting my time with your case, but I need more to work with." Sandra attempted a different approach. She was desperate to break through the stubborn silence of her client. "The case the prosecution will use to convict you is based on evidence quite damaging." Sandra paused and read Beth's apprehension.

"They plan to suggest you were involved with Andy Thompson because you were a drug addict and a prostitute?"

Beth flashed a look of disbelief at Sandra. "That's not true!"

"It doesn't matter if it's true. All they need to do is cast the shadow of doubt and the jury will draw their own conclusions." Sandra sighed. "Maybe you were dealing drugs for Thompson and things got ugly so you murdered him." Sadly, Sandra wanted to reach across the table to offer comfort to her young, naïve client. "How do you think Sam is going to feel when he hears these things?"

As much as Sandra hated to resort to using this kind of emotional blackmail, she would stop at nothing to break Beth down. "Andy Thompson was shot and you were there. I need a strong reason to use as your defense. Tell me why." Beth looked down at the table, her face was pale and drawn. "Obviously you are willing to take the rap for someone. Tell me who!" Sandra watched Beth cover her face with her hands. "Tell me about the night you left Aidan two years ago."

Rolling her eyes, Beth grew impatient. "We've been over this again and again."

Sandra stood and hit the table with her clenched fist. "We'll continue to go over it until we get it right. Who raped you the night you left?" Sandra saw Beth wince.

"I already told you." Beth rang the buzzer to signal the guard. Sandra reached to hold Beth's hand. "Tell me again."

"Andy Thompson," Beth whispered. "He pulled the gun out because I tried to run away from him. He was forcing me back to Aidan."

The guard unlocked the door and Beth turned to face Sandra. "He was shot. It was an accident. We struggled and the gun, which doesn't have my prints on the trigger, went off. I was never involved with drugs or prostitution. All I want is for the trial to end so I can try to piece together a life."

Sandra's frustration escalated as Beth stepped out of the holding cell. "That's what I want for you, too."

* * *

It was dawn the day of the trial and Sam dragged himself out of bed knowing he was on the losing end of a tug of war battle between sleep and awake. He opened the window shade and observed the peacefulness of the late summer morning. It was the kind of glorious morning that made mockery of the gloomy state of affairs in store for the day.

He ran his hand through his hair and fumbled in the darkness to find a pair of shorts and a tee shirt. He laced his running shoes and stepped outside to tally some serious miles. He beat the pavement ruthlessly as it helped to feel the rush of adrenaline. Lately, he felt so isolated and powerless.

As he jogged down Elm Street, he passed the familiar shops lining the Main Street of Jane Arbor. Once they felt safe and friendly. Now, the alienation he felt was staggering. His entire life he had felt a sense of belonging in this town, but not any longer. Even his dad had become a victim of the narrow-minded, small town prejudice that could turn on one of it's own faster than the blink of an eye.

A pang of guilt swept through Sam as he thought of the hardware store in nearby Aidan. Business was suffering because his father supported Sam in his unwavering belief of Beth's innocence. Sam knew his dad wouldn't have it any other way. Sam gazed at the quiet storefronts and a sense of confidence began to fill him. When this trial was over, and the truth was known, then a lot of people would need to do some serious groveling.

* * *

Seated in his familiar place in the courtroom, Sam clenched his fists together, anxious to get this thing under way so it would finally be behind them. As in the preliminary trial, there was standing room only. Feeling isolated among the room full of people, his attention was fixed on the door Beth would soon enter. It seemed like an eternity, but finally the door was pushed open. His heart leaped in his chest when he feasted his gaze upon Beth. Her eyes were downcast as she was led to the bench where she'd sit with Sandra Parker.

When Beth looked up briefly and her gaze rested upon Sam, his throat tightened as restrained emotions fought to be acknowledged. Before he could read her thoughts, she looked away.

Sandra entered through a side door and sat next to Beth. Sam watched as Sandra leaned over and the two exchanged words. Sam scrutinized the jury as they curiously observed Beth. How in the hell could twelve people of various ages and backgrounds determine the guilt or innocence of someone they didn't even know? Someone as sweet and caring as Beth.

Richard King was next to make his appearance. He moved toward the prosecution table with quick, confident strides. His manner exuded arrogance as he waited for the trail to begin.

A low beat of indistinguishable words spoken by over one hundred people simultaneously pulsed through the air.

The crowd hushed immediately when the bailiff entered and called for all to rise as the Honorable Bentley T. Walker followed behind. The bailiff declared that the State of Michigan Federal Court was now in session.

The trial began with the lengthy opening statement from the prosecuting attorney. In his convincing, confident manner, Rich King presented a strong case against the defendant known as "The Cop Killer." He vowed to provide clear and precise evidence to prove Elizabeth Brockton did indeed gun down Officer Andrew Thompson in cold-blooded fashion on the night of February 12th.

As Rich King completed his speech, Sam attempted to ignore the cold, tight ball of nerves radiating from the back of his neck to his shoulders. If he were a member of the jury, he wouldn't have a problem believing the vivid picture of Beth as a cop-hating, unscrupulous killer.

Sandra Parker walked over to the jury box and paused momentarily to make eye contact with Beth before she started the crucial opening address for the defense. In sharp contrast to Rich King, Sandra presented herself in a compassionate manner, accusing the system of using her client to cover up a botched investigation and misusing evidence to pin the entire crime on Beth. She cited Andy Thompson as a bad cop who was involved in so many wrong doings it would embarrass the entire police department, all the way to the state level, if Beth were not used as the scapegoat. As Sandra concluded her remarks, the queasiness in Sam's stomach suddenly changed to waves of hope, only to be dashed when Rich King called forth his first witness, Lena McCray.

Sam studied Beth's aunt as she sat in the witness chair. Lena briefly acknowledged Beth before turning back to the prosecuting attorney.

"Ms. McCray, do you recall the night Elizabeth disappeared over two years ago?"

Lena glanced around the room and wrung her hands. "Yes."

"Could you describe what happened?"

Lena swallowed hard. "Beth came to my house, she had been badly beaten, in near shock. She wouldn't tell me what happened. She was adamant I drive her up north to her grandmother's home in Pineville." Lena took a deep breath before continuing. "We picked up her grandmother, Rose Brockton. I dropped them off at the hospital in Essexville."

"Did you stay at the hospital?"

"No. Rose asked me to go back to her house to wait for any news. When she returned the next morning, she told me Beth needed time to recover, but she would get better."

Sandra frowned. "Did Rose Brockton give you any information about what had happened to Elizabeth?"

Lena stirred in her chair. "No, she was quite secretive about everything. She told me once Beth recovered, she would need to stay up north because of what had happened in Aidan."

"You just took her word for it that everything would be all right?"

"Beth and I were never close." Lena sighed. "We had a strained relationship, not at all like the one she shared with her grandmother. I knew when I left, Beth was in capable hands. She didn't need me there."

"Did you keep in contact with your niece afterwards?"

Sadly, Lena looked at Beth. "I never saw her again until this past November at my sister's, Beth's mother's, funeral."

"Do you know who hurt her the night she left?"

"At first I thought it was her mother."

Sandra let the words settle and glanced at the jury. "Why would you assume her mother had beaten her?"

Again, Lena shifted her weight, appearing more nervous than when she first sat down. "Whenever Linda drank she became abusive.

There were many times when Beth would come to my house seeking protection from her mother."

"Did Elizabeth ever seek refuge at your home from someone other than her mother?"

Lena turned toward Beth once more. "Once, years ago. Beth came to my house nearly hysterical. Her shirt had been torn and she was terrified. I asked her what was wrong and she begged me not to let him hurt her."

Sandra again faced the jury, then directed her question at Lena. "Did she tell you what had happened?"

"Linda and her boyfriend were fighting. They were drunk at the time. Beth stepped between them and tried to defend her mother. Linda stormed out of the house and when she returned, she found her boyfriend forcefully kissing Beth. Beth was fighting to get away, but Linda started hitting Beth as if she was the one to blame. Linda and her boyfriend broke up afterwards."

"Who was Linda's boyfriend at the time?

In a quiet voice, Lena responded. "Tom Hutchins."

"Will you please speak up?"

"I said Tom Hutchins."

Quiet, whispered tones filled the room. Sandra turned away from the witness and stated brusquely she had no further questions for the witness.

Sam's blood pulsed quickly. He wanted Sandra to do something, but she sat calmly and deferred questioning the witness until the prosecution had presented its entire case.

Rich King called his first witness to the stand. All attention focused on Sally Cantrell as she was sworn in. "Ms. Cantrell, how did you know the defendant?"

Sally nervously cracked the gum in her mouth as she scanned the faces of the crowd seated in the courtroom. "I worked with her mother, Linda Brockton, at Max's Tavern."

"Did you know Elizabeth Brockton well?"

"I only saw her come into the bar to give her mother a ride home. I was not on close personal terms with her, if that's what you're asking."

"What was your relationship with her mother?" Rich asked.

"We worked together, but did not socialize outside of work. Linda had a real drinking problem. She kept mostly to herself."

"When Elizabeth came in to pick her mother up from work, did she ever make contact with anyone else in the bar?"

Sally relaxed a bit and appeared more confident as she continued. "Oh, she sure turned every man's head in the bar. She was just like her mother. Whenever either of them entered the room, every man with a pulse would give them their full attention." Sally scoffed and continued without further provocation. "Linda would end up with just about anyone who paid her any attention." Sally frowned when she inspected her nails. "Oh yes indeed, Beth was exactly like her mother."

Sandra stood and called out, "Objection, the witness is speculating." Judge Walker turned to Rich King. "Sustained."

Rich smiled warmly at Sally. "What was your relationship with Andrew Thompson?"

Sally's gaze darted around the court. "Andy and I were involved in a relationship."

"Were you involved in this relationship when he was shot?"

Tears sprang to her eyes and she glared at Beth with contempt. "Yes."

"Did Officer Thompson ever talk to you about Beth Brockton?" inquired Rich.

"Yes. He was obsessed with finding her."

Rich passed Sally a box of tissue and patiently waited while she wiped tears from her eyes.

Sam glanced at the jury, their faces reflected sympathy to a woman who was having an affair with a married man. Who gave false testament with conviction. This was exactly the reaction the prosecution wanted.

"Did he say why he wanted to find her?"

"He said he thought she was involved in Tom Hutchins' death."

Again, a low hum of astonishment droned in the room as Sandra stood to address the judge. "Objection, Your Honor, this is purely speculation."

Sally spoke above the whispers, her voice angry. "Before Andy was shot, he told me he was going to arrest her for killing Tom."

The judge banged his gavel. "Miss Cantrell, enough! The objection is sustained."

Rich pushed himself away from the stand and declared in his self-assured manner he had no further questions at this time. His face was smug and he knew the jury would take the information and use it to the prosecution's advantage.

The judge called for a short recess. The trial would continue after lunch.

* * *

Sam walked around the building during the break. He clenched his hands into fists when he realized Beth looked as if she were losing hope. He was afraid their "happily ever after" was developing a huge fissure so large, it might be impossible to repair. He questioned whether he shouldn't attend anymore of the trial. He didn't want to know anything further about what might have happened. It wasn't looking good for Beth right now.

He checked the time and it was ready to restart the trial. He didn't hesitate to enter the courtroom. He knew he'd support Beth until his heart told him otherwise.

When all were seated, the Judge checked some paperwork on his desk and addressed the court, "I'm afraid something has come up I must attend to. Counselors, can we postpone until the end of the week?" Sandra and Rich King agreed Thursday morning would work and so it was announced that the trial would reconvene then.

* * *

As scheduled, the trial proceeded on Thursday morning. The third witness for the prosecution was called to the stand. She stated her name was Marcy Hamilton and her occupation was a registered nurse. When she declared she would tell the truth, Sam saw her nervously look at Beth.

Rich queried. "Ms. Hamilton, do you recall seeing the defendant when you were a nurse at Pineville General Hospital?"

"Yes. She was my patient during her hospital stay."

"What was the nature of her illness at the time?"

Marcy glanced at Beth. "She was admitted to the hospital after she had been beaten and raped,"

Rich referred to his notes. "What was the extent of her injuries?"
"She required surgery to repair a broken jaw and plastic surgery to reconstruct her cheekbone."

"What was her mental state at the time?"

Sandra jumped to her feet, objecting. "Your Honor, the witness is not a trained psychiatrist."

"Sustained."

Rich King paused to redirect his question. "Did the defendant suffer from amnesia at the time of her hospitalization?"

"Yes. She was treated for amnesia as well. She didn't remember any details of the attack."

"At any time during her hospital stay did her memory return?" "Yes, before she was released."

"What name did she use at the time of her release?"

"Alisa Rose." Marcy's reply was nearly silent.

"Did you ever have reason to believe she was using an assumed name and did not have amnesia as indicated?" Rich demanded.

"Objection, Your Honor!"

Judge Walker directed his attention to Rich King. "Sustained! Counselor, Mrs. Hamilton is not qualified to answer this line of questioning."

"My apologies, Your Honor. I'll rephrase the question" He turned to Marcy. "Did Ms. Brockton, or Ms. Rose as the case may be, ever reveal her identity to you?"

"I worked the night shift at the time, and on several occasions, Miss Rose had terrible nightmares. I stayed with her because she was terrified someone was trying to locate her. I tried to reassure her no one would harm her at the hospital, but she said she wasn't safe anywhere, no matter where she hid."

* * *

After the lunch break, there was lengthy testimony from the original officer who found Andy Thompson's body. He gave an account of the crime scene.

Next, more incriminating evidence from the crime lab technician revealed that Thompson's blood, gunpowder and cocaine residue were found on Beth's clothing. The evidence of footprints had matched her shoes, her scarf found in Andrews Thompson's hand, as well as her fingerprints on the barrow of the gun that killed Andy Thompson, was described in a scientific, technically long-drawn-out method.

When it appeared the jury had enough for the day, Rich King called his last witness, Officer Jack Walsh.

Sam's mouth went dry when he saw the pained look on Jack's face as he repeated the damaging testimony he'd presented at the preliminary trial regarding statements Beth made when he found her at the bus station on her way to Chicago.

"What exactly did she say when you told her you were taking her back to Jane Arbor," Rich asked.

Jack sighed. "She asked me to let her go to Chicago so no one else would get hurt."

"Why didn't you let her go?" Rich questioned.

Jack turned his attention to Beth. "If I let her go, who knows what would have happened to her."

"How long have you known the defendant?"

"Since childhood. We grew up on the same street."

"Were you close friends?"

"Yes."

"Were you always her protector?"

Jack leaned back in his chair. "I always watched out for her. She had a rough childhood with no parental support."

"Why would she need to be protected?"

Jack frowned as if he were puzzled by the question. "She would come to school with bruises and cuts. Some of the kids made fun of her. I made sure they didn't."

"So, you were like her body guard." Rich paused and nodded to the jury as if to make a point.

"More like a big brother," Jack announced.

"Officer Walsh, keep your comments related to the question," the Judge warned.

"When Elizabeth came back to Aidan for her mother's funeral, you began to investigate the reason why she had left town two years before."

Jack nodded. "Correct."

Rich paused. "You received a warning note to back off the questioning. Why didn't you?"

"The note only supported my theory Beth was in some kind of trouble. I knew she needed my help."

"Do you think Ms. Brockton was responsible for the accident when you were run off the road and almost killed?"

Jack sat forward in his chair. "No! She would never hurt me. She was not in Aidan at the time."

"What if she was only trying to warn you off the questioning and for stirring up circumstances about her disappearance? She had no alibi for that night! Nor for the night Tom Hutchins was murdered." Rich said in a negative manner.

Jack's voice grew stronger. "I don't care. She didn't do it."

In an accusing voice, Sandra jumped to her feet and pointed a finger at Rich King's smug, arrogant face. "Objection. Your Honor, counsel is purposely planting leading information unrelated to this case! This is all speculation."

The judge removed his glasses to rub his eyes. "Sustained. Mr. King, I'm not going to ask you again to revel only the facts of this case. Do you understand?"

Rich appeared humble as he addressed the judge. "Yes, Your Honor."

His expression didn't change as he turned back to Jack. "What did you find in the trunk of Officer Thompson's car at the scene of the shooting?"

Jack sat upright. "There were hundreds of thousands of dollars' worth of drugs, cash and weapons in his trunk."

"Is it normal to find such items in a police officer's trunk?"

"Not unless he was involved in an undercover drug case."

"Was Officer Thompson involved in such a case at the time of his death?" Rich appeared humbler to the court.

"I'm not privy to that information," stated Jack.

Rich paused. "Was Elizabeth Brockton involved in drug dealings with Andy Thompson?"

Sandra stood once more. "Objection. There is no basis for this accusation."

Judge Walker observed the witness with interest. "Overruled. I want to hear the answer. You may answer the question, Officer Walsh."

Jack cleared his throat. "Not to my knowledge."

Sam watched as Rich King stared directly into Jack's unwavering eyes. "Have you questioned her involvement? Say as a front?"

Jack was the first to look away. "When I couldn't find any other reason for her leaving town in such a hurry, I tossed the theory around, but there's no way Beth could be involved in something like that."

Rich confronted Jack with his hands on his hips. "Officer Walsh, surely in your line of work you see things every day that aren't what they seem. You have admitted you were like her big brother. Are you sure you're still not trying to protect the defendant?"

Jack bolted forward and all could see his temper flare. "Hell no!"

Swiftly, Rich turned away from his witness and whispered to his assistant, loud enough for Sam to hear. "Bulls eye! We have a murder weapon, we can place her at the scene of the crime, and we have a motive, and just enough questions to plant the seed of suspicion in the mind of the jurors."

The case for the prosecution rested. Court adjourned for the day. Sam watched as Beth was led from the room. He couldn't help notice her resigned body language, as if she was defeated. He had to talk to her, to reassure her everything would be all right. He struggled through the crowd to the front of the courtroom to catch her before she disappeared through a security door. When Sam called out her name, Beth paused, mid-stride, but didn't turn to acknowledge him as she was escorted out the door.

* * *

Outside, she covered her eyes against the blinding sunshine as she stumbled against the guard who escorted her to the waiting police car stationed at the rear of the building.

The guard shielded her from the hecklers and journalists crowded and pushed against the police barriers, in an aggressive attempt to get a glimpse of the famed Cop Killer.

As the car door closed, Beth shut her eyes to block out all sounds and sights of her surroundings. She ached to be back in the cell. Slowly she accepted the space as her shelter from the outside world, which now seemed harsh and bleak. Would there be a place for her in that world again?

* * *

Although Sandra pulled a forty-eight-hour marathon the weekend before the trail resumed, she still had questions regarding the gaps left in the case for the defense of her client. Beth had yet to reveal any new information. In fact, Beth seemed more withdrawn now than during the past six months Sandra had known her.

When the trial resumed the following week. Sandra called Lena McCray to the stand as her first witness. "In your prior testimony, you made reference to the fact Elizabeth was abused by her mother, Linda Brockton. If you knew of this alleged abuse, why didn't you interfere for the sake of your niece's safety?"

Lena held her head up a notch. "I made every attempt to persuade Linda to seek help for her alcohol addiction and her abusive nature. It broke my heart to find Beth with bruises and cuts from the effects of abuse."

"Yet you allowed it to continue, even though you were aware the abuse was taking place."

"No! I sheltered Beth from Linda on several occasions. I begged Beth to move in with me, but she was fiercely loyal to her mother. I finally confronted Linda when I realized she wasn't going to make any effort to change. I let her know if she hurt Beth one more time, I would contact child welfare." Lena paused. "Afterwards, Linda never hurt her again, as far as I know."

Sandra continued to her next point. "How did you handle the situation with Tom Hutchins after the incident with Beth?

"I contacted him right away. I told him if he didn't make amends then I would tell the captain at the police station what he'd done. He seemed genuinely sorry for the way he scared Beth. He promised to join Alcoholics Anonymous, which he did. He broke off his relationship with Linda when he realized she would not join him at the meetings. He apologized to Beth for his behavior. From then on he became a changed man. He volunteered for drunk driving awareness groups, which he continued until his death." Lena's voice faltered. "Tom contributed a large sum of money toward Beth's college education. Beth thought the money came from her father's GI bill which wasn't enough to send her to the university."

Lena paused to take a breath. "Tom and Beth never became close, he made amends, and she was quick to forgive. She had no reason to harm him."

Jack was the next witness, giving a moving description when Beth was a little girl and she'd come to him when her mother was on one of her drinking binges. Beth stayed at his house where his mother cared for her. He described the events that led up to the death of Andy Thompson. How he found her bedroom riddled with bullet holes, how someone tried to break into the motel she was staying at in town the night before her mother's funeral, and finally, the state Beth was in when he found her at the bus station.

Mug shots of Beth were introduced to demonstrate the beating she'd endured. Sandra closely observed the reactions of each juror as the photos were passed between them. When she was assured each member of the jury had studied Beth's battered face, she returned her full attention to Jack. "Did Beth tell you she shot Officer Thompson?"

"It was proven Andy Thompson broke into Beth's apartment and abducted her. She told me she was trying to escape, but he caught her and pulled out a gun. There was a struggle and the gun went off. It has not been determined who pulled the trigger."

Sandra noted how the mood of the jury was shifting. "Can you shed some light on the night Officer Hutchins was killed?"

Jack was clearly uncomfortable. "Tom called me at home to ask me to meet him when his shift was over. He said he had discovered something he needed to tell me right away." Jack bowed his head. "He was killed on his way to meet with me."

"How did he die?" Sandra asked with sympathy.

"Autopsy concluded he died from an overdose of Fentanyl."

When Jack stood to exit the courtroom, he paused next to Beth and gave her a weak smile and a slight nod of encouragement.

Sally Cantrell was next to testify. When Sandra approached the witness, she concealed a slight smile. Sally was dressed the part of a saloon girl. Her bleached white hair was fluffed to the point it defied the laws of physics. Her tangerine lipstick matched the nail polish on her one-inch fingernails, which was mild in comparison to the bright orange sundress she wore. Add black nylons and white sandals, and you had a total picture of fashion disasters sited in most women's magazines.

Sandra backed away just a bit to avoid overexposure to the strong perfume Sally sported. She couldn't afford to get a migraine this early in the trial. The day promised to be tedious enough as it was. She inhaled slowly and gripped the edge of the wooden partition that housed the witness.

"Ms. Cantrell, in your prior testimony, you referred to Linda Brockton as having loose morals, yet you admitted your involvement with Andy Thompson. How is being involved with a married man any different?"

Rich King sprang to his feet and barked, "Objection, Your Honor, Ms. Cantrell is not on trial."

Judge Bentley T. Walker peered over the eyeglasses perched at the end of his nose. "Counselor, please direct your line of questioning to the case at hand."

Forcing calm, Sandra addressed the judge. "Your Honor, I'm attempting to establish discrepancies in the witness's testimony."

"Overruled, but I caution you to keep the questions relevant to this case."

Sandra felt her cheeks flush warm. She was used to dealing with the predominantly male oriented rules in the field of law, but it still aggravated her beyond measure.

Judge Walker turned to the witness. "You may answer the question."

Appearing uncomfortable, Sally looked back at Sandra. "What Andy and I had was much more than a casual affair. We had planned to get married as soon as his divorce was final."

"The divorce was never filed."

Sally rolled her eyes. "Don't I know it! I told Andy if he didn't start the proceedings after the holidays, then we were through. He promised he would."

"You stated Beth Brockton turned heads whenever she entered the bar where you worked. Did you ever see her involved with any man at the bar?"

Sally fidgeted a bit and adjusted her short dress. "I didn't need to see the obvious. I can tell when a female is on the prowl. Beth had that certain look about her."

"Did you actually witness her carrying on romantically with any man at the bar?"

Sally paused. "No."

"Did Andy Thompson ever confide in you about his involvement with drugs?"

"No."

"Did you ever see Beth involved in a drug transaction with Andy Thompson?"

Sally crossed her arms. "No."

"Why are you sure Beth was using or selling drugs?"

"Because Andy told me she was always badgering him for free hand outs." Sally swallowed hard as her eyes grew large. Sandra followed Sally's gaze when she glanced quickly at Bill Tanner well hidden in the middle of the courtroom. He must have entered earlier as there would be some commotion associated with his arrival. Tanner returned her stare with the look of death.

"Then you admit to having knowledge about Officer Thompson's involvement in drug dealings?"

Flushing, Sally turned to the judge. "I knew he used coke once in a while to settle his nerves, but he wasn't involved in dealing drugs."

"Ms. Cantrell, I'm sure you're aware that perjury is a serious offense." Sandra faced the jury for a moment, then turned back to address Sally. "Did Andy ever hit you?"

With less of an edge to her voice, Sally replied weakly, "No."

"What about the night on Nov. 30th, the day before Thanksgiving. You were treated at Jane Arbor University Hospital for abrasions and a broken nose. You told the resident who treated you Andy Thompson hit you. I repeat the question, did Andy Thompson ever hit you?"

Sally's voice choked. "Yes. When he was high he became mean and nasty."

Judge Bentley rapped his gavel and pointed it at Sally. "I will not tolerate false testimony in my court. Do you understand you are under oath? Any more deliberate untruthful testimony and I'll charge you with perjury. Do not delay the proceedings again."

Sally nodded her head to affirm she understood, covered her face with her hands and began to cry.

Sandra waited until the sobbing died down. She continued in a softer tone. "Why was Officer Thomson obsessed with finding Beth Brockton?"

Sally raised her head and dabbed the tissue at the smeared mascara under her eyes. "He told me how he thought Beth was involved in the death of Tom Hutchins, but I didn't believe him."

"Why not?"

"I think the reason he wanted to find her so badly was because he was had a thing for her."

"Were you jealous?"

"What women wouldn't be if they thought she was involved with her man?"

"Why did you think they were having an affair?" Sandra inquired.

"Andy talked about her all the time. He was obsessed with finding her after she disappeared. He became agitated whenever her name was mentioned. After she came back to town for her mother's funeral, all Andy talked about was Beth Brockton. I was sick to tears of hearing her name."

"Did Andy ever mention he thought Beth was responsible for Officer Jack Walsh being run off the road?"

Sally bowed her head and looked forlorn. "Jack Walsh came into the bar on Nov. 30th and asked me questions about the disappearance of Beth a few years back. Andy went crazy when he found out I talked to Jack. I never told Jack anything, but Andy didn't believe me. That's when he broke my nose."

Sally looked into Sandra's eyes somberly. "He said he'd kill that bastard Walsh if he came sniffing around asking anymore questions. A few nights later, I thought it was more than a coincidence when Jack was nearly killed when his car was run off the road."

After Sally was dismissed as a witness, Judge Bentley stood and the bailiff announced there would be a one-hour lunch break.

* * *

In the quiet of a boardroom in the bowels of the old courthouse, Beth rested her head on the long table and closed her eyes to shut out the voices of the men who stood guard outside the locked door. If only it was as easy to shut away the jabbing thoughts in her mind, she might find some hope in the progress of the trial thus far. It was hopeless to believe she and Sam would be together again. Yet, an unsolicited image of the cabin flaunted her desolate thoughts. Just for a moment, she allowed herself to imagine herself as she basked in the luxury of Sam's arms, with the fire glowing warmly in the fireplace. When her lips began to tremble as his pressed to hers in a soft kiss, Beth jumped to her feet and quickly dashed the foolish visions away. It made no difference what her hopes or dreams were. It didn't matter anymore because they were probably lost forever. She wiped tears from her face.

The door opened and Beth didn't bother to turn to see who entered. She jumped when Jack sat next to her and took her hand in his.

She opened her mouth in protest, but Jack intervened. "Beth, you need to stay strong. Sam and I believe in you one hundred percent." She pulled her hand from his, but Jack didn't allow her to speak. "You haven't lost Sam's love. He remains dedicated to you and would do anything to prove your innocence. You need to tell the entire truth about what happened, every detail. He is behind you and nothing you reveal will change his love and loyalty to you and your future together."

Jack saw a flash of hope through the tears in her eyes as she sat a bit taller and some color touched her cheeks.

"I have to go. Be strong, Beth and know this will soon be over." He kissed her on the forehead before he slipped from the room.

* * *

Sam watched closely as Beth walked across the courtroom to be seated once more. He could tell she'd been crying. It was difficult to get a handle on how well she was holding up. His eyes followed the profile of her face. Other than the slightest hint of dark smudges under her eyes, she was as lovely as ever. Before she was seated, her gaze met his. He couldn't read what she was thinking. He saw only sadness, but his heart swelled to bursting when he detected a slight smile..

He reluctantly looked away from her when someone patted him on the knee. Sam looked over to find his father sliding into the seat beside him. "Dad! You shouldn't be here," Sam whispered, concerned the trial might be too emotional for his dad's health.

"Of course I should. No need for you to go through this on your own." John Andrews craned his neck and acknowledged his friends and acquaintances. "I closed the store. No need to stay open with most of the town here."

It took Sam a moment before he could say thanks. It meant so much for the love and support of his dad.

The jury filed in, followed by the usual procession of the attorneys, court recorder, bailiff, and finally the judge.

Sandra flipped through her notebook before she addressed the next witness, Nurse Marcy Hamilton. Marcy's eyes were bright with anticipation.

"You stated you and Beth became close during her hospitalization. Did she ever confide in you who she thought might find her, and why?"

"No. I stayed with her when she was frightened. Not much was said."

"How long was she in the hospital?" "A little over a month."

"Did you ever see her after she was released from the hospital?"

Marcy glanced nervously at Beth, who moved forward stiffly in her chair. "Yes." Marcy squirmed in her chair, looking uncomfortable

"When?"

"I saw her again five months later.

"Under what circumstances? Did you see her socially?" asked Sandra.

Marcy nodded her head no. "I saw her again in the hospital."

"Was she an inpatient?"

Quietly, Marcy responded. "Yes."

Thoughtfully, Sandra consulted the notes Chris, her assistant, had passed to her at the lunch break. "Why was she in the hospital?"

Marcy paused and averted her gaze. "She was admitted to deliver a baby."

Instantly, excited gasps escalated in the room where just moments ago there was dead silence. Judge Bentley rapped his gavel to quiet the crowd. Sandra whirled around long enough to flash Beth a look of displeasure before she faced the witness once more.

Sam clenched his fists together, his stomach muscles tightened as a wave of uncertainty staggered him. His gaze darted to Beth as she covered her mouth with her hand as if to prevent herself from crying out.

Once the room had returned to a hush, Sandra asked, "Was the baby full term?"

"Yes," Marcy replied meekly.

Mentally, Sam calculated the math and frowned when it didn't add up logically.

"Then the baby could not have been conceived at the time of the rape," stated Sandra.

"That's correct. When she was hospitalized following the rape, there were some complications which required follow-up testing. I was with her when an ultrasound was performed. Together we saw her baby on the screen." Marcy wiped a tear from her cheek. "She was nearly two months pregnant when she first arrived at the hospital."

Softly, Sandra continued the interrogation. "Did Beth ever reveal who the father of the baby was?"

"No, but when she saw the baby on the ultrasound screen, she wept and whispered, "Sam."

Sam felt his heart lurch to his throat and he jumped forward in his seat, but felt his father's hand firmly restrain him and guide him back to his seat.

"Did you see the baby after the delivery?"

"Yes. She asked me to stay with her when they brought the baby to her after the delivery."

"Was the baby healthy?" Sandra asked.

Sam observed the devastating expression on Beth's face and was afraid to hear the answer.

Marcy cleared her throat in an obvious attempt to steady her faltering voice. "Oh yes. I watched while she held her beautiful baby daughter for some time. I learned from the words Alisa whispered, they would not see each other for some time."

Again, the silence in the room grew suffocating. Sandra allowed the words to settle before she continued. "What happened to the baby?"

"The baby was released to Rose Brockton the next day. Alisa stayed in the hospital a few days longer." Quietly, Marcy added, "I never saw her again."

"I have no further questions, Your Honor." Sam watched Sandra march to the table where she glared at Beth and leaned over to speak in whispered tones, although there was no need to speak softly, since the room was loud with the buzz of excited chatter.

"Beth, what in the world is going on?" Sandra demanded as Judge Walker pounded his gavel.

Beth was pale and shaken. "You must put me on the stand right now. I'll tell you everything."

Sandra turned to step away, but Beth grabbed her arm. "Please, Sandra! For my baby's safety."

Sandra whispered in low, harsh tones. "I'm not prepared to question you now. I can request a motion for a recess. It will give us time to prepare."

Beth jumped to her feet and faced Sandra. "We have no time to prepare. Put me on now."

Judge Walker continued to bang the gavel in an attempt to quiet the crowd. "Ms. Parker, do you have another witness?"

Reading the pleading look of desperation in Beth's eyes, Sandra reluctantly pulled her hand free from Beth's grip and addressed the judge. "Yes, Your Honor. I would like to call my next witness, Elizabeth Rose Brockton."

A burst of surprised chatter filled the room followed by silence. Suddenly the air in the room was stale and suffocating as all eyes were centered on Beth while she walked to the bench to be sworn in. All could see her hand tremble as she raised it, swearing to tell the truth. All could see the pale terrified look on her face.

Sam refrained from jumping to his feet to confront her with some questions of his own. He watched her cautiously sit in the witness box. All ears strained to hear her state her name in a near whisper. She shirked back when the booming voice of the judge demanded she speak clearly.

Pouring a glass of water, Sandra passed it to her client. Beth took a sip, her hands shook so badly the water sloshed in the glass.

Beth stared at the faces of the crowd who watched her. Her eyes grew large and glazed.

Suddenly her gaze met Bill Tanner's, and for a moment, Beth could only hear a buzzing sound in her ears. She began to stand, yet she knew she was faced with no other choice but to remain seated.

She forced her eyes away from the warning glare Bill Tanner directed at her. Her eyes rested on Sam's gentle, loving face. Tears clouded her sight until Sam was a blur. She directed her attention at Sandra.

"Beth, describe how Andy Thompson was shot."

Slowly Beth began the story. "He was hiding in my apartment when I came home from work. I was in the kitchen putting groceries away when I saw wet boot prints on the carpet leading to the back bedroom." Beth stopped to catch her breath. "I knew I wasn't alone. I tried to run to the front door, but he reached me before I could get away." Beth then described the events before and after Andy Thompson was shot.

"Why did you try to leave the state?" Beth stared at Sandra blankly. "Beth, who were you afraid of? Who were you running from?" Again, Beth searched the faces in the courtroom.

"Young lady!" boomed the Judge. "Answer the questions or I will hold you in contempt of court."

"Beth, why was he taking you back to Aidan?"

Beth couldn't seem to form the proper words; the room began to spin around her. Judge Walker hit the gavel with a bang. "You are wasting the court's time, young lady."

In a daze, Beth turned to Sandra. "He was taking me back to. . . because. . ."

Sandra traced the look of confusion and terror in Beth's gaze when it met the menacing, threatening expression of Bill Tanner. She redirected her attention to Beth and moved slightly to block Beth's view of Tanner.

"Beth, describe what happened the night you left Aidan."

Beth sipped the water. "I worked later than usual at the theater." Sandra watched Beth's gaze grow distant as she continued. "It was after two in the morning when I drove by the bar where my mother worked. I stopped to see if she needed a ride home." Beth clasped her hands together to keep them from shaking uncontrollably. "I found my mom passed out in a booth. We were alone in the bar. I attempted to wake her, but she wouldn't move, so I decided to leave her there to sleep it off." Pausing, Beth looked at Sandra for reassurance.

"What happened next?"

"I turned to leave, but I heard angry shouts coming from the back storage room. It sounded like someone was in trouble so I opened the door to see if I could help." Beth stopped.

Cautiously, Sandra continued questioning Beth. "What did you find when you opened the door?"

"Three men." Her voice trembled and all could see how difficult it was for her to continue.

"What were they doing?"

Beth frowned and saw the picture in her mind clearly. "Two men were holding guns to another man's head. He had been badly beaten. The other two were threatening him. One said something about traitors not getting a. . . a second chance."

"What happened then?"

Beth placed trembling fingertips to her lips and cleared her throat. "One of the men shot him in the head." Beth covered her face with her hands. She could still hear the loud piercing sound of the bullet rip through flesh and bone, could still visualize the vivid color of blood.

Gently, Sandra covered Beth's hands with her own. "Who were these men?"

Beth looked at Sandra as if she pleaded for this burden to be lifted. "One of the men I didn't recognize."

"Which one?"

"The man who was shot. I don't know who he was."

"Was one of the men Andy Thompson?"

Beth nodded, her eyes large with fear.

"Answer the question."

"Yes, one was Andy Thompson."

"Did Andy Thompson shoot the man?"

"No."

Sandra sensed Beth was closing down. "What did you do then?"

"There was so much blood, I knew he was dead. I screamed. . . it was stupid, but I screamed." Beth closed her eyes. "I ran out of the tavern to my car. All I thought about was finding Jack. I knew he was the only person who could help me."

Beth covered her face once more and tried in vain to block away the visions of that horrible night. "One of the men followed me. I. . . he chased me in his car, easily catching up to me. He forced my car to a stop. Then. . . he pointed a gun at me through the window, yelling at me to open the door or he would shoot." Beth's voice broke as tears flowed down her cheeks. "He made me drive to my house where he forced me inside. I struggled to get away. I fought him as best I could. He hit me so hard I blacked out for a moment."

Sandra handed Beth a box of tissue. "You're doing great, Beth. Stay with me," she whispered.

Beth wiped her eyes. "When I regained consciousness, he was dragging me up the stairs. I hit him again and kicked him in the face." Beth swallowed hard. "He went crazy then. I think he was on drugs. He laughed hysterically, screaming how he was tired of the way I ignored him at the bar and it was time for me to realize how much he cared for me. He continued to drag me up the stairs to my bedroom." Beth quickly glanced at Sam's solemn face then back to Sandra. "I told him I loved Sam, and nothing could ever change my feelings. He hit me again, breaking my jaw. He torn at my clothes, he. . ." Beth stopped and shook her head.

"Did he rape you, Beth?"

"Yes," she cried.

Sandra turned to observe the faces in the courtroom. Before where she had seen contempt and narrow-minded judgment toward Beth, she witnessed expressions of sympathy and sadness.

Sam appeared as pale and shaken as Beth. All was quiet except for the soft sound of Beth's sobs.

"Afterwards, he begged me to forgive him. He said he would make it up to me. He helped me get dressed, I could hardly move. He demanded I leave town until he figured out what to do." She paused and looked Sam in the eye. "I told him to go to hell."

Beth shuddered before she continued. "He pointed his gun at me and cocked the trigger. I screamed at him to go ahead and shoot me. Instead he shot at everything in my room. He stopped when he saw a picture of Sam. Pulling me to my feet, he dragged me to the picture, screaming if I ever told anyone about what happened, he would kill Sam and my family. He told me to leave town right away and never see Sam again." Beth said in a raspy voice. "Before he left, he shot Sam's picture, screaming if I didn't stay away, he would kill Sam."

Beth searched Sam's face, not able to read his thoughts. "That's why I sent our baby away. I couldn't let him find out about her. I knew somehow he would try to use her to hurt me."

"Beth, who did this to you?"

Beth stared at Sandra blankly. "What?"

"Who hurt you? Was it Andy Thompson?"

"No."

"Who was it?"

From the heavy weight upon her, Beth could feel her shoulders slump. "It was. . .Bill Tanner." Her voice trailed off as the room grew quiet. Several eyes turned toward Bill Tanner who was seated next to the police commissioner in the center of the courtroom. A bright red flush crept up above his collar and onto his face.

Calmly, Bill Tanner straightened his expensive silk tie and pulled at the cuffs of his crisp linen shirt. Calmly, he raised himself to his feet as he pointed a gun randomly at an elderly women seated at the end of the aisle. Slowly he moved toward the frightened women and yanked her to her feet. She pleaded with him to let her go, but he placed the gun against her temple and pulled her along with him toward the front of the courtroom.

As he made his way toward Beth, he screamed at the women he held hostage to shut up.

He stopped in front of the witness box and pushed the terrified women aside in exchange for Beth. He roughly wrenched her to him and used the gun to gently move the strands of curls that had fallen across her face. The contempt in her eyes only fueled his anger.

"I warned you," he whispered as Beth struggled against him. He dragged her with him toward the security door. "If I go down, you're coming with me."

Sandra stepped toward Tanner. He yelled and pointed the gun in her direction. "Stop right there, Counselor."

One of the deputies stepped forward and aimed a gun at Tanner. Before he could order Tanner to drop the weapon, Tanner shot him.

Beth screamed out in terror as the guard crumbled to the floor.

Jack stopped pacing in the hallway outside of the courtroom when he heard the gunshot, followed by screams.

Cautiously, he opened the door a crack to see the drama unfold. He dropped unnoticed to the floor. Crawling along the side aisle next to the benches, he slowly inched his way toward the front of the room. Beth helplessly struggled, but Tanner's grip tightened around her.

She planted her high-heeled shoe onto the top of his foot with all the force she could. Tanner yelped in pain. He landed a blow across her face with his hand and dragged her along.

"You idiot!" he yelled as he hit her again. Beth struck at him as she struggled to get away.

Sam leaped over the bench in front of him and stepped forward, but Tanner pointed the gun at Sam.

"Let her go, Tanner." Sam demanded.

Tanner chuckled deep in his throat as his finger tightened on the trigger.

Beth screamed, "No!" She hit his arm and the gun was aimed at the ceiling. A loud shot misfired into the air and hit a hanging light fixture. As shattered glass filtered over them, the spectators screamed and panic ensued. There was a mad scramble as people ducked for cover behind the benches.

Suddenly, Beth glared at Tanner as her fear dissolved to hatred. His eyes filled with rage as he struck her with the butt of the gun. She stumbled and fell to the ground. Tanner aimed the gun at her, ready to fire. "I warned you."

Jack sprang to his feet and shouted, "Drop the gun!" He pointed a gun at Tanner's chest. Tanner turned his gun toward Jack and fired a shot, but missed as Jack rolled on the ground out of harm's way. Tanner turned the gun toward Beth and cocked it.

Jack steadied his aim, fired and hit his mark.

Sam pushed his way to Beth's side and knelt beside her as he gently observed the ashen pallor of her face. Quickly, he grabbed a towel someone shoved at him. He placed it against the gash on her head. A dark blue bruise was already spreading dangerously close to her temple.

Sandra knelt beside him. "Is she all right?"

"Call for an ambulance, " he shouted. Sam looked into Sandra's worried eyes, then back to Beth. Her eyes opened long enough to hear Sam whisper, "It's over now, baby. Everything will be all right."

* * *

Early the following morning, Sam rushed to beat the closing elevator doors. He grinned at an elderly couple inside. He pressed the button for the third floor of the hospital. He inspected the bouquet of pink roses he carried and inhaled the soft, fragrant scent.

When he rounded the corner, his heartbeat quickened as he stopped in the doorway to make sure Beth wasn't asleep. He smiled broadly when he found her seated in a chair next to the bed, already dressed. Her smile lifted his heart to unbelievable heights as he stooped to kiss her.

"Hi," he murmured against her lips.

"Hi," she whispered back. Sam placed the flowers in her lap to free his arms so he could hold her against him. Beth looked at the flowers and then into Sam's eyes. "Thank you, Sam."

He smiled as his heart filled with love for her. "Are you ready to leave?"

She nodded. "I am so ready."

Sam pressed the button to alert the nurse. He observed the bandage that concealed the stitches near her forehead, but the dark bruises were still apparent. "How do you feel?"

"A little shaky, but so anxious to get out of here."

Sam detected the worry in her eyes. "What's wrong?" he questioned.

Her voice was so quiet Sam had to lean forward to listen. "I'm afraid to trust this happiness inside of me."

"Never again, my love." Tenderly, Sam pressed his lips to hers. "Hopefully you'll get used to it real soon, because there's so much more to come."

* * *

On the drive from the hospital to Aidan, Sam stopped the car next to a roadside picnic area over-looking a small brook.

He led Beth to sit and enjoy the peacefulness for a moment. In his arms, she closed her eyes to let the warmth of his love and the sunshine radiate down on her.

Excitedly, Beth looked into his eyes. "I hardly slept all last night after Sandra's visit."

Sam smiled when he recalled the great news that Charlie, the bartender at Max's Tavern, had come forward with information to clear Beth's name once and for all. Following the death of Bill Tanner, Charlie signed an affidavit stating he witnessed Officer Tom Hutchins entering the storeroom at Max's Tavern to discover a huge drug deal in progress. Officer Hutchins left the bar in a rush, trailed by Andy Thompson.

At Tanner's request, Charlie followed Andy to the police station where Tom Hutchins was poisoned. Furthermore, he followed Andy while he trailed Tom's car before he died of the overdose. Charlie watched as Hutchins drove by Tom's car as it came to a stop. Charlie stated in his testimony that on several occasions he witnessed Hutchins and Tanner dealing drugs and weapons to the tune of millions of dollars.

Never was Beth Brockton a part of the transpired dealings. He had never come forward before as he knew he'd be marked as a dead man. Charlie hired Sandra Parker as his lawyer to work out the legal issues he now faced.

Sandra was certain the case would be thrown out of court and Beth would not have to appear again to face prosecution. Sandra met with Rich King and he seemed equally confident the case was as good as finished. It would only be a formality to go to court once more to have the judge officially close the case.

"I still can't believe it's finally over." Tears filled Beth's eyes. "There's so much lost time to make up for. Where do we begin?"

Sam tried to ignore the hard lump in his throat. He gently kissed her forehead and wrapped his arms tightly around her. "Right here, Baby, right now."

* * *

The drive to Aidan was full of mixed emotions for Beth. It had been so long since she called this town her home. When Sam stopped the car in front of the hardware store, he met her questioning gaze. "There is nothing left to hurt you, Baby."

He sensed her apprehension and gently squeezed her hand. "I promised my folks we'd stop by so they could see you're okay." He opened the front door to let her into the store first. It was dark and quiet and it took a moment for her eyes to adjust.

The lights went on when she stepped inside. She nearly jumped a foot when everyone yelled, SURPRISE!

When Suzy, Jack, Bradley and Mary Kathryn greeted her, Beth smiled through tears of joy. Jack's eyes filled with tears as he held her against him. Both were too choked up to speak, but words were not needed.

"Gram!" Beth cried.

Rose stepped forward to hug her close. "I'm so happy to see you, honey."

When Helen Andrews walked toward them, Beth covered her mouth to stifle a squeal.

"Look what I found." In Helen's arms, a small toddler stared at Beth warily. There was no doubt when everyone looked at the dark, curly ringlets that capped her head, and the deep blue "Andrew's eyes" fringed with dark lashes, this child belonged to anyone but Sam and Beth.

Hesitantly, Beth touched the soft skin on Samantha's cheek. The child smiled broadly and reached out to Beth. Samantha wrapped her chubby arms around Beth's neck to hug her. She looked at the tears streaming down Beth's face and scrunched her sweet little face into a frown. Samantha pointed to the bandage on Beth's face.

"Boo-Boo." The baby puckered her lips to place a clumsy kiss on Beth's face. Beth laughed through her tears and everyone joined in.

There was not a dry eye in the store as Sam embraced Beth and Samantha. "Shes's beautiful." Beth looked into Sam's proud eyes, also brimming with tears.

"Is this really happening, or is it a dream?" she asked, her voice shaking with emotion.

He buried his face against her ear and whispered, "It's finally the beginning of our dreams together."

EPILOGUE

August, 2024

Beth closely watched Samantha as she shoveled scoops of wet sand into a bright green plastic pail, dumped it into a pile, and started the process over. Samantha called the heap her princess castle. Beth smiled as her heart swelled with love, knowing only through the eyes of a parent, could she actually see a castle, too.

Beth sat in the damp sand with her feet at the water's edge. The cold Lake Superior waves rushed up to touch her knees and then dragged the sand out from beneath her.

"Look, honey, here comes another freighter." Beth pointed to a blur in the distance.

Samantha dropped her pail and shovel and joined Beth to search the horizon for the ship. Beth smiled when Samantha's face lit up with delight. "Boat!" Samantha exclaimed excitedly.

Beth kissed her precious daughter's soft cheek and marveled at the joy she found in the simplest touch or loving expression from her child. During the last months, Beth had never taken for granted the everyday pleasures she had missed.

So much had happened in one short year. She would gladly experience it again. There was no regret. There was so much to make up for. Tenderly she placed her hand on her flat stomach and was in awe she and Sam expected another baby in early Spring.

Before she and Sam married, she sought out counseling to assist her to rid herself of the fear, the panic and the low self-esteem she carried since childhood.

The wedding was beautiful at a vineyard near Lake Michigan. She wanted a small wedding, but Sam's parents wouldn't hear of it.

The entire town of Adian showed up to celebrate the brave women who exposed the town of evil and to celebrate the town hero who stood by her side unconditionally. Everyone wanted to celebrate the love story that would stand the test of time.

Sam was in Washington D.C. for a job interview with an environmental agency. He worked laboriously to seize this opportunity to achieve his ultimate goal.

She gazed at the clear water of Lake Superior and suddenly felt a bittersweet rush of emotion. She'd prefer not to move from the home where she had felt safe and loved for the first time in her life. Where she felt serenity she'd never felt before. Yet, to share Sam's dreams with him would be a wonderful, too.

Samantha wrapped her arm around Beth and leaned against her.

"When Daddy home?"

Beth noticed the pouted lower lip and touched a finger to her little girl's nose. "He'll be home tomorrow."

Samantha sighed. "Come now."

Beth reached for the picnic basket. "I know, sweetheart. Is it time for our tea party?"

Samantha's wistful expression quickly turned to glee. "Tea party! Yay!" She busily set her dolls and teddy bear on the blanket to join the party.

Beth ran her hands up and down her arms as a sudden, foreboding sensation settled over her. She felt as if she and Samantha were no longer alone. She squinted to search the beach in each direction, but there was no one to be found.

Acting on protective instinct, she picked up Samantha to shield her as she stood to see if anyone was near.

Her heart pounded as she walked toward the house and searched the deck. Her gaze fell upon a tall figure leaned against the rails and she cried out, "Sam! You scared me!"

Samantha squirmed to get down. "Daddy!' she squealed and ran up the slight hill to meet her dad who was already half way down to greet them. He picked Samantha up, tossed her into the air and caught her.

"How's my favorite munchkin?" he asked as he kissed her.

Samantha squeezed him around the neck. "Daddy."

Sam kissed her cheek once more. "I missed you so much. That's why I'm back so soon." He set her down on the sand and she took his hand to lead him to the picnic.

"Tea party?" she babbled.

"Looks yummy," he said with love and emotion in his voice.." Samantha ran back to the blanket to set a place for her daddy.

Sam smiled into Beth's eyes warmly. "I missed you, too." They held each other close as they slowly walked toward the beach.

Beth stifled a laugh as Sam nibbled on tiny flower shaped sandwiches and sipped apple juice from a miniature teacup.

Afterwards, Samantha continued the construction of her castle. Sam removed his shoes and socks, rolled up his pants, and rested back on the blanket. He pulled Beth close to him.

"How are you feeling?" He searched the brightness in her eyes.

"I feel wonderful." She lowered herself to kiss him. "Why are you home so soon? Did the interview go well?"

Sam gazed over the water. "It went too well."

Puzzled, Beth reached to smooth the hair from his eyes. "Did you get the job?"

He brushed light kisses on her fingertips. "As a matter of fact, I did."

"Why aren't you more excited? It's what you've always dreamed of."

Sam sat up and pulled her to face him. "There's a difference between thinking, and knowing what you want." He paused. "At first, it was a great feeling to be there in the thick of the inner workings of the agency, but as the week wore on, it became apparent these people never spend time with their families. All they do is work, and when work is done, they go out for late dinners to discuss work further."

He played with a lock of her hair that had blown across her face. "I don't like the idea of not being with you and Samantha. The city was crowded, dirty, and noisy and did I mention the traffic? All I wanted to do was come home to our dream."

He placed his hands on either side of her face and held her gently. "I want to imprint the image of your face in my memory forever, just the way it is right now."

The blue sky matched the sparkle in his smile and the rhythmic pulse of the waves that lapped gently against the beach beat in sync with her heart. His gentle gaze radiated love back to her. "Never before have I seen such peacefulness in your eyes," he whispered. "Never before have I felt such love in my heart."

When he lowered his lips to hers, she tasted the sweetness of his response and the promise of forever.

They glanced at their daughter as she continued to make the biggest pile of sand mess they'd ever seen. Sam chuckled deep in his throat and turned to Beth.

"Everything I want is right here."